Highlander Healed

Courageous Highland Hearts
Book Three

JAYNE CASTEL

WINTER MIST
PRESS

Highlander Healed, by Jayne Castel

Published by Winter Mist Press

ISBN: 978-0-473-63775-0 (paperback)

Edited by Tim Burton
Cover design by Winter Mist Press
Cover photography courtesy of www.shutterstock.com
Dagger vector image courtesy of www.pixabay.com

Visit Jayne's website: www.jaynecastel.com

Only one woman could help him heal from the wounds of the past. A laird, his chatelaine, and a love that conquers all.

Jean Munro wishes she were pretty and charming like her sisters—but that hasn't stopped her from developing an infatuation with a man who has sworn off love.

Robin Mackay has developed a hard and bitter shell. Three years have passed since he suffered a terrible betrayal by his wife and brother. Robin is haunted by their treachery.

Deciding to take fate into her own hands, Jean applies for the role of chatelaine in Robin's broch. Against his better judgment, the laird agrees—and the two begin a dance as old as time.

Jean learns there is more to the object of her desire than she realized, while Robin begins to wonder if the walls he has built around his heart are strong enough to withstand one small, determined woman.

But starting again after such betrayal is never easy. Can Robin truly put his past behind him and learn to trust again?

HIGHLANDER HEALED is Book Three of the Courageous Highland Hearts series. This steamy and emotional follow-up to Jayne Castel's bestselling Stolen Highland Hearts series follows the lives of four battle-hardened Highland warriors and the courageous sisters who capture their hearts.

Historical Romances
by Jayne Castel

DARK AGES BRITAIN

The Kingdom of the East Angles series
Night Shadows (prequel novella)
Dark Under the Cover of Night (Book One)
Nightfall till Daybreak (Book Two)
The Deepening Night (Book Three)
*The Kingdom of the East Angles: The Complete
Series*

The Kingdom of Mercia series
The Breaking Dawn (Book One)
Darkest before Dawn (Book Two)
Dawn of Wolves (Book Three)
The Kingdom of Mercia: The Complete Series

The Kingdom of Northumbria series
The Whispering Wind (Book One)
Wind Song (Book Two)
Lord of the North Wind (Book Three)
The Kingdom of Northumbria: The Complete Series

DARK AGES SCOTLAND

The Warrior Brothers of Skye series
Blood Feud (Book One)
Barbarian Slave (Book Two)
Battle Eagle (Book Three)
The Warrior Brothers of Skye: The Complete Series

The Pict Wars series
Warrior's Heart (Book One)
Warrior's Secret (Book Two)
Warrior's Wrath (Book Three)

The Pict Wars: The Complete Series

On the Empire's Edge Duet
Taming the Eagle

Novellas
Winter's Promise

MEDIEVAL SCOTLAND

The Brides of Skye series
The Beast's Bride (Book One)
The Outlaw's Bride (Book Two)
The Rogue's Bride (Book Three)
The Brides of Skye: The Complete Series

The Sisters of Kilbride series
Unforgotten (Book One)
Awoken (Book Two)
Fallen (Book Three)
Claimed (Epilogue novella)
The Sisters of Kilbride: The Complete Series

The Immortal Highland Centurions series
Maximus (Book One)
Cassian (Book Two)
Draco (Book Three)
The Laird's Return (Epilogue festive novella)
*The Immortal Highland Centurions: The Complete
Series*

Stolen Highland Hearts series
Highlander Deceived (Book One)
Highlander Entangled (Book Two)
Highlander Forbidden (Book Three)
Highlander Pledged (Book Four)

Guardians of Alba series
Nessa's Seduction (Book One)
Fyfa's Sacrifice (Book Two)

Breanna's Surrender (Book Three)

Courageous Highland Hearts series
Highlander Defied (Book One)
Highlander Tempted (Book Two)
Highlander Healed (Book Three)

Epic Fantasy Romances by Jayne Castel

Light and Darkness series
Ruled by Shadows (Book One)
The Lost Swallow (Book Two)
Path of the Dark (Book Three)
Light and Darkness: The Complete Series

***

For Timbo.

***

*"For there to be betrayal,
there would have to
have been trust first."*
—Suzanne Collins

1

FORTUNE FAVORS THE BOLD

Castle Varrich
Strathnaver, Scotland

Samhuinn, 1438

"FORTUNE FAVORS THE bold."

Repeating the words under her breath, and trying to ignore the nerves twisting her guts, Jean Munro drew in a deep breath and gathered her courage. The time for meekness, for lingering in the shadows, was over.

Tonight, she would be brave.

Eilidh was off getting them some roasted chestnuts. Now was her moment to move. Squaring her shoulders, Jean set off toward where Robin Mackay, laird of Melness, stood.

Weaving her way through the crowd of revelers guised as angels, devils, wulvers, and selkies, Jean kept her gaze upon the man standing alone on the far side of the bonfire.

The chieftain wasn't in costume tonight. Standing apart from the revelers, he watched the dancing flames of the Samhuinn bonfire, which burned upon the hill before the gates of Castle Varrich. His handsome face, set in harsh lines that made him appear older than his years, didn't shift from watching the fire.

Jean's stride faltered. The laird didn't look like he welcomed company.

She glanced down then at the guise she'd donned for the festivity. Like her sister Eilidh, she was dressed as a fairy—in a long cream-colored shift with wings made of linen stretched over willow wands, a crown of flowers about her head. But unlike her younger sister—who would have looked good even in a sack—Jean felt self-conscious and a trifle silly.

Wiping her damp palms upon her shift, she pressed on. "Fortune favors the bold," she whispered to herself once more.

Lord, she hoped so. She'd longed for Robin Mackay from afar for months now—an unrequited yearning that was slowly driving her mad.

Drawing up next to the chieftain, Jean plastered a bright smile on her face, in an attempt to mask her nervousness. "Good eve, Mackay," she greeted him, raising her voice to be heard over the whooping of the revelers, and the wail of the accompanying Highland pipe. "It's a pleasure to see ye."

The laird of Melness started slightly, as if he really had been leagues away, and turned. His features softened when his hazel gaze alighted upon her.

"Greetings, Lady Jean." He inclined his head then. "That's a bonny guise ye are wearing."

Jean swallowed, as the urge to tell him she felt uncomfortable and foolish in this garb reared up. However, she managed to quash it. Her stepmother, Laila, had once told her that a woman mustn't put herself down in front of a man she wanted. "If ye don't think ye are desirable, how will he, lass?"

That advice checked her now, even if her cheeks warmed. "Thank ye," she murmured. "Eilidh insisted we both dress up as fairies this year."

His mouth lifted just a little at the corners, although his gaze remained somber. "I can't recall the last time I donned a guise for Samhuinn."

Indeed, Jean remembered that he hadn't worn one the year before. Robin Mackay of Melness cut a solitary figure, yet he always came to Castle Varrich for the fire festivals and meetings, at the clan-chief's invitation. And whenever he did, Jean had made a point of talking to him.

He wasn't an easy man to draw into conversation, yet he was well-mannered enough not to ignore her attempts. And after a few stilted exchanges, he'd responded to her. They'd had some wonderful talks over the past months—exchanges that she relived, word for word, afterward.

Jean's stomach fluttered as anxiety overtook her. She longed to see more than polite reserve upon this man's face. She'd tried to get him to dance with her once—at her sister Neave and John's wedding—but he'd made it clear he wouldn't. It had taken a lot to ask him, for she wasn't an overly confident dancer herself at the best of times. His refusal had stung.

"How are things at Melness?" she asked when a pause stretched out between them. It was always like this with Robin. If she didn't make conversation, the man would happily remain silent. Having grown up with three chatty sisters, Jean wasn't comfortable with long silences.

"Busy," he replied. "But at least the harvest is behind us now."

"The Mackay tells me Melness broch is fine indeed," she said, eager to keep him talking.

"Aye, my great-grandfather built it ... the broch stands like a great watchtower looking out to sea."

Jean smiled at this description. "I imagine ye are loath to leave it?"

"No," he replied, his gaze shuttering. "These days, I'm happy to be away ... the walls hold too many memories."

Jean drew in a sharp breath. She couldn't believe it. After nearly two years of acquaintance, Robin Mackay had actually referred to the tragedy that had befallen him.

"It must be difficult," she replied, her voice lowering. "At times."

"It's *always* difficult," he said roughly. Robin paused then, his jaw tensing, before continuing. "The past never leaves me. Shadows lurk around every corner, reminding me of her ... of him."

Jean tensed. She hadn't expected such a raw answer and was momentarily at a loss at how to reply. An awkward silence fell before she cleared her throat. "One day it will," she assured him. "Ye just need time."

He met her eye, his gaze sharpening. "Do I?"

Jean started to sweat. This wasn't going well at all. Their exchange had started amicably enough, yet had suddenly taken a sharp turn. Nonetheless, she couldn't give up—not when she'd been looking forward to seeing him for months now. Somehow, Robin Mackay had taken up residence in her head, and she couldn't turf him out. "Don't ye ever get lonely?" she asked.

Robin flinched at the question, and mortification rolled over Jean. She wished she could claw the words back, but it was too late. Her mouth had run away with her.

Tense moments followed, and then the laird shook his head. "No," he replied, stepping away from her. "Sorry, Lady Jean... if ye will excuse me ... I must talk to the clan-chief."

Her lips parted to answer, but he was already moving past her, heading into the crowd.

Swiveling around, Jean watched him go.

Heart pounding, she inwardly cursed her clumsiness. Why couldn't she be more like her sisters? None of them planted their feet in their mouths when they spoke to men. Tears pricked her eyelids. God's bones, she was charmless and gauche. At this rate, she'd die a spinster.

She'd been feeling restless of late. Life at Castle Varrich was good, but she often awoke with the nagging sense that she was merely marking time here. Somehow, she knew her destiny lay elsewhere. She wanted it to be with Robin Mackay.

A creeping sense of desperation had shadowed her usually positive outlook over the past months. Both Jean's elder sisters were now happily wed—soon folk would start to wonder if any man would ever offer for *her*. None had shown any interest thus far. Potential suitors swarmed around Eilidh on evenings like this, ignoring her plainer elder sister.

Jean had tried not to care about her lack of wooers. Instead, she told herself it didn't matter, for she knew whom she wanted: Robin Mackay. He'd seemed to enjoy their chats in the past, but that last question had been a step too far. The man had virtually bolted.

"So much for 'Fortune favors the bold'," she muttered, blinking rapidly as her vision misted.

All her boldness had done was to scare the man she wanted away.

Drawing in a deep breath, Jean weathered the sting of rejection. Ever practical, she then tried to rationalize Mackay's behavior. *He wasn't running from ye*, she told herself. *Ye just touched on a sensitive topic, that's all.*

Aye, all wasn't lost. The chieftain of Melness would remain at Castle Varrich for another day at least. Before he departed, she would do her best to smooth things over between them.

Jean's spine straightened then, her jaw firming. She wasn't a lass easily defeated. Whatever it took, she would win his trust.

Robin Mackay strode through the crowd.

To his right, he spied Niel Mackay. The clan-chief was speaking to his cousin John. Like Robin, the chieftain of Achness had made a trip to Varrich for Samhuinn. The cousins were both guised as wulvers: beasts that were half-man, half-wolf. They were laughing over something, teasing each other. Next to Niel, Beth stood with their bairn, Angus, asleep in a sling across her front.

Something tugged deep in Robin's chest. The sight of Niel and Beth with their child—and the knowledge that they were so happy and in love—just made bitterness twist its blade tighter into his heart.

Sometimes, it seemed as if the whole world was merry and bright, while he walked under gloomy skies. The sun never warmed him, not inside.

Ever since Liosa.

Ever since Gordon.

Robin didn't approach the clan-chief. His excuse to Lady Jean had been just that: a means of escape.

Instead, he headed for the gates to the keep. The castle loomed above the revelers, its bulk outlined against a star-strewn sky.

Resisting the urge to glance over his shoulder, for he knew the lass would be standing there, watching him go, Robin clenched his jaw and quickened his pace.

He'd been insufferably rude.

He hadn't meant to be, but when Jean had gazed at him with her guileless grey-green eyes and asked him if he ever got lonely, he'd felt as if she'd just punched the air out of his lungs.

He'd told her he didn't, but it was a blatant lie.

Loneliness dogged Robin Mackay's steps, every waking moment. It gnawed at his belly, stole his peace, and whispered cruel words in his ear. But he couldn't tell Jean Munro that. The lass would think him a raving lunatic. She was young and innocent of the ways of the world—and she seemed to hold a fascination for him.

A fascination he couldn't return. He'd never make himself vulnerable again, would never trust like a blind fool.

I must stop coming to these festivals, he told himself ruefully. Indeed, he should spare the folk of Varrich and Tongue the sight of his miserable face. He visited the clan-chief often, for he was committed to keeping their clan strong, and would do what he could to prevent the likes of the Gunns and the Sutherlands from eating away at their borders. But being at Varrich would just encourage Jean Munro to seek him out.

As much as he hated the place these days, he would need to start spending more time at Melness. At least there, no one would ask him questions he didn't wish to answer.

2

AN UNEXPECTED OFFER

"WHY THE GRIM face, Robin?" Niel Mackay's voice echoed across the table. "Didn't ye find Iver's story amusing?"

Like everyone else seated upon the dais, Jean's gaze settled upon the laird of Melness. Iver Mackay had just shared a tale about the rivalry between his three younger brothers. The incident—which involved a pretty lass, drunken boasts, and a tavern fight—made the other chieftains roar with laughter. John Mackay of Aberach, Connor Mackay of Farr, Iver Mackay of Dun Ugadale, Breac Mackay of Balnakeil, Hugh Mackay of Loch Stach—and Robin Mackay of Melness—were all there today. Relations between the Mackay chieftains were the strongest they'd been in years.

However, despite that the others were still wiping tears of mirth from their eyes, the laird of Melness had yet to crack a smile.

"Did ye go too hard on the ale last night, eh, lad?" Hugh Mackay suggested with a wink. "Ye appear a little peaky."

Robin pulled a face before taking a gulp from his tankard of ale. "I'm well enough," he replied gruffly. "Just a little weary. Life has been busy at Melness of late."

Jean picked up her pewter goblet of bramble wine and took a sip. It was dark and spicy, and warmed her stomach. The noon meal the day after Samhuinn was a merry affair. Most of the clan-chief's guests had stayed on, and men and women packed the great hall of Castle

Varrich, lining long trestle tables, while upon the dais, Niel Mackay hosted his chieftains. Wine, mead, and ale flowed—and the rich aroma of boar stew drifted through the humid, smoky air.

"Have ye found someone to replace Lachlan yet?" John Mackay asked from across the table.

Robin shook his head.

Jean studied his handsome, yet stern, face. She shouldn't stare so—especially after the embarrassment of the eve of the night before—but Jean couldn't help herself. She'd lain abed after the bonfire, listening to the whisper of her sister's breathing, while she went over the brief exchange between her and Robin. And every time she thought on how that conversation had ended, her breathing constricted, heat pulsing like a stoked ember in her breast. Aye, she had to find a way to make things well between them again.

"Lachlan?" Niel asked, holding up his goblet so a passing servant could refill it with wine.

"My steward," Robin replied. "He died last summer, but I've yet to find a worthy substitute."

"It can't be that difficult, surely?" Beth asked, flashing Robin a sympathetic smile.

Robin grunted, making it clear that the task was harder than Lady Mackay thought. "Lachlan served both my father and grandfather ... his loyalty was unequaled." The laird paused there. "I doubt I shall ever find such a man to manage my household again."

"Ye could always take on a chatelaine," Neave piped up. Jean's sister then favored Robin with a wink. "I'm sure a woman could do the job just as well as a man."

Observing her older sisters gently tease Robin, Jean stifled a pang of envy. She didn't enjoy feeling jealous of Beth and Neave—but there were times, especially of late, when she did.

They were both so confident, so at ease with themselves, and in love with men who worshipped them. Jean rarely spoke up at the table when the chieftains were present. She was outspoken with her sisters but feared stumbling over her words or blushing when men other than Niel or John were present.

And when it came to Robin Mackay, she couldn't be trusted not to make a complete goose of herself.

Even so, the subject of conversation intrigued her.

He needed a chatelaine.

She hadn't known Robin had lost his steward. He hadn't said anything about it when she'd asked him about Melness the eve before. Of course, their conversation had ended shortly afterward.

"Neave has a point," Niel said, leaning back in his carven chair and observing Robin over the rim of his goblet. "Widen yer search a little, man."

Robin took another gulp of ale before shrugging. "Maybe."

"Ye could send word to my father?" Beth suggested. "We have two unwed cousins at Foulis … capable women. Ye could take on one of them."

Robin's jaw tightened. "There's really no need. I just—"

"Nonsense," Niel cut him off with a wave of his hand. "Ye can't manage yer household *and* oversee yer lands, Robin. Leave it to us to find some suitable candidates for ye to interview."

"That won't be necessary … *I* shall be happy to fill the position," Jean spoke up.

The moment the words left her mouth, she clamped her lips shut—shocked at her own audacity.

Hades, what am I doing?

One instant she'd been listening to the exchange, and the next she was offering her services. The offer hadn't been planned—it had merely burst from her.

Jean had no experience as a chatelaine. Aye, she helped Beth with the running of Castle Varrich, but she'd never been in charge before. Heat blossomed across her chest, and she was grateful for the high-necked kirtle she wore, which would conceal her embarrassment. Hopefully, the blush wouldn't creep up her neck to her face though.

Everyone at the table swiveled to look at her.

Gripping the spoon she'd been using to eat her stew, Jean stared back at them and fought the urge to cringe.

It was too late now; she'd made the offer. If she took it back, she'd appear an utter fool. And despite that she was embarrassed to be the center of attention, a part of Jean thrilled at her bravery.

This was her chance to bring herself closer to Robin. If she was working for him, they'd *have* to spend more time together.

Gathering her nerve, Jean forced herself to shift her attention to Robin—and to her dismay, the man was staring at her as if she'd just sprouted a forked tail and devil's horns.

Humiliation prickled across her chest, and—curse it— her cheeks heated up.

"It makes perfect sense," she continued, breaking the surprised silence that had settled across the table. "I'm highly capable … and available."

Jean glanced over at Beth then, marking the shock on her eldest sister's face. Likewise, Eilidh wore a stunned expression, as if she couldn't believe what she was hearing. She'd have to deal with an interrogation from them both later.

Sucking in a deep breath, Jean shifted her attention back to Robin.

The laird of Melness's hazel gaze was narrowed now, which didn't bode well.

Jean's grip on her spoon tightened. It took all her will not to drop her gaze and mumble an apology.

"I thank ye for the offer, Lady Jean," he said, his voice low yet firm. "But ye are too inexperienced for such a role."

Jean's stomach dove at these words, and the treacherous heat upon her cheeks started to burn. Humiliation pulsed through her.

Niel Mackay cleared his throat. "Jean is serious beyond her years, Robin … the lass would manage yer broch well." Beth cast her husband a look of chagrin, yet Niel continued, his attention still upon his chieftain. "The solution to yer problems is sitting at this table. I'd suggest ye consider Jean Munro for the position of chatelaine.”

Silence fell. There was an edge to Niel’s voice—one that Jean had heard before. He’d turned out to be a fair-minded and well-loved clan-chief, yet the man could be mercurial. And he didn’t take kindly to not being heeded.

His support surprised Jean, yet she shot him a grateful look all the same.

“Ye won’t find any chatelaine better than Jean,” Neave added. “I think it’s a wonderful idea.” Unlike Beth and Eilidh, Jean’s offer hadn’t rendered her mute with shock. Her gaze twinkled as she met Jean’s eye, before fastening her attention on Robin Mackay.

Jean pitied the man. Neave was the most persuasive of all the Munro sisters, and she favored Robin with a charming smile. “Ye are clearly busy at the moment,” Neave continued, even as the laird of Melness’s mouth pursed. “Ye don’t have time to interview prospective chatelaines.” Neave swept an elegant hand in Jean’s direction. “And now ye don’t need to.”

Another hush descended. Meanwhile, the conversation at the tables beneath the dais grew increasingly raucous. A harpist, seated in the gallery on the opposite side of the hall, had begun to play, and one of Neil’s men was singing, off-tune. Some of his friends joined in.

However, no one at the clan-chief’s table paid that any mind. Instead, their gazes flicked between Robin Mackay and Jean Munro.

Eventually, the laird of Melness cleared his throat. “I don’t understand why ye would want such a position, Lady Jean,” he said, meeting her eye directly now. “Surely, a lass of yer age and rank should be looking for a husband, not offering to run my household?”

His expression was genuinely perplexed, although Jean noted the tension around his mouth, the shadow in his eyes.

She started to sweat. *He knows I hold a fascination for him.*

It shouldn't have come as a great surprise, for Jean sought Robin out every time he visited Castle Varrich, and her questions the eve before had likely made her interest in him plainer still.

Fighting embarrassment, Jean cleared her throat. "I'm not like my sisters," she murmured, deliberately not looking at any of her siblings as she replied. It was a sweeping comment, yet true: she wasn't a beauty like Neave or Eilidh, and nor did she have Beth's sensuality or self-assurance. She was plain, mousy, Jean. The serious one. The one that blended into the background. "I don't wish for a husband, but to make myself useful."

Jean dropped her gaze then, silently whispering a prayer to Mother Mary to forgive her for her lie. *Of course,* she wished for a husband. Yet to admit to the table that she desired Robin Mackay would both humiliate her and ruin her chance of being taken on as his chatelaine.

"Ye are useful here, Jean." Beth finally spoke up then, and there was no mistaking the hurt in her voice.

Jean's breathing hitched. She glanced up, favoring Beth with an apologetic look. She didn't want to wound her eldest sister—Beth had always been good to her—but now that she'd made the offer, and Niel and Neave had both supported her, she dug her toes in. "I know," she murmured. "But this is what I want."

It was a pity then that the man she wished would view her as a future wife, now wore an expression as if someone had just spat in his stew.

Jean swallowed hard, in an attempt to dislodge the lump that had risen in her throat.

Fortune favors the bold, lass, she reminded herself as she tried to ignore the warning that chattered in the back of her head. Nothing in her life would change if she sat in the shadows.

Let Robin Mackay be the one to reject her.

3

CORNERED

ROBIN MACKAY INHALED deeply, aware that all eyes were on him.

Farther down the table, Jean sat watching him. Her grey-green eyes were wide upon her serious face.

God's blood, Jean Munro ... what are ye doing?

The last thing he needed was this lass as his chatelaine. If he and the clan-chief had been alone, he'd have told him that Jean had developed a fixation upon him.

Why else would she have made such an offer?

He could see making it had embarrassed her, as had his less than enthusiastic response. There was a flush to her cheeks, and she sat rigidly upon the bench seat. She'd offered an excuse of sorts, yet he didn't believe her. Of course, she wanted a husband—all lasses did.

Jean was attractive, although she didn't draw attention to her comeliness. She was dressed in a loose, high-necked kirtle today, and she'd pulled her brown hair into a severe bun. It was as if Jean Munro didn't want men to notice her. Nonetheless, she would surely have suitors.

But Robin *wasn't* alone with Niel and had no wish to humiliate Jean. As such, he said nothing. All the same, he didn't want to take her into his household. He hadn't been exaggerating earlier. Lachlan's death had made life even more wearying than usual at Melness. Despite his advancing age, the steward had gone beyond the duties required of him in the past three years, knowing that the laird was distracted. However, one morning Lachlan hadn't risen from his bed—and when servants went looking for him, they found he'd died peacefully during the night. It was an easy death, one few people lived long enough to receive. And auld Lachlan had been a good soul; if anyone deserved such an end, it was him.

Yet, following his death, the broch had been shambolic.

Robin really did need someone to replace him.

"What will it be then, Robin?" Niel asked, a hint of irritation in his voice. The clan-chief was clearly tiring of this subject, and of the long silences at the table. "Are ye going to accept this fine offer or not?"

Glancing Niel's way, Robin caught the glint in his blue eyes. Indeed, he was losing patience.

Robin was aware that his reticence was bordering on petulance. As far as Niel was concerned, there was no good reason why he'd reject Jean's generous offer. The lass was clearly competent. Robin was coming across as needlessly obstinate.

A wave of fatigue swept across him then. Satan's cods, this conversation was both vexing and exhausting. He should have made his excuses and left for home after breaking his fast earlier that day—anything to avoid being cornered.

"Very well," Robin muttered. It was an ungracious reply, yet he couldn't help it. He'd slept badly the night before—and when he had finally managed to drop off, he'd dreamed of Liosa and Gordon: they'd been abed together, talking softly as lovers do after coupling. And they'd been laughing—at him.

The cuckold. The fool.

Unsurprisingly, by the time dawn had broken, Robin's mood was black.

Glancing back down the table, Robin met Jean's eye once more. She wore a determined look, although her gaze gleamed with pleasure as she favored him with a nod.

"Ye won't regret this, Mackay," she assured him, her mouth lifting at the corners in a shy smile.

Robin's fingers tightened around his tankard before he raised it to his lips and took another large gulp.

Too late. I already do.

The moment they were alone, Eilidh rounded on Jean. "What in Hades are ye doing?"

Jean met her younger sister's gaze for the first time since she'd offered to become the chatelaine of Melness broch.

Eilidh's large oaken-colored eyes, the same shade as her hair, gleamed with tears.

Jean's belly clenched. She'd been ready for anger, but she hated to see the hurt on Eilidh's face. Considering her reply carefully, she walked over to one of the high-backed chairs flanking the hearth in the women's solar. She then settled herself into her usual seat and picked up the embroidery she'd been working on. "I wish for a change."

"Really?" Eilidh lowered herself into the chair opposite. However, she didn't pick up the basket of wool she'd been winding onto a spindle. Instead, she continued to stare at her sister as if she were a stranger. "This is the first I've heard of such a thing." She paused then, her delicate features tensing. "I thought we shared *everything*, Jeanie?"

Their gazes fused for a long moment before Jean looked down at her embroidery hoop. She was embroidering a cluster of meadow flowers onto a pillowcase, although she currently felt too churned up to concentrate on such an intricate task.

He agreed!

Aye, Robin Mackay hadn't appeared overjoyed by the prospect of her becoming chatelaine of his broch—and Niel had virtually bullied him into accepting—but what mattered was that he *had* agreed.

"Don't ye like it here?" Eilidh's question roused her from her thoughts.

Glancing up once more, Jean sighed. "Of course, I do."

Eilidh's smooth brow furrowed. "Then why are ye leaving?" Her slim hands clasped together on her lap, her fingers twisting together. "Beth needs ye ... as do I."

Jean heaved in a deep breath before releasing it slowly. She'd been prepared for this. All her sisters knew how to twist the knife. She was surprised that Neave had taken her side in this, but since she'd moved away to Achness, the cord had been cut between Neave and her siblings. She could see Jean wanted to spread her wings—and wished to encourage her.

Eilidh and Beth wouldn't be so easy to convince.

Stubbornness coiled under Jean's ribcage then, and trying to ignore Eilidh's wounded expression and glittering eyes, she replied, "Beth is a capable chatelaine of Castle Varrich ... and ye are a great help to her. Neither of ye needs me here."

"I do!" Eilidh knuckled away a tear that escaped, sliding down her smooth cheek. "I've never been without ye, Jeanie."

"Eilidh." Jean set her embroidery hoop aside and went to her sister, kneeling before her and taking her hands in hers. "Do ye remember how upset we were when Neave left for Achness?"

Her sister nodded, her throat bobbing.

"But we had to let her go ... so she could live her life. And now, we've come to accept things. Neave is happy at Achness with John. The four of us were never meant to remain under the same roof forever."

Eilidh's eyes filled with fresh tears. "But it was different with Neave ... she was getting married."

Jean bristled at this detail. "And I've taken up a position as chatelaine. Both are worthy paths."

"We've always been so close," Eilidh sniffed. "What shall I do without ye?"

Jean favored her with a sad smile. "Ye will thrive ... as ye already do." She reached out and wiped away another tear that had escaped. Eilidh's long lashes now sparkled with droplets. "We will always have a special bond." She paused there, considering her next words carefully. "But we are nothing alike."

Eilidh frowned. "What do ye mean?"

"Ye are a rare beauty for one thing ... everywhere ye go, men's gazes follow." Her sister flushed at this, yet Jean pressed on. "I saw Iver Mackay watching ye during the noon meal ... ye definitely have an admirer there."

Eilidh's cheeks started to glow like hot coals. "Nonsense, he was not."

"He was ... and ye are fortunate indeed." She wasn't exaggerating. The young laird of Dun Ugadale was a striking man: tall and muscular with a shock of white-blond hair that made him stand out in a crowd. Jean had spoken to him a few times over the past two years and had noted that the chieftain was both articulate and charming. She didn't understand why Eilidh wasn't actively encouraging him. "The fact remains that the time is swiftly approaching when a man will offer for ye ... I am not so fortunate."

Eilidh's large brown eyes widened further still. "What?"

Jean made an irritated sound in the back of her throat, rising to her feet and returning to her chair. "How many men have wooed me of late, Eilidh?"

Her sister stared at her, understanding dawning. "Ye believe no man wants ye?" Her tone was incredulous. "That's a ridiculous notion."

Jean snorted. "Is it?" She picked up her embroidery hoop once more and stabbed her needle into it. "Suitors aren't exactly lining up, are they?"

"No ... but that's only because ye don't encourage them." Eilidh's voice trailed off then before she pressed on. "The only man I've seen ye show interest in is Robin Mackay."

Jean tensed. Deliberately not looking up, she took a quick, neat stitch. "We get on well," she replied stiffly. She'd always been strangely reluctant to admit her feelings for Robin Mackay to her sisters, and she kept the truth to herself even now. "He's a pleasant conversationalist."

Eilidh gave a loud, unladylike, snort. "Don't lie to me, Jeanie. I've seen the way ye look at him. That's why ye offered to become his chatelaine, isn't it?"

Heat rolled over Jean. Curse it, had she been that obvious?

Clenching her jaw, she raised her gaze to find her younger sister watching her. Eilidh wore an expression she knew well: mouth slightly pursed, eyes narrowed.

There wasn't any point in denying her words, yet she wouldn't admit the depth of her feelings either. "It matters not," she said, her tone clipped now. "Robin Mackay isn't interested in me."

"If that's the case, is it wise to live under the same roof as him?"

Jean scowled. "Excuse me?"

Eilidh sighed. "He's still *married*."

Jean's breathing hitched. Somehow, she'd forgotten that. Robin's wife had run off with his brother, but that didn't mean their marriage was severed; in the eyes of the church, he was still wedded. Queasiness assailed her then.

"If he isn't free to wed ye, don't ye risk getting yer heart broken?" There was an edge to her sister's voice, a shadow in her gaze that took Jean aback. Suddenly, it was as if Eilidh were a much older sibling. It was almost as if she spoke from experience—which was ridiculous for Eilidh had never been in love. Eilidh enjoyed male attention and was a natural flirt. Men gathered around her at dances and festivals like wasps to honey, yet she always seemed to flit away from them, just out of reach.

"Fear not, I shall keep my heart well-guarded," Jean replied. It was too late for that. Every time she spied Robin Mackay, her stomach dived as if she'd just jumped off a high wall. If he was present, her gaze constantly strayed to him. But she was aware he didn't return her fascination. The man was damaged, wary of women, and she could hardly blame him.

And, even if he did see her in a different light, it would still be impossible, she reminded herself. Eilidh's comment had been sobering indeed. She'd thrown herself into this situation without much thought. But pride dictated that she plow on.

"So ye really want to be a chatelaine?" Eilidh arched an eyebrow, her direct gaze demanding honesty. "To spend yer days managing a broch?"

"Aye," Jean answered softly. Despite her confusion at present, she really did wish to take on the role. "As much as I love ye and Beth … and enjoy my life at Varrich … I've been restless of late. I meant what I said. I don't want to wait around for a man to offer for me. Instead, I wish to do something constructive with my life." She paused then, her mouth curving into a smile. "And I'm certainly bossy enough to do the role justice."

~ 30 ~

4

I'M READY

ROBIN ATE HIS supper without tasting it. Objectively, he knew the bread, cheese, and cured sausage were good, especially washed down with cool ale, yet these days he got little enjoyment from eating. He ate only because he had to.

Around him, conversation rumbled across the table. Unlike the feast at noon, this meal was a more intimate one. Most of the chieftains had already departed for their brochs, all except Connor Mackay of Farr, John Mackay of Aberach—and Robin.

Connor was teasing John about his appetite, for he'd just swiped the last sausage. The pair of them were good-humored men, always with a ready smile. But then both Connor and John had something to smile about: they were wed to women they adored, loyal wives who loved them fiercely in return.

Robin's meal churned in his gut, and he put down the piece of bread he'd been about to take a mouthful of.

It's been nearly three years. When are ye going to let this go?

Reaching for his goblet of wine, Robin took a large gulp. He always drank too much when he thought about Liosa and Gordon—and for some reason, this trip to Castle Varrich had stirred up memories more than usual.

He remembered bringing his wife here for Samhuinn, a year after they'd been married. He'd been so proud of her: the golden-haired beauty on his arm. He'd shown Liosa off at every opportunity. But God had punished him for his vanity—in the cruelest way possible.

Taking another swallow of wine, Robin let his gaze travel down the table, to where Jean Munro sat next to her youngest sister, Eilidh. The two lasses had been conversing, but upon feeling someone's gaze upon her, Jean looked his way.

Her cheeks grew pink when she saw he was watching her.

The lass looked uncomfortable, and rightly so. This whole situation was awkward.

Robin hadn't spoken to her after gracelessly accepting her offer. However, he would need to, for practicality's sake.

"I can't believe Roy Gunn slipped our net," John Mackay's voice drew Robin's attention then. He looked away from Jean to see that the laird of Achness's mood had sobered. He was talking to the clan-chief now, a groove etched between his dark brows. "It's like the bastard went up in smoke."

"Ye dealt him a serious wound," Niel replied. "I wouldn't be surprised if he dragged himself off somewhere and bled to death."

Robin's mouth thinned.

Roy Gunn was one of the Gunn clan-chief's younger brothers. He was estranged from his kin and clansmen these days and had been working in the nearby village of Tongue under another name. However, earlier in the year, Roy had developed an obsession with Neave Munro, and when John Mackay had thwarted him, he'd tried to kill him.

The attack had ended with John stabbing him in the side.

Roy had fled, and they'd hunted him. But the man had vanished. There had been no sign of him in the past months.

"The Mackay's right," Robin spoke up, meeting John's eye. "He's likely dead and rotting in a hollow somewhere."

John nodded, although the tightness to his jaw revealed that he remained unconvinced. "Aye ... maybe."

"Ye think he'd make another attempt to kill ye?" Connor asked then, his pine-green eyes narrowing.

John's mouth pursed. "I doubt he'd be that foolish … but the man's an agitator, a danger to the uneasy peace between us and the Gunns. I'll only relax when I *know* he's dead."

"Aye, it's an uneasy peace all right," Niel murmured. The clan-chief leaned back in his chair, his fingers drumming on the carven armrest. "Although the Gunns are behaving themselves at present."

"They will … as long as ye hold William Gunn," Robin pointed out. "It's the Sutherlands ye need to keep an eye on."

The clan-chief cocked a dark eyebrow, yet reluctantly nodded.

The year before, Niel had taken the youngest of the Gunn brothers captive after the Battle of Harpsdale. While his brother remained at Varrich, Tavish Gunn was unlikely to start stirring things up. Instead, the Sutherlands had been more of a worry of late.

Indeed, Robert Sutherland held a longstanding grudge against John Mackay.

Just a few months earlier, John and his men had fought a group of Sutherland raiders before driving the survivors off his lands. Rumors now circulated through the Highlands that the Sutherland clan-chief sought reckoning—again.

"Perhaps the Gunns will one day unite with us against the Sutherlands," Connor mused, swirling the wine in his goblet. "There is certainly hope now that the rift between our clans will be healed."

Robin frowned. He wasn't so sure—although Connor Mackay had married a Gunn, so his comment wasn't entirely surprising.

Niel snorted in reply, while John grinned at Connor's comment. Niel's cousin was a warrior of renown and had lost a hand and an eye defending Mackay lands, but he was rarely serious for long. "I hear ye and William Gunn have become friends, Niel … Ewan Reay tells me ye played Ard-ri with him last week?"

"Captain Reay has loose lips," Niel muttered. However, he didn't deny John's words.

Robin's gaze widened. "Ye have befriended him?"

The notion of their clan-chief being civil to a Gunn was ridiculous. Niel Mackay had spent ten years locked up on Bass Rock plotting his revenge against the enemy clan—and he'd had it. But marriage had mellowed the clan-chief, as had becoming a father.

Even so, Robin couldn't imagine him ever trusting a Gunn.

Niel snorted before taking a sip of his wine. "John is exaggerating, as usual," he muttered. "William Gunn isn't any good to us dead, is he?"

Supper ended, and the clan-chief's kin and retainers rose to their feet, filing out of the great hall.

Robin wished to join them, yet first he had to speak to Jean Munro.

Moving around the table, he intercepted her as she was about to step off the dais. "Lady Jean," he greeted her brusquely. "We return to Melness at first light tomorrow ... Ye will need to be ready."

He'd expected her to be flustered by his directness. Women always needed days to prepare for trips—Liosa always had—and longer still to ready themselves for a move. He'd anticipated excuses and a request to delay their departure—one he intended to deny.

But Jean Munro surprised him.

Favoring him with a smile and a nod, she replied, "I *am* ready, Mackay."

He frowned. "Have ye packed?"

"Aye ... my maid helped me this afternoon. I don't have many possessions."

"Do ye have a mount? I didn't bring any extra horses with me."

She nodded once more. "I have a pony ... a hardy garron my father gifted me."

Her response disarmed him. He'd been ready to put her in her place, to show her how grossly unprepared she was for the task ahead. Jean might be a practical lass, and a great help to her eldest sister, but she had no idea of the responsibilities awaiting her.

Auld Lachlan had made the stewardship of Melness broch look easy, but in the months since his death, when Robin had taken on many of his tasks, it occurred to him just how skilled Lachlan had been, and just how hard he'd worked.

As serious-minded as she was, Jean Munro was a poor choice—and even more so, for he suspected the lass had an ulterior motive in offering her services.

She had to know from the beginning that there could be no future between them.

Robin wasn't a widower, for his wife still lived, so he wasn't even legally allowed to wed again. But even if he'd been free to take another wife, he wouldn't.

As such, he'd have to keep Jean at arm's length. In the past, he'd enjoyed conversing with her on his visits to Varrich, but their amicable rapport would need to cease now. The lass had grown bold of late—and had clearly forgotten her place.

"Good," he said abruptly. "Make sure ye are saddled up and ready to go once the sun crests the eastern walls tomorrow."

Not waiting for her answer, Robin swiveled on his heel and walked away.

"Are ye sure this is what ye want?"

Jean glanced up from where she was sorting through the saddlebags she'd packed, to see Beth standing in the doorway. Her sister's cheeks were flushed; she looked as if she'd just come from the stifling heat of the kitchen, where she spent many hours a day.

Beth had her hands on her hips, and her chin jutted in a gesture that Jean knew well. Her sister was readying herself for a fight.

Heart sinking, Jean turned from the saddlebags upon the bed, preparing to do battle. "Aye, it is," she replied firmly. "So don't try and convince me otherwise. I've already had Eilidh chew my ear off."

"And rightly so." Beth took a step forward. They were alone in the bed-chamber, for Eilidh had returned to the women's solar after supper while Jean packed a few last minute items. "This has come from nowhere, Jean. I can't help but think ye haven't given yer decision much thought at all."

"I have," Jean answered, stubbornness rising within her.

Beth wasn't her mother, but she often spoke to her as if she were. In many ways, Jean and Beth were similar, both physically and in character. They were small, curvaceous, and strongly built, unlike Neave and Eilidh who were slender and elegant. And they both could be bullishly stubborn.

If they locked horns, neither was prepared to back down.

"This *is* what I want, Beth," she informed her sister. "Can't ye just be happy for me?"

Beth's hazel eyes shadowed. "Ye know I only want the best for ye, lass," she murmured, hurt lacing her voice now. "But this is so sudden. I had no idea ye wished to be away from here."

Jean sighed. "I'm not running away … I just want a challenge. I will make an excellent chatelaine."

"I have no doubt," Beth replied, her tone dry, as her brow furrowed. She was scrutinizing Jean's face as if trying to read her thoughts, and appeared truly perplexed by her younger sister's behavior. "But remember, if it doesn't work out … if ye find yerself regretting this decision … ye can always return here. No one will think any less of ye." Beth paused then, her expression softening. "Ye have been such a help to me, Jeanie … I hope ye know how grateful I am?"

Jean smiled and went to her sister, pulling her into an embrace. Beth hugged her back, fiercely.

"Aye ... thank ye," Jean murmured, feeling tears prick her eyelids. Events had moved so swiftly today that she hadn't fully understood the implications of leaving. She would miss her sisters—terribly, in fact. "I shall remember that."

5

A COOL WELCOME

"WE SHALL SEE ye soon?" Eilidh was doing her best not to weep as she drew back from hugging Jean.

"Of course," Jean assured her. "The laird of Melness usually visits Varrich at Yuletide." She cast a glance left then to where Robin Mackay sat astride his courser. She'd hoped for an assurance that they would, indeed, return in two months for the festive season. However, the man remained mulishly silent. His handsome face was set in harsh, disapproving lines this morning.

Jean had heard that before his wife and brother's betrayal, he'd once been a kind, easy-going man—and indeed, she'd caught numerous glimpses of his true nature during their conversations—but all traces of softness were gone from his face this morning.

Jean tensed. Maybe she should have heeded her sisters' warnings.

Pride and stubbornness were about to get her into trouble, and yet she couldn't back down. Not with all her sisters and brothers-by-marriage looking on.

Quite a crowd had amassed in the bailey this morning as the first rays of sunlight crested the high walls. The dawn was chill, and their breathing steamed in the crisp air. No doubt, there would be frost beyond these walls: the first of the year.

"Write often, Jeanie." Neave stepped forward, flashed Jean a wide smile, and clasped her in a hard hug. "I want to hear all about yer new life."

Jean cleared her throat to dislodge the lump that made it difficult to speak. "Of course I will ... as always."

Ever since Neave had moved away, Jean had ensured she sent her weekly missives.

Neave's enthusiasm bolstered her spirits and quietened the nagging voice in the back of her mind that warned her she was being foolhardy. Nonetheless, Neave's attitude wasn't mirrored by her sisters. Beth and Eilidh both wore fixed smiles, their gazes shuttered. They had given her their well-wishes, yet they still worried for her.

Robin Mackay made an impatient noise in the back of his throat. "Come, Lady Jean ... we must be away now."

Catching the irritation in his voice, Jean hurriedly hugged Beth. She then nodded to Niel and John. The clan-chief and his cousin waited a few steps back from the sisters, giving them a respectful space to say their goodbyes.

Jean turned and clambered gracelessly onto the back of her garron. Dusty was a placid-natured bay gelding. The pony was well-suited to her, for, unlike her two elder sisters, Jean had never been a confident rider. Dusty was unfailingly gentle with her.

The pony was burdened like a pack-mule this morning, with several bulging saddlebags containing all her most prized possessions. She didn't have an extensive collection of beautiful kirtles; instead, Jean rotated between four plain ones. However, she'd packed a number of books—'borrowed' from her father's library—and embroidery and sewing supplies. She already had one nephew, but it wouldn't be long before her elder sisters gave her more bairns to sew clothing for.

"Go well, Jean," Beth called out as she turned Dusty toward the gates. Robin Mackay was already riding through them, although his escort of six warriors waited for her to go ahead of them so they could bring up the rear.

"Thank ye." Jean flashed Beth a brave smile. "I shall see ye all soon."

And with that, she dug her heels into Dusty's furry flanks and urged the garron into a jolting trot.

Outside the walls, a frost lay heavily across the land, glittering like a sprinkling of stardust. Jean was grateful for the heavy fur-lined cloak she wore, and the warm boots she'd donned for the journey.

As the crow flew, Melness was the closest of all the chieftains' strongholds to Castle Varrich—even so, it would take them all day to reach their destination, for they would have to travel south, skirting the Kyle of Tongue, before riding north up its far shore.

Dusty picked his way carefully down the steep, windy path from the clan-chief's holding.

Jean's eyes stung, and her throat ached from the urge to cry, yet she swallowed hard and focused on her surroundings to distract herself.

Lord, how she hated goodbyes.

It was indeed a bonny late autumn morning as they departed. The clear, pale light made everything stand out in sharp relief. The sweeping outlines of Ben Hope and Ben Loyal—the two mountains that watched over Castle Varrich—rose into the morning sky, sculpted and majestic against the pastel-blue sky to the south. And as Jean descended the rocky outcrop and her gaze shifted west, she admired the sparkling expanse of the kyle; it would be their constant companion throughout the day's journey.

At the foot of the outcrop, they turned left, heading toward the shore of the kyle. And on the way, Jean spied figures making their way out into the fields.

Among them, she saw a familiar, lanky figure with wild dark hair: William Gunn.

Had Eilidh been with her, her sister would have stared unabashedly at the prisoner, for she'd developed a fascination with the youngest of the Gunn brothers since his capture over a year earlier. Sometimes, Jean had suspected Eilidh would make up reasons to go into Tongue village, just so she could take a stroll by the fields and catch a glimpse of the enigmatic prisoner.

Jean didn't understand her sister's interest. Gunn was a scowling, unkempt individual clad in layers of ragged leather and wool. And unlike the other men who worked the fields, he wore heavy chains about his ankles. The shackles gave him a strange shuffling gait, yet the man still managed to appear haughty.

He glanced their way now, his gaze sweeping over the party, before taking a hoe one of the cottars passed him.

A day of back-breaking work lay ahead for William Gunn. Yet she supposed it was preferable to rotting in a damp cell. Castle Varrich's dungeon sat at the base of the outcrop, carved into the rock. Over the winter, it would have been unbearable.

Turning her attention from the cottars, Jean looked ahead to where Robin Mackay led their party.

He didn't turn or speak to her. His broad shoulders, emphasized by the fur mantle he wore, were set in tense lines.

Nerves fluttered up under Jean's ribcage. Not for the first time since offering her services to the laird of Melness, misgiving stole over her. Had she, indeed, just made a grave mistake? She and Robin had enjoyed a friendship of sorts over the past months. But now the man had turned into a cold stranger.

He'll warm to ye again, she reassured herself. *Once ye show him how well ye can run his broch.*

Drawing herself up in the saddle, Jean promised herself she'd make a success of her new life.

I'm a Munro ... I don't give up easily.

Jean's breathing caught when she spied Melness broch for the first time.

She'd heard it was a bonny spot, but she hadn't expected it to be quite this spectacular. Robin Mackay had likened his broch to a great watch tower looking out to sea—and when Jean spied the stronghold for the first time, she could see why.

Many brochs she'd seen were squat structures, sturdy round-towers, like Achness broch, where Neave and John resided. But Melness was different. It soared high, at four stories, and battlements ringed its flat roof like blunt teeth. The landscape here was largely barren, due to the harsh winds that gusted in from the sea. Melness broch perched on the western shores of Tongue Bay, where tawny-green hills sloped down to a pale-gold beach.

Urging Dusty into a canter, Jean followed the chieftain and his men down the well-worn path toward the tower.

The fine weather certainly helped her first impression of Melness—a sparkling, frosty morning had stretched into a chill, yet sunny, day. Not a breath of wind had chased them as the company circuited the southern end of the kyle and headed north.

They'd halted briefly at noon and consumed a light meal of bread and cheese, purchased at the village of Kinloch. Jean had hoped the chieftain's mood would improve during the morning, but Robin ate his meal apart from her and his men, talking with no one, his gaze trained upon the glittering kyle.

Jean had wanted to approach him, to attempt conversation, but there was something about his stance that warned her against doing so.

Instead, she'd eaten her bread and cheese in silence, listening to the rumble of conversation of the men behind her.

And now, a few hours later, as the day dimmed and the gloaming approached, they'd arrived at Melness.

A cluster of squat, white-washed cottages spread out beyond the southern and western edges of the holding's walls. Smoke rose lazily from sod roofs, and the aroma of roasting fish greeted Jean as she slowed Dusty to a walk. Villagers emerged from their homes as they approached, waving, and calling out to their chieftain.

Robin Mackay raised a hand to acknowledge them but didn't speak. Instead, he headed toward the open gate and raised portcullis.

It wasn't long before the villagers spotted Jean.

Their gazes widened, and some of them even shared looks of surprise. Of course, they'd be wondering who she was.

The stares made her uncomfortable, yet good manners meant that Jean raised a hand and waved, flashing them a smile.

No one smiled back. Their gazes weren't hostile—however, they *were* guarded. Perhaps they'd warm up when they discovered she was the new chatelaine.

Or they could turn on me.

Jean gnawed at her bottom lip and tried to quieten the doubts that had whispered to her all day, telling her she'd bitten off more than she could chew. Robin was right. She was young and untested—and she'd never run a household on her own before.

She'd brazened it out until now, yet she was about to be put to the test.

What if I can't cope?

Feeling a little queasy, Jean shifted her attention to Robin Mackay's broad back and followed him to the barmkin, the defensive enclosure around the base of the tower.

A tall man with shaggy brown hair and peat-colored eyes came out to meet the chieftain. Dressed in heavy braies and a chainmail hauberk, a dirk at his hip, the man carried himself with the unconscious arrogance of a warrior.

"Greetings, Mackay," the man stopped before Robin as he swung down from the saddle.

"MacVane." Robin handed his courser over to a stable lad who'd darted out to meet them. "All is well?"

"Aye. Did ye pass a good Samhuinn?"

The chieftain grunted. "Good enough."

The warrior spied Jean then, his gaze widening. He glanced back at Robin. "Who's this?"

Robin turned to where Jean was attempting to dismount elegantly—something she rarely managed. His expression was veiled. "Captain Daniel MacVane ... meet the new chatelaine of Melness broch ... Lady Jean

Munro." The chieftain's voice was as expressionless as his face, and hot, prickling embarrassment swept over Jean.

Mackay couldn't have sounded less enthusiastic if he tried.

Recovering swiftly from his surprise, the captain favored Jean with a nod. "Welcome to Melness, Lady Jean."

"Thank ye," she murmured.

Another stable lad appeared then and took Dusty's reins from her. "Can ye please make sure ye give him an apple after ye rub him down?" she asked, smiling. "He likes a treat after a long ride."

The youth arched an eyebrow, yet nodded, leading the garron away.

Jean kept a smile fixed upon her lips, although she was cringing on the inside. She wasn't sure how a chatelaine was supposed to behave, although the stable lad's reaction warned her she wasn't conforming to expectations. Was she over-eager? Maybe she should appear more aloof.

"MacVane leads the Melness Guard," Robin told Jean, meeting her gaze for the first time since they'd left Castle Varrich. "Ye shall work closely with him."

Glancing in the captain's direction once more, she didn't miss the way the man's mouth quirked.

Jean dropped her gaze to her dusty boots.

Beth made running a holding appear seamless. From the moment she'd assumed control of Niel's household, the servants had respected her. Yet Beth was a clan-chief's wife—Jean didn't have the same status. If she wanted the residents of this broch to respect her, she would have to work for it. However, she had no idea where to start.

"Da!" A high, girlish voice carried across the barmkin then, drawing all their attention. "Welcome home!"

Jean's chin kicked up, and she glanced left to see a waifish figure—a young lass with golden hair—standing upon the steps before the broch.

Momentarily forgetting her embarrassment and sense of inadequacy, Jean looked back at Robin Mackay. "*Da?* Ye have a daughter?" She'd conversed several times with him of late, yet not once had he mentioned this important detail.

Jean's skin prickled then, disquiet rippling over her. What kind of man didn't speak of his daughter?

Robin nodded, his brow furrowing. "Go inside, Grace," he said, not unkindly. "I'll be in soon."

The girl gave a timid nod, her gaze darting shyly to Jean for a moment before she ducked her head and flitted back into the shadowed doorway to the broch.

The chieftain then turned back to Jean. "Aye, Grace has just turned eight ... and is in need of instruction." No emotion showed on his face as he spoke of his daughter—not a trace of warmth, or irritation. It was as if he were talking about a piece of furniture and not his flesh and blood. "She will also be one of yer responsibilities."

6

DID YE THINK THIS WOULD BE EASY?

"SHE'S A BIT young, isn't she … to run yer household?"

Robin glanced up from where he'd been reading over the accounts, his gaze spearing Danny MacVane's. The captain leaned against the window frame of the chieftain's solar, arms folded across his chest. A heavy ledger sat open before Robin. He'd be handing it over to Jean on the morrow but wanted to make sure everything was in order before he did so.

The fewer questions she needed to ask him going forward, the better.

"Aye, she's young, but wise beyond her years," Robin replied, careful to keep his voice neutral. He didn't feel like admitting he'd been trapped into taking Jean Munro on as chatelaine. The captain would think he was turning daft for agreeing to something he didn't want. "Jean has helped her sister manage Castle Varrich … she'll fit in well here."

Actually, Robin thought the lass was well out of her depth and was hoping she'd come to her senses in a day or two and ask to be relieved of her duties so she could return to Varrich.

However, he didn't feel like admitting that either.

MacVane had led his guard for a few years now; the man was doggedly loyal. However, the captain's expression this evening was unconvinced. "Will Lady Jean be able to handle Grace? The lass has gotten a bit wild of late."

Robin's mouth thinned. He didn't like talking about this daughter and tried to spend as little time as possible with her. Every time he looked her way, he was reminded of Liosa: the lass was the mirror image of her bonny mother. Looking upon his daughter also dredged up gut-wrenching memories, ones that still twisted like a blade.

Ones he wished to bury forever.

Leaning back in his chair, Robin raked his hands through his short hair. He was tired this eve, and his nerves felt stretched tight after the events of the past day. Getting to his feet, he crossed to the sideboard. "Wine?" he asked, glancing the captain's way.

MacVane shook his head. "I'm about to take my watch on the walls ... wine will only send me to sleep."

Robin nodded, pleased the captain took his duties seriously. He could always rely on MacVane. However, *he* wouldn't be abstaining this evening. He needed something to take the edge off.

Pouring himself some sloe wine, Robin returned to the desk. He then took a deep draft from his goblet. "Jean will be good for Grace," he admitted after a pause. "She can continue her education."

After Liosa's departure, Grace had indeed run a bit wild. Robin had little time for her, and there were no bairns her age within the broch.

Robin's gut tightened then. Guilt. He was aware that it must have been a lonely life for his daughter, and Jean would provide the lass with much-needed companionship. Liosa had taught the lass her letters, and Robin recalled Jean telling him she and her sisters could all read and write.

Robin took another large gulp of wine, welcoming the soothing heat. Perhaps bringing Jean here wasn't a mistake after all. His new chatelaine could keep Grace occupied. She could give her the time and attention he couldn't.

"This is yer bed-chamber, Lady Jean."

Standing inside the small, damp stone room, Jean forced a bright expression and turned to the lass who'd just shown her inside. "Thank ye, Kenna … this will do nicely."

Kenna—a small, wiry lass with a mane of red hair and a scattering of pretty freckles across a pert nose—gave her a cautious smile in return. "I've just added another brick of peat to the fire … for the nights grow chilly."

Indeed, a fug of blue smoke filled the chamber. Jean would need to open the tiny window to get rid of the smoke, or she'd spend the whole night coughing. The glow of the hearth and the light of a stubby candle by the bed illuminated the room. Usually, such light made interiors look more inviting, yet there was no hiding the dampness of the stone walls and the drabness of the simple furnishings.

"I appreciate that, Kenna." Jean moved across to the canopied bed. Her saddlebags sat upon it; although she was weary, she'd need to unpack before going to bed. "I shall see ye tomorrow morning."

"Aye, the laird has left instructions that ye are to continue to join us in the kitchen at mealtimes."

This comment made Jean tense. She glanced over her shoulder to see that Kenna's gaze was downcast, her thin shoulders rigid. Jean was new to this role, yet she knew that stewards and chatelaines didn't sup with the servants. And so did Kenna, it seemed.

"Doesn't the laird wish me to eat with him and his daughter?" Jean asked, struggling to hide her disappointment. Once again, she felt at sea. It was going to take a while to find her feet here.

"Mackay takes his meals alone … as does Grace," Kenna replied.

Jean's brow furrowed. *What an odd, and decidedly lonely, habit.*

It would make her role harder too. As chatelaine, wasn't she supposed to discuss the running of the broch with the laird daily? Mealtimes provided an excellent opportunity to keep him updated.

Jean's frown deepened then. And why didn't he take his meals with his daughter? The poor lass must feel forgotten.

However, tonight wasn't the time to tackle such things. Jean was bone-weary after the day's travel. She'd just taken a supper of mutton stew and dumplings in the kitchen, where she'd met Brighde Neilson—the cook—and the rest of the servants. In addition to Kenna, her mother, Fiona, also served the laird, while a burly lad, Brian, did a lot of the heavy physical work within the broch.

"I shall bid ye good eve then, Kenna," Jean said after a pause.

Nodding, the lass turned and left the chamber.

Alone, Jean let out a heavy sigh. Her throat started to ache. Mother Mary, she suddenly felt so alone. She was tired and overwhelmed. Events had moved so fast that she hadn't been able to prepare for her new role.

Coughing, she walked to the window and rolled up the heavy sacking that protected the chamber from the elements. She really needed to clear the air in here.

Outside, the world lay in darkness. A still, clear night followed a bright day. Her window looked north, out to sea, where the water gleamed as if oiled, reflecting the hoary crescent of the moon.

The tightness in her throat intensified, and her vision blurred.

Eilidh.

This was the first night in her four and twenty winters that she'd slept apart from her sister. Like twins, they'd been swaddled together as bairns and had always shared the same bed. Every eve, the two sisters huddled under the covers and talked over the day's events.

It seemed too quiet in this depressing box of a chamber without her sister's chatter.

Such was Jean's eagerness to become Robin Mackay's chatelaine that she'd deliberately not let herself think of the implications of being separated from her younger sister. Eilidh hadn't been given time to get used to the idea either. In the space of a day, Jean had uprooted herself and moved away.

Swallowing hard, she desperately tried to dislodge the lump that had risen in her throat.

"Goose," she whispered to the night. "Did ye think this would be easy?"

Sniffing, she turned from the window and moved to the bed.

Desperate to distract herself, she unbuckled the first of her saddlebags and began removing the contents. A small iron railing sat in one corner of the chamber—and it was just as well that Jean hadn't brought many clothes with her, for there was barely space upon it for her kirtles and winter and summer cloaks.

On the way up from the kitchen, Kenna had told her this chamber had once belonged to the steward. Lachlan had slept in this room for nearly fifty years, and yet no trace of the old man remained.

A chill entered the chamber as Jean worked, but she welcomed the cold. It kept her alert. She couldn't retire until every item was put away; unlike Eilidh, who didn't mind if she lived surrounded by chaos, Jean was neat and orderly in her ways.

Her chest constricted. It had been a mistake to think about her sister. She was at a low ebb this evening as it was.

Blinking hard, Jean dug into the last of her saddlebags, carefully withdrawing one of her prized belongings: a small looking glass. Spotted with age and edged with flaking gold, the glass was once her mother's. When she died, each of the sisters had taken one of her treasured possessions as a keepsake: Eilidh wore her mother's jade ring upon her right hand.

Jean glimpsed her reflection in the glass and scowled.

"Heavens, I'm a fright," she muttered. Her face was pale and tired. The day's travel had left her hair and clothing disheveled. Frizzy strands had worked free of the tight bun she'd asked her maid to put up for her that morning.

No wonder the folk here were bemused by her. She didn't *look* like a chatelaine.

With a sigh, Jean placed the looking glass upon the nightstand next to the bed and emptied the rest of the saddlebag. Then she readied herself for bed.

This, too, felt odd—wrong. For years, she'd shared a maid with her three sisters, although when Neave moved away to Achness, Greta had gone with her. After that, a shy lass named Clara had served Jean and Eilidh at Varrich. Clara helped her dress in the mornings and did her hair; and in the evenings, the maid helped her ready herself for bed.

Now, Jean would have to do all those things herself, for it seemed Robin Mackay didn't intend to provide her with a maid.

"Ye aren't useless, lass," Jean chastised herself as she fumbled with the laces of her kirtle and wriggled out of the garment. "Ye have two good hands and sharp wits … ye'll just have to get used to looking after yerself."

Underneath her kirtle, she wore a long, floor-length lèine, although she hesitated to strip it off and sleep naked as she usually did. Jean felt vulnerable enough in her new environment and, as such, preferred to remain partially clothed.

She undid her hair and gave it a few deft swipes with a brush before crossing to the window. Rolling the sacking back down, leaving a gap so that smoke could escape overnight, Jean then knelt before the bed and clasped her hands together for her evening prayer.

The flagstones beneath her knees were ice-cold, yet she persisted. Unlike her sisters, Jean was devout, and she never missed an evening prayer.

"Dear Lord," she murmured, closing her eyes. "The evening comes. The day is done. Let peace wash over this household throughout the dark of night and in the few still hours of the next morning. Wipe away our troubles. Cleanse us of worry and doubt. Through Ye, may Yer magnificent good be our protection forever more. Amen."

Jean breathed a sigh and opened her eyes. As always, prayer calmed her.

She climbed into bed and blew out the candle. The bed ropes creaked as she tried to get comfortable upon the lumpy mattress, but the linen and blankets smelled clean enough. Nonetheless, she felt odd. Eilidh wasn't wriggling around, yanking at the covers.

A heavy sensation settled upon her breastbone then, yet Jean desperately fought it. She was strong; she wouldn't falter. Tomorrow was a new day—and she would start afresh.

7

THE KEEPER OF THE KEYS

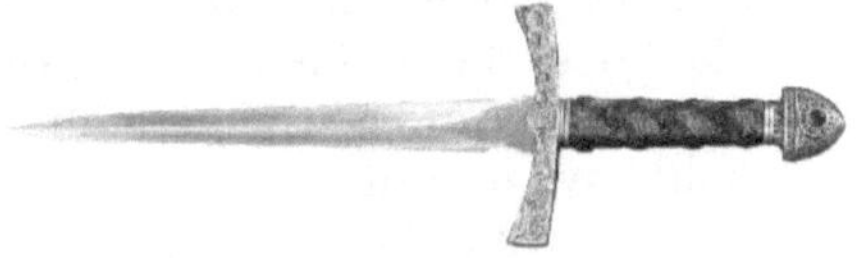

"I HOPE YE slept well, Lady Jean?"

Jean glanced up from slathering butter and heather honey onto a wedge of bannock, to see that Kenna was smiling shyly at her. The lass's expression was a trifle awkward, her gaze immediately dropping when Jean looked her way.

"Aye, thank ye." In truth, Jean hadn't. The lumpy bed and a racing mind had kept her awake for most of the night. And when the chill from the window had gotten too much, she'd been forced to get up and lower the sacking completely. Fortunately, the peat brick had burned down by that stage.

Jean shifted uncomfortably upon the bench seat then, aware that everyone at the table was observing her. Before her arrival at Melness, she'd never taken meals with servants. It felt awkward—for all of them.

An uncomfortable silence fell. Eventually, Kenna's mother, Fiona, broke it. "Ye must find this broch a little shabby, Lady Jean ... after living at Foulis and Varrich?"

"Not at all," Jean replied, favoring the servant with a smile. "And please ... just call me Jean."

Fiona's brow creased as if she wasn't comfortable with the request. However, Jean had a practical nature: there wasn't any point in the servants addressing her as 'Lady' Jean when she took her meals with them.

Silence fell at the large scrubbed table that dominated the kitchen. Jean took a mouthful of bannock and focused her attention on the wooden plate before her. She could almost taste Fiona's curiosity. No doubt she itched to know why a clan-chief's daughter had taken such a position.

Once again, nervousness spiraled up within Jean.

What would they think if they knew the real reason? Now she was here, her plan to get to know Robin Mackay better seemed filled with flaws. She would have her hands full just learning how to be a chatelaine.

Romance would have to wait.

"We're grateful to have ye here, Jean," Brighde spoke up then, smiling at her as she wiped floury hands on her apron. "It's been a difficult few months since auld Lachlann died." She paused then, her gaze shadowing. "He held this place together."

Jean smiled, grateful for the cook's warmth. She didn't appear as uncomfortable as the other servants. Upon meeting Brighde Neilson the eve before, she'd immediately taken a liking to her. Green-eyed, with raven-black hair and milk-white skin, Brighde was at least five years Jean's elder. She was small and curvaceous and carried herself with confidence. Today, Brighde wore a form-fitting green kirtle that matched her mossy eyes. The scooped neckline revealed a lush swell of cleavage; Jean had caught Brian staring at it more than once while they consumed their bannocks.

"And I look forward to getting to know ye all," Jean replied shyly. Suddenly tongue-tied, she glanced back down at her half-eaten bannock. What was she supposed to say now? She didn't want to come across as bossy or, worse still, foolish.

"I imagine you'll need to talk to us about our roles and daily routines," Brighde said, coming to her rescue. "But that can wait ... the laird has asked that ye go up to his solar after breaking yer fast."

Jean nodded, grateful for the cook's assistance. Robin Mackay had locked himself away since their arrival at Melness, but she couldn't start work without receiving instructions from him.

"We're out of bannock in the hall, Brighde." A man's voice intruded then, causing Jean to swivel around. Captain MacVane lounged in the doorway, arms folded over his chest. He wore a half-smile that made Jean suspect he'd been listening in on their conversation. "Instead of ordering our new chatelaine around, ye should be making sure my men don't start work with empty bellies."

The cook's eyes narrowed, her chin lifting as she stared the captain down. "Another round of bannock is on its way," she replied, her tone clipped. Then, to demonstrate her point, she flipped the large round cake she'd been cooking upon the griddle onto a platter and thrust it out to him. "Here ... since ye are here, ye might as well take it out."

MacVane grinned. Wordlessly, he stepped forward, took the platter, and then winked at Brighde. Silence followed him as he returned to the hall.

"Insolent churl," Brighde muttered, grabbing her last ball of dough, and flattening it—with more force than was necessary—into a cake. She slammed it down on the griddle. "I hope he chokes on it."

Noting Jean's look of surprise, Fiona smiled. "Don't mind them ... Danny's day isn't complete unless he's riled up Brighde. In truth, I think she secretly enjoys it."

The cook's answering snort, followed by a muttered oath, denied these words.

Jean looked down, swallowing a smile. Despite the initial awkwardness, she was relaxing among the members of her new household. Nonetheless, she couldn't linger down here. Robin was waiting to talk to her.

Pushing aside the remnants of her bannock, she rose from the bench seat. "I'd better go upstairs and speak with the laird."

Jean left the kitchen, which was a stone annex built onto the back of the tower, and entered the hall beyond. Feet crunching on rushes that looked as though they needed changing, she crossed the circular space. MacVane and his men sat at long trestle tables, finishing their morning meal. A large hearth burned at one end of the hall, and a great shield and axes hung above the mantel, iron gleaming in the firelight.

She took the narrow circular stairs from the hall up to the first floor of the broch. The chieftain's solar was located here. Kenna had given Jean a brief tour of the tower the eve before, explaining that the first floor housed the solar and the library, while the second floor housed the sleeping quarters for the chieftain's kin and steward. The third floor held the guest chambers, and the laird's quarters took up the entire fourth level of the broch.

Reaching the door to the solar, Jean gave it a brisk knock.

"Enter," a man's voice greeted her.

Jean heaved in a deep breath, squared her shoulders, and pushed the door open. Today, she needed to start in the manner she wished to continue: with confidence and purpose. She needed to be like Beth. Her sister had stepped into her role as clan-chief's wife and chatelaine of Varrich with grace and self-assurance. Niel Mackay could be an intimidating man—far more so than the chieftain of Melness—but Beth had been indomitable.

Jean stepped into a chamber that smelled of leather and peat smoke. Robin Mackay was seated behind a large oaken desk in one corner, scribbling something with a quill into a leather-bound ledger. His fingers were stained black with ink; he'd clearly been at work for a while.

Jean couldn't help it; her gaze roamed over the laird. Dressed in a cream-colored lèine, open at the neck, with a quilted grey gambeson on top, and chamois braes, Robin Mackay cut a virile figure. However, the daylight filtering in through the open window highlighted the deep lines on either side of his mouth and his furrowed brow.

I wonder what he looks like when he smiles, Jean thought. In the time they'd known each other, the most he'd managed was a slight lifting of the corners of his lips.

A chill breeze filtered in through the window, yet Mackay didn't seem to notice, for a fire roared in the large hearth. Sheepskins covered the icy flagstones, and a great boar's head hung above the fire. The beast seemed to glare at Jean, its great, yellowed tusks gleaming.

Swallowing, she pulled her woolen shawl tightly around her and stepped forward. "Ye wished to see me, Mackay?"

Robin glanced up, his hazel eyes settling upon her. He looked tired, she noted. Had he slept badly too? The thought made warmth filter through her, an odd kind of kinship, before she chastised herself. She needed to be practical, not fanciful.

"Aye," he said, rising to his feet. "I take it ye find yer lodgings to yer liking, Jean?"

It was a question, yet Jean sensed she wasn't supposed to complain about the damp, squalid chamber, and so she held her tongue. Instead, she nodded. She'd do her best to freshen the room up herself as soon as she had the time. A wash of lime and some dried herbs to scent the air would work wonders.

Satisfied, Robin turned and removed a heavy set of iron keys from the wall behind him. "Lachlan wore these at all times," he said, handing the keys to her. "The man could never sneak up on ye with his keys jangling at his waist. They unlock every door in this broch and all the outbuildings. Look after them well."

Jean deftly tied the keys to the belt about her waist. They were heavy, although she imagined she'd get used to the weight soon enough. "I will guard them with my life," she promised. "And I assure ye, I won't try to sneak up on ye either … I prefer the direct approach."

She flashed him a smile, but Robin didn't return it. Instead, the chieftain nodded brusquely before motioning to the ledger still open on the desk between them. "Lachlan kept a record of the accounts in here. I've just finished updating it this morning … so ye should find everything ready."

Feeling a little embarrassed that he hadn't responded to her teasing, Jean peered down at the neat rows of numbers. Her pulse quickened. She'd never looked after accounts before, although she'd helped Beth and Neave

take inventories of the spence and the granary at
Varrich. This couldn't be much more complicated, could
it?

"Ye are to keep the ledger in the library and update it
regularly," Robin went on briskly. "We have monthly
deliveries of grain, as well as provisions from Inverness.
Ye are to take responsibility for storage."

Jean nodded eagerly. Fortunately, she liked
organizing stores; it was a task that suited her orderly
nature. "And my other duties?" she asked.

Robin closed the ledger and passed it to her.
Clutching the heavy leather-bound volume to her breast,
Jean watched him expectantly.

"I receive few visitors these days, so ye won't have
much to do there," he replied. "However, the daily
function of the broch will be yer responsibility."

"Do ye have any special instructions for when ye are
absent from Melness?" she asked.

"When I'm away, Captain MacVane will take charge.
If he isn't available, one of the other warriors will act as
steward. Yer ken is the household." He paused then. "I
have been blessed with loyal servants ... however, Fiona
is prone to prattling rather than working ... ye'll need a
firm hand with her ... and with Brian. The lad can be an
idler."

Jean took this in with a nod. The news that MacVane
would take responsibility for Melness broch during his
absences disappointed her. When the clan-chief was
away, Beth assumed control of Castle Varrich. Did
Mackay not think her capable?

Jaw firming, Jean resolved to show him that she was.

"In addition to yer chatelaine duties," Robin went on,
walking to the open window and looking out, "ye are also
to take charge of my daughter." He fell silent then, the
sounds of hammering from the barmkin below drifting
into the solar. "Grace has learned her letters, but she
needs instruction on more womanly matters. Ye shall
teach her to sew, embroider, and weave."

"Of course," Jean replied, even as her mind started to
scramble. Mother Mary, her days would certainly be

busy here. "I'm happy to teach her such things." She paused then. "I can also teach her French … and how to play the harp, if ye wish?"

Robin glanced over his shoulder. "Such accomplishments should help her find a husband when the day comes." His expression was carefully veiled. It was as if he wasn't talking about his daughter but of someone of no importance to him. There was no emotion in his voice or warmth in his eyes.

Jean didn't understand it. Robin Mackay had failed to mention his daughter before her arrival, almost as if she was of no relevance.

Surely, he couldn't be so unfeeling?

"I look forward to meeting Grace properly," Jean said, favoring him with a brittle smile. The tension between them hadn't eased as she'd hoped. Robin's manner remained reserved, distant, and the silences between them were awkward.

"Come." The laird moved away from the window. He passed Jean and headed purposefully toward the door. "I shall introduce ye to her now."

8

NEVER TO BE SPOKEN OF

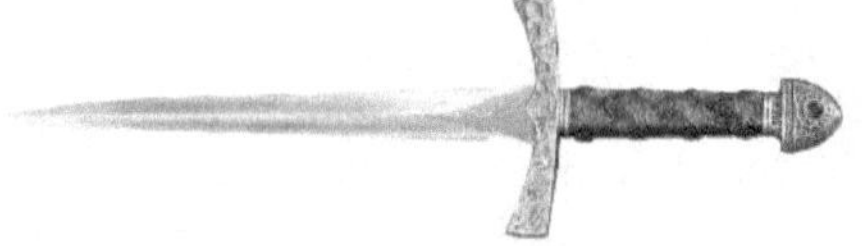

JEAN HURRIED OUT of the solar, following the chieftain across the landing. Throwing open the door opposite, he led her through into the library—a similarly sized chamber to his solar, yet much more inviting. A small bookcase filled with precious leather-bound books sat against one wall, while a pair of high-backed chairs faced a glowing hearth. An oaken table dominated the room, with an empty cup and a dish scattered with crumbs on it.

And upon a window seat filled with colorfully embroidered cushions sat Grace Mackay. She was reading a small book, although, upon spying her father, promptly dropped it, her large hazel eyes flying open wide.

"Da!" The lass leaped off the window seat, cheeks flushing in pleasure.

Jean's chest constricted; it was clear Robin didn't venture into the library often.

"Morning, Grace," he said briskly. "I'd like ye to meet Lady Jean ... she will be taking over Lachlan's duties ... *and* she will be yer new tutor."

Grace nodded, her gaze swiveling to Jean. The curiosity on her face was plain; she'd spied Jean's arrival the afternoon before and likely wished to know all about their new chatelaine. The lass gave a neat curtsy. "Good morning, Lady Jean."

Jean smiled back. "Please ... just call me Jean." She then glanced over at Robin. "I've asked all the servants to address me so," she explained, noting his frown. "I'm a chatelaine, not the lady of the keep."

Robin Mackay's frown deepened. However, he gave a brusque nod and stepped back. "Well, I shall leave ye two to get better acquainted. Ye shall spend some time every morning with Grace ... and again later in the day once yer other duties have been seen to." His attention flicked to the empty cup and dish upon the table. "And get Kenna to clear the table ... both she and Fiona have gotten lax of late."

With that, the laird turned on his heel and exited the library, leaving both his chatelaine and daughter in silence.

Grace Mackay was watching her, intelligent gaze bright.

Jean smiled back, even as she wondered how she was supposed to find time to run this broch if she was to tutor and be companion to his daughter for large chunks of the day.

Stifling a sigh, she moved to the table and picked up the cup and dish.

"Kenna is supposed to do that," Grace pointed out.

"Aye, but since I need to speak to her, I might as well take these down to the kitchen," Jean replied. She glanced over at the book Grace had abandoned when they'd entered the library. "What were ye reading?"

"A book of psalms." Grace pulled a face then. "I know them all by heart ... but the rest of the books in here"— she gestured to the bookcase behind Jean— "are too boring."

"Well, ye are in luck ... for I'm a keen reader and have brought some of my favorite stories with me. I shall fetch them shortly." Jean grinned at her as she made for the door. "In the meantime, find us some parchment, ink, and a quill. We shall start the day with some writing."

Jean watched the lass write out a sentence, her face scrunched in concentration. It was clear she was out of practice, yet her calligraphy was neat enough.

"Who taught ye to write?" she asked, breaking the companionable silence in the library. They were nearing the end of their morning lessons, and Jean was eager to go downstairs and talk to Brighde. Even so, Grace Mackay had proved to be a delightful child: earnest and eager to learn.

The lass glanced up, her pretty face tensing. "Ma did."

Jean immediately regretted the question. She'd assumed there had been a tutor in the past.

"Well, she did a fine job," Jean replied, injecting a bright tone into her voice to cover up her embarrassment. Best she pretended that she didn't know about Grace's mother.

"Ma loved to read and write," Grace replied, glancing back down at the sheet of parchment. "I miss her."

Jean swallowed. She wasn't sure how to reply. She couldn't just sit in silence, so she eventually murmured, "Of course ye do ... every lass needs her mother."

Something in her voice must have betrayed her, for Grace looked up, curiosity lighting in her eyes. "Where's yer Ma?"

Jean favored her with a soft smile. "She died ... a few years ago now." She paused then, even as a familiar sadness tightened her throat. "But I still miss her. She was a wonderful woman."

Grace stared back at her, a myriad of emotions playing across her face. The lass was hungry for connection; Jean had sensed her loneliness the moment she'd set eyes on her the day before. "Ma said she loved me," she said, her voice catching. "But then she went away."

Jean's breathing caught. Hades, did the lass know why? She had to tread carefully, lest she inadvertently revealed something she shouldn't. She'd need to talk to Robin later and find out exactly how much Grace knew.

"Ye must feel alone here," Jean replied after a pause. "I know I would have ... if I'd grown up without my sisters."

Grace's gaze widened. "How many sisters do ye have?"

"Three ... two elder and one younger. Our household growing up was a noisy one. I'm sure my poor father despaired."

It was the wrong thing to say, for Grace's chin started to tremble, tears gleaming in her eyes. "My father also despairs," she said huskily. "After Ma left, he stopped smiling. He never talks to me now ... he doesn't even look at me." The lass drew in a shaky breath. "Maybe it's my fault Ma left."

Jean's breathing hitched, pressure building under her breastbone.

The poor lass. Jean's heart ached for her. How could Mackay be so insensitive? Aye, she would need to talk to him about Grace—and soon.

This couldn't be allowed to continue.

Drawing a deep breath, Jean knocked on the door to the solar.

A long day was coming to a close, and she'd just come from the kitchen and a delicious meal of roast mutton. Now her stomach was full—as was her head, for Brighde had spent the meal explaining the daily running of the kitchen—she was tempted to continue upstairs to her chamber, where she would collapse upon her lumpy bed in exhaustion.

But first, she had to talk to the laird.

After her brief meeting with Robin Mackay that morning, the chieftain hadn't spoken to her again. She'd seen him only once: crossing the barmkin toward the stables, deep in conversation with Captain MacVane.

But all day, as she learned about this broch, and of those who resided within its walls, the words she'd exchanged with Grace in the morning haunted her.

The lass was suffering—and her father needed to know.

"Aye," a gruff male voice called out.

It wasn't a welcoming tone, yet Jean exhaled sharply and pushed the door open, stepping inside the solar.

The chieftain sat alone at an oaken table in the center of the space. He'd finished his supper yet lingered over a goblet of wine. The sacking had been lowered over the window, for an icy wind gusted off the sea this evening, and the fire guttered in the hearth.

Glancing her way, Robin Mackay frowned. "Jean," he greeted her brusquely. "Ye aren't to collect my dishes … let Kenna or Fiona do that."

"Kenna will be up shortly to take yer dishes away," Jean informed him.

She'd already had a 'talk' with the mother and daughter earlier that day, gently letting them know that they weren't to leave dirty dishes lying around in future. Kenna had flushed with embarrassment, while Fiona had scowled. Jean had realized with a sinking heart that she risked making herself unpopular; even so, Fiona was a strong-willed woman used to doing as she pleased. The chieftain was right: instead of gossiping, she needed to be attending to her duties. When she'd gone downstairs with Grace's dishes that morning, Fiona was still lounging at the table, chattering away to Brighde, while the cook attempted to clean up around her.

Robin frowned. "Why are ye here then?"

"I wish to talk to ye … about Grace."

His frown deepened. "Is something wrong?"

"Aye." Jean moved forward, although Robin didn't rise from the table. "Yer daughter blames herself for yer wife's departure." The words were bald, and she hadn't meant them to come out quite so bluntly. But Jean wasn't the type to bandy words.

Nonetheless, it was clear Robin Mackay hadn't appreciated her candid observation. His features tightened, and his mouth compressed. He then slammed his pewter goblet down on the table, wine sloshing over the rim, and got to his feet. "What are ye doing discussing my wife with Grace?" he demanded, his voice cold.

Jean started to sweat. "I wasn't," she assured him. "We were talking about me actually … and my sister and parents. Grace merely came out with it. I didn't ask her."

"Ye are not to speak of Liosa Mackay with my daughter. Ever," he replied, biting each word out. "Is that clear?"

Jean stared back at him. His wintry anger unnerved her, yet underneath her discomfort, she could feel her own temper quickening. "And I shall not," she answered, her tone hardening. "But are ye going to continue to let yer daughter blame herself for what is clearly not her fault?"

Robin muttered an oath under his breath before shoving back his chair and moving toward her.

Jean held her ground, even as he drew close, his gaze pinning her to the floor. She hadn't realized Robin Mackay was this easily vexed, and was now sorely regretting being so open with him. However, there was a part of her that didn't wish to back down. He was being unreasonable.

"Grace has no cause to believe such," he ground out.

"Perhaps she wouldn't if ye would talk to her."

He glared down at her. A nerve jumped under his eye. "My relationship with Grace is none of yer business," he growled.

Jean's belly clenched. She hadn't wanted to upset him, yet she clearly had. Aye, the man was being unreasonable, but she could sense the hurt boiling just beneath. She'd unwittingly awoken a sleeping dragon. "I'm sorry, Mackay," she murmured. "I spoke hastily … it won't happen again."

Silence fell, and their gazes remained fused.

Nearby, the fire popped and hissed, and when Robin Mackay finally spoke, his voice was low and hard. "The things that took place under this roof between me, my brother, and my wife, are never to be spoken of. Grace knows little of what happened … and it shall stay that way."

Jean nodded. She wished to back away from him, anything to distance herself from his simmering fury, yet her feet seemed to have grown roots.

"Ye are a woman used to having her own way. That much is clear," he continued, his jaw flexing. "At Varrich, ye had a special status, being the clan-chief's sister-by-marriage ... but here ye are my *servant*." Jean flinched at the way he bit out that word, but Mackay hadn't yet finished telling her off. "Here, ye shall mind yer tongue and do yer duties, Jean. And unless an emergency drives ye to my door, ye are *not* to bother me in the evenings. Do I make myself plain?"

Jean stared back at him, a lump rising in her throat. "Aye," she whispered. The man couldn't have made himself plainer.

Robin stepped back then, his expression shuttering. "Now that's settled, I shall bid ye good eve."

9

FOOLISH WHIMSY

ROBIN LISTENED TO Jean's soft footfalls receding as she climbed the stairs beyond his solar toward her bed-chamber.

"Chac," he muttered. *Shit.* Plucking his goblet off the table, he drained the remaining wine in one gulp.

What had just come over him? He'd never spoken to a woman like that before, not with such biting fury. Not even Liosa—even when she'd baited him. Not even on that fateful day when she'd deserved it.

He'd barely recognized himself as he loomed over his chatelaine. She'd stared up at him, wide-eyed, while he told her off. And yet she hadn't shrunken back from him.

Jean Munro was no coward.

But he was a bastard.

The urge to go after her and apologize reared up, yet he quashed it. Let her think him cruel; it was better that way.

He couldn't have her knocking on his door in the evenings. Something about Jean's manner made him wish for her to linger in his company; it had since the first time she'd sat down next to him in the great hall of Castle Varrich.

But he didn't want her company—and he didn't want her prying into his past.

Yer daughter blames herself for yer wife's departure.

Robin's breathing caught, and his chest began to ache.

In truth, Jean's admission had been a slap to the face. Aye, he avoided his daughter these days, for good reason, yet he'd never blamed her for what happened with Liosa. It wasn't the lass's fault.

He should tell her so.

"Chac," he muttered once more. He then dragged his hand down his face and carried his empty goblet over to the sideboard, refilling it with sloe wine. He was drinking too heavily in the evenings of late, yet wine was the only thing that blunted the memories.

He couldn't talk to Grace about her mother. If he did, he wasn't sure what he'd say, what awful truths would spill from his lips. His silence protected the lass, yet Grace wouldn't understand that.

And neither did Jean.

Aye, he'd been harsh with her—unnecessarily so—but his chatelaine had to be put in her place. He couldn't keep her on if she continued to pry.

The past needed to stay buried, and he would see that it did.

Blinded by tears, Jean stumbled into her bed-chamber and made her way over to the bed. The ropes creaked as she sank down onto the mattress and covered her face with her hands.

"Daft woman," she berated herself. "Ye have overstepped."

Aye, but Robin Mackay has the manners of a goat, her pride hissed back. *How dare he speak to me thus?*

Indeed, she had transgressed, but her motives had been good, for she'd hated seeing Grace so upset, believing that her father blamed her for her mother's departure. She'd thought Robin would wish to know, but instead, she'd enraged him.

Panic seized her then, cutting through the hurt and indignation.

What if he sends me away?

Squeezing her eyes shut, she imagined the humiliation of returning to Castle Varrich, and having to tell Beth and Eilidh she'd been thrown out.

Eilidh would be sympathetic, yet Beth would give her that look: the one she'd favored Jean with many a time over the years. Affection mingled with frustration. Jean knew she, like Neave, had a habit of interfering in others' business. There was no malice in it—only a genuine need to help others—but Robin Mackay merely saw her as a mouthy meddler.

Jean opened her eyes, her gaze traveling around her squalid wee bed-chamber. Not for the first time, loneliness assailed her. She wasn't used to being away from family, being apart from those who loved and understood her. She drew in a deep breath, clenching her hands upon her lap so tightly that her fingernails bit into her palms.

What a goose I am!

Her father had often told her that a rash act could lead to remorse, and he was right. Girlish infatuation for Robin Mackay had clouded her judgment. She was working for a man who barely tolerated her.

Her dreams of courtship and love seemed foolish whimsy now.

She'd gotten herself into a right mess.

Jean got up from her bed and crossed to the hearth. Kenna had been up here earlier and lit the fire and a candle. It was a cold night, and the brick of peat hardly seemed to take the bite off the air. Jean wouldn't be opening the window tonight. She'd just have to suffer the cloying smoke.

She took hold of the poker and stabbed at the fire, watching as golden sparks flew up the chimney. Her jaw set then, resolve filtering through her.

She couldn't let loneliness and regret drag her down.

Mackay might not want her here, but she wouldn't let a few harsh words cow her; besides, Grace needed a companion and tutor. The lass had been sorely neglected.

Jean had learned a valuable lesson today, one she'd heed.

Life wasn't sonnets and vows of undying love. Beth and Neave were lucky indeed to have found men who worshipped them, but fortune didn't shine on Jean as it did her elder sisters. Instead, she would make the most of what God had given her: sharp wits and resourcefulness.

"I'll show ye, Mackay," she muttered to the crackling hearth. "I'll be the best chatelaine the Highlands has ever seen."

Captain Danny MacVane inclined his head, a groove forming between his eyebrows. "Ye want me to look at the accounts with ye?"

Jean shifted uneasily and gripped the heavy ledger to her breast. "Aye … if ye wouldn't mind … just this once."

MacVane's frown deepened. "Ye should really ask the laird … he looked after that side of things after Lachlan died."

"I'd rather not." Jean lifted her chin, eyeballing the Captain of the Melness Guard. "I'd appreciate yer assistance, Captain."

The noon meal had just ended, and she'd seized the opportunity to talk to MacVane as he lingered by the hearth in the hall with a tankard of ale. She'd waited until he was alone, for she didn't want his men gawking at her while she showed her ineptitude. In truth, she'd spent the last two days poring over the accounts, but had difficulty understanding some of the abbreviations both the former steward and Mackay used. And pride dictated she didn't approach the laird about it.

With a sigh, MacVane set down his tankard. "Very well … let's have a look."

Smiling, Jean slid onto the bench seat next to him and opened the ledger at the most recent entries. "The numbers all make sense to me," she admitted, running a fingertip down the right-hand column. "But what do those abbreviations in the two left-hand columns mean?"

MacVane frowned, leaning forward. Jean tensed, heat flooding across her chest. What if the captain couldn't read, and she was about to unwittingly embarrass him? Most soldiers didn't learn their letters, for they had no use for it. But surely MacVane would have refused to help her if that had been the case?

"The column on the far left tells us the subject of the entry," the captain said after a pause, and Jean let out the breath she'd been holding. "'Gr' is for the granary stores. 'Bl' is for building projects."

"Wait … I need to write this down," Jean muttered. Pulling out a thin wooden tablet from the back of the ledger and a stub of charcoal from a pouch at her waist, she hurriedly scratched out the abbreviations and their meanings. "Go on."

MacVane indulged her, going through each one before he explained that the middle column was for a description. Here too, there were many abbreviations used—and he deciphered them for her as well.

Jean nodded and scribbled, eagerly taking every word in.

Although her encounter with Mackay, and his rebuke, still stung, she was determined to prove to him that she could run his household seamlessly.

When they were done, Jean sat back and flashed MacVane a wide smile. "Thank ye, Captain … ye've been a great help."

MacVane studied her face, his mouth curving. "Ye are a surprise, Jean Munro," he admitted.

Jean carefully replaced her wooden tablet inside the ledger and closed the heavy volume. "How so?"

"I wasn't sure ye'd last a day here." He paused then, his smile widening. "But ye have more pluck than I thought."

Jean's mouth pursed. She wasn't sure whether to be flattered or insulted by his words. "All of the women in my family are stubborn," she admitted, deciding she'd take it as a compliment. "We don't give up at the first hurdle."

MacVane grinned. "Glad to hear it."

"Even so … I did need yer assistance. Thank ye, Captain."

MacVane nodded before pushing himself to his feet. "Ye're welcome, Jean … and call me Danny."

Jean watched him leave the hall. MacVane's stride was loose-limbed, arrogant; it matched his personality. However, he'd just proved he wasn't all swagger—as Brighde swore. There was a thoughtful man under that brash exterior, and a kind one too.

Picking up the ledger, Jean headed toward the stairs. Now that she could decipher the accounts, she needed to spend an hour or two studying them. The grain merchant was due later in the afternoon, and she wanted to be ready for him.

For the first time in days, Jean mounted the stairs with a smile gracing her lips.

She hadn't mastered her new role yet—but she would.

10

WE SHALL BE WAITING

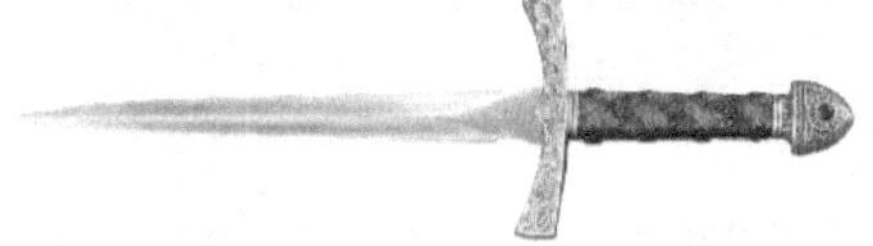

"ISN'T IT TOO cold and wet to go to market?"

"Nonsense, lass. Ye have yer cloak. We don't want to miss this one. With Yule approaching, there will be vendors from all over the Highlands there today."

Jean and Grace crossed the barmkin, heading toward the gates that led out to the village. They both carried baskets under their arms, wore fur-lined boots, and had donned woolen cloaks for their walk. Emerging from beyond the broch's sturdy walls, Jean blinked as a stinging wind—laced with sleet—chapped her cheeks.

It was indeed bracing, now that they'd just passed from autumn to winter, Jean liked to get Grace out of the broch whenever possible. She'd been at Melness around a moon; soon the ground would be frozen, and snow would lie for weeks on end. They had to seize the opportunity while they still had it.

Leaving the broch behind, they walked down the incline into the village. Melness was a small hamlet, around half the size of Tongue, yet it was indeed bustling this morning. There was a market in the small dirt square at the heart of it, where farmers hawked fresh cabbages, turnips, and onions. Geese honked in an enclosure as Jean and Grace passed by. A man wrapped in swathes of fur, his nose red from the cold, was haggling with the farmer over the fattest of the geese, their indignant voices drifting over the market.

"We always had roast goose for Yule at Foulis," Jean remarked to the lass with a smile, even as a pang of homesickness tugged at her chest. "Although at Varrich, the clan-chief prefers suckling pig stuffed with apples and chestnuts.”

“I’ve never been to Castle Varrich.” A wistful expression settled across Grace’s delicately featured face. She’d pulled up her hood, and fur framed her pink cheeks. “Ma told me it is magnificent.”

“It is … a great fortress perched high upon a rocky outcrop.”

Grace’s lips parted. “Ye must have a bonny view from up so high?”

“Ye do … in one direction, ye look across the Kyle of Tongue, and then in another, ye can spy the outlines of the mighty Ben Hope and its twin, Ben Loyal.”

The lass nodded, taking in Jean’s description. “Yuletide must be special indeed there.” Grace then glanced back at where the man now handed a silver penny across to the beaming farmer.

“We haven’t had roast goose for a while,” Grace murmured, her tone subdued. “Not since Ma left.”

“How does Melness celebrate Yuletide then?”

The lass’s face shadowed. “We don’t … really. The servants dine together in the kitchen, but Da and I eat alone.”

Jean resisted the urge to frown. “Ye don’t dine together at Yuletide?”

Grace shook her head. “Not anymore.”

Digesting this, Jean tensed. It didn’t matter how he grieved what had befallen him, Robin Mackay had no right to make his daughter suffer.

“This Yuletide, ye and I shall eat together,” she assured the lass. “And I will ensure Brighde roasts a goose for the occasion.” She smiled then. “Would ye like to help me make wreaths and decorations of ivy and mistletoe for the broch?”

Grace grinned, the shadow on her pretty face disappearing. “Aye, Jean!”

Jean’s smile widened at the lass’s enthusiasm. “Then that is what we shall do.” She paused. “However, it’s too early to collect such things. Today, let’s visit the soap seller. I noticed we're almost out … do ye prefer lavender, rosemary, or rose?"

Grace squealed, the happy sound cutting through the howl of the wind. "Rose!"

It occurred to Jean then that it was the first time she'd seen the lass show real joy—and a kernel of warmth germinated under her breastbone at the sight. The lingering ache of loss that had arisen in her breast at the thought of Yuletides passed with her sisters eased a little. She could make new memories here, with Grace. "Come on then." She hooked her arm through Grace's, and they wove their way through the milling crowd, heads bowed against the wind. The soap seller hunched under a flapping awning. However, his expression brightened when he spied their approach. "I wonder if he has any Damask rose … that's my sister Eilidh's favorite."

Behind a stall selling candles and lanterns, a man and a woman watched Grace Mackay and her companion chat animatedly with the soap merchant. A particularly violent gust of wind barreled through the market square then, blowing back Grace's hood.

Watching her, Liosa Mackay's throat tightened. There was no mistaking the lass's bright yellow curls. "It's her," she whispered, her fingers clenching around the candle she'd been pretending to admire.

"Aye … she's a beauty, just like her mother."

Liosa glanced up at the broad-shouldered man next to her. Gordon's hazel eyes glittered as he peered across the market. Like her, he wore a deep cowl to hide his face, but she was standing close enough to see his expression.

They'd taken a risk coming back to Melness, and mingling with the folk at market, but it was worth it. Fortunately, the weather had been their ally, for the locals were too busy clutching at their cloaks and hurrying to get their shopping done, to pay much attention to the other folk in the crowd.

Liosa turned back to watch her daughter charming the soap merchant. A small woman wearing a heavy winter mantle accompanied Grace. No doubt, Robin had hired a maid to look after the lass.

"She's growing so tall." Liosa's voice caught then. Her vision blurred, and she hurriedly blinked, fighting back tears. She couldn't weep, not now. Instead, she needed to act. She and Gordon had been living at Hexham, upon the Anglo-Scottish border, for a while; it had been a long journey up to the Highlands. She couldn't bear to turn away now, to leave empty-handed. "This is our chance," she whispered, putting down the candle and stepping back from the stall. The chandler selling these wares had just finished speaking to someone and was moving toward her. "We can follow them and wait until Grace's companion is distracted."

"No, mo ghràdh," Gordon said softly. "There are too many people around. Someone will see ... and look ... there are Robin's men-at-arms in the crowd."

Liosa's gaze swept right, her jaw tightening when she spied a handful of men from Melness garrison weaving through the press. Liosa's gaze narrowed as she recognized Danny MacVane among them. Curse him. Unlike the chandler, the captain would recognize Liosa and Gordon on sight.

Liosa's chest started to ache. "I don't want to leave her here," she muttered between clenched teeth.

Gordon shifted close. An instant later, his hand fastened upon her shoulder, squeezing gently. "I understand ye wish to see her ... but we take a great risk straying this close to the broch. We can't linger."

"I know," Liosa whispered back. However, she didn't move. Indeed, Gordon spoke sense, yet she still railed against leaving without Grace. She'd never loved her husband, not during their courtship or after the wedding. She'd merely wed Robin to escape her bullying father—but her daughter was precious to her. After their wedding, Liosa had met Robin's younger brother. Big, buff, with a swagger she couldn't resist, Gordon Mackay should have been the first-born, not his dull, soft-hearted brother.

It was inevitable that she and Gordon would become lovers. She had no regrets about taking up with him—only that Robin had discovered their affair.

Only that she'd been forced to leave Grace behind.

"Ye shall have her back," Gordon continued, his tone soothing. "But we must plan this properly, or we risk failure. Winter is almost upon us … and Grace isn't likely to be seen outside the village for a while. But come spring, she will venture farther afield … and we shall be waiting."

"Spring." The ache in Liosa's chest deepened. "But that's months away."

His grip upon her shoulder tightened. "Ye have already waited three years, love," he murmured. "What are another few months?"

11

DELIBERATE DISOBEDIENCE

"I NEED YE to sort out the spence this morning, Kenna," Jean instructed, ushering the lass into the alcove at the far end of the kitchen. "We must make sure we have everything for Yuletide."

Kenna rolled up her sleeves and nodded. Floor-to-ceiling wooden shelves surrounded them. The scent of dried herbs mingled with the ripe odor of maturing cheese.

Halting, Jean ran a critical eye over the space. She'd taken a look in here shortly after her arrival at Melness but had been too busy to focus on it since. The larder was a dusty, chaotic jumble. "And make sure ye wipe down all the shelves."

Jean emerged from the spence to find Brighde chopping turnips for the noon meal, the rhythmic banging of a knife against wood echoing off the kitchen's stone walls. "I'm going down to the village," she greeted the cook. "Do ye want me to pick ye anything up?"

Brighde shook her head. "Wrap up well … it's freezing out there."

"It's not that warm in here either," Jean pointed out, shivering. "When ye see Fiona, tell her to add an extra brick of peat to the hearths in all the bed-chambers."

Satisfied the servants were all dealt with for the moment, Jean left the kitchen and went upstairs, retrieving her fur mantle from her chamber. A short while later, stepping outdoors, she whispered a curse under her breath.

Brighde hadn't been exaggerating. God's bones, it was cold enough to freeze her innards this morning. As it often did this far north, winter had hit with the force of a mailed fist. Even on days when the sky was clear and the wind didn't howl, the sun held no warmth.

But there was no sun today. The sky was the color of wood smoke, and the wind howled like a banshee, bringing with it stinging needles of hail. Yule was only three days away; she wouldn't have been surprised if snow arrived before then.

Jean didn't want to venture beyond the sheltering walls of the broch, yet she'd promised Grace they'd make decorations for Yule. There was an old, gnarled oak behind the kirk, on the southern edge of the village, and now that the leaves had dropped, she'd spotted drualus—mistletoe—growing amongst its boughs. There were also holly bushes growing on the edge of the kirkyard and ivy creeping over the shady edge of the kirk itself.

She should be able to fill her basket soon enough. Drawing her fur-lined cloak tightly about herself, she quickened her pace.

Keys rattling at her side, Jean set off toward the gate. However, she was halfway across the barmkin when a movement to her right caught her eye. Her step faltered, and she halted, swiveling to see a warrior, stripped to the waist, practicing with a battle-axe.

Jean knew she really shouldn't stand there and gawk like a half-wit, yet she couldn't help herself. In the two months she'd been at Melness, she'd pushed her infatuation to the back of her mind. But it didn't change the fact that Robin Mackay was a sight to behold.

She'd heard his weapon of choice was the axe. Her father had always favored a claidheamh-mòr—the great Scottish broadsword that had to be wielded two-handed—but the chieftain of Melness swung his axe with deadly precision.

Mackay currently had his back to her. Sweat gleamed off his naked skin. He struck, undercut, and thrust with the axe, throwing his entire bodyweight into it, and rotating with each strike as the axe blade whistled through the air.

Jean was captivated. She couldn't help it; her gaze slid across his broad shoulders and down the muscular columns on either side of his spine to his narrow waist. His braies sat low on his hips. Upon first meeting Robin, she'd thought he was stocky in build, yet seeing him shirtless, she realized he was all muscle.

Her mouth went dry.

He practiced with the axe with single-minded determination, as if he fought an invisible enemy. The man didn't seem to notice the freezing wind that whipped across the yard. However, as he swiveled around in a vicious undercut, Robin Mackay realized that he had an audience of one.

His gaze swung left, pinning her to the spot. Face warming, Jean considered gripping her basket close and hurrying on toward the gates.

However, pride won over embarrassment, and she flashed him a tight smile.

She'd barely seen the laird of Melness since their argument in his solar. And she hadn't set foot into his private space either. Robin hadn't asked to see the ledger she was now in charge of; in fact, he hadn't asked for any updates at all. She'd been hurt at first, although it had been a relief to settle into her role without him taking note of her lack of experience.

"Ye have some skill with an axe," Jean greeted the laird as she approached him.

Breathing hard, Robin received her compliment with a nod. "The Mackays of Melness always fight with axes ... a legacy handed down by our Norse forbears."

"Da told me a broadsword is better in battle," she replied. "He says they're nimbler and give greater reach." The comment was bold, yet she was interested to know his thoughts.

"Aye, they do," Robin panted, wiping sweat off his brow with the back of his forearm. "The axe also leaves yer hands more vulnerable than a sword does."

"So why use it?"

He cocked an eyebrow. "An axe has more force than a sword," he replied. "When blood-lust ignites, there is nothing more frightening that a crazed axe-man." Perhaps noting Jean's surprised expression, his mouth then lifted, just a little, at the edges. "It's also more adaptable. Ye can use it to hook shields and blades, ye can block with the shaft, or break noses with the butt-end." He hefted up the weapon to show her.

Jean suppressed a shiver. "Sounds brutal."

"It is."

Silence fell between them, and then the laird's gaze slid to her basket. "Where are ye off to?"

Of course, he would know she wasn't heading to the morning market, for that was Fiona and Kenna's role. All the same, Jean often took walks, despite the worsening weather. Her days were busy, and she spent most of them with Grace or the servants. Her brief excursions gave her time to plan for the coming day.

"I'm off to gather drualus, ivy, and holly," she replied, "for Yuletide decorations."

His brow furrowed. "Shouldn't ye be getting the likes of Kenna and Fiona to do that?"

Jean kept a smile firmly in place, despite the irritation that stabbed through her. "I needed to take a break."

Mackay's frown deepened. "We don't do much for the Long Night, here at Melness ... I don't want my broch looking like a forest glade."

Jean fought the urge to frown. "I promised Grace we would make decorations." She paused then before her mouth quirked. "Fear not, I shall not go overboard ... and I certainly wouldn't dream of putting any decorations up in yer solar."

Robin Mackay's jaw tightened, and Jean realized she'd been too pert. However, she'd been unable to help herself. His grumpiness, especially at this time of year, vexed her.

"Go on then," he said, jerking his chin toward the gates. "Don't let me hold ye up." Dismissing her, he

turned away, swinging his axe in a wide arc before
expertly changing hands and repeating the swing.

Mouth thinned, Jean marched out of the barmkin
and down the incline into the village. "*We don't do much
for the Long Night,*" she grumbled, mimicking his
rumbling tone. "No, ye wouldn't … miserable bastard."

Robin Mackay might have been an entrancing sight
as he practiced, half-naked, with his axe, yet the man's
attitude rubbed her the wrong way. It was just as well
they saw little of each other. She had sympathy for the
tragedy that had befallen him, she really did, but the
man made it difficult to empathize with him at times. He
could be a terrible curmudgeon.

Before coming here, she'd thought his wife a she-devil
for what she and his brother had done to him—and she
still didn't condone their treachery—but Grace painted
her mother as a loving, albeit a little lofty, woman, who
had lavished time and attention upon her only child.

Her descriptions stood in stark contrast to the laird's
treatment of his daughter. Since her arrival at Melness,
she'd barely seen him speak more than a handful of
words to Grace.

It was shameful. Maybe she'd been wrong about
Robin Mackay being a decent man. The amiable
conversations they'd shared at Castle Varrich—and
indeed the connection she'd thought had developed
between them—seemed a distant memory.

Fuming, she stalked through the village to the
kirkyard. Out here, the wind barreled in from the sea,
pushing at her. Jean kept walking, heading toward the
ivy-covered wall of the kirk. She was tempted to pop
inside for a prayer, but Father Malcolm, the village
priest, was a surly man. Since her arrival at Melness,
she'd only ventured into the kirk once.

Stopping before the kirk, Jean started to pull ivy from
the wall before shoving it into her basket.

"It's Yuletide," she muttered to the buffeting wind.
"I'll not let him rob joy from the season." Yule was a
special time of year for Jean, as it was for all the Munro
sisters; growing up with their mother had made it so,

with lavish decorations, singing, and a decadent feast prepared for both the Long Night and the day that followed.

Grace deserved to enjoy this time of year too.

"What do ye think, Jean?"

Glancing up, Jean's gaze traveled to where Grace had just finished placing the last of the holly wreaths they'd made together amongst the row of white candles that lined the trestle tables in the hall. A smile curved her lips. "I've never seen such a bonny Yuletide display," she admitted.

Grace grinned back. "In truth?"

"In truth." Indeed, the lass had taken great care to make the tables look as festive as possible—and had even sprinkled aromatic sprigs of rosemary and pine amongst the candles for a special touch.

Warmth settled over Jean as she surveyed the hall. When she'd first arrived at Melness, this had been a slightly grubby, unadorned space. However, on this—the eve of the 'Long Night'—it was warm and welcoming. And the toothsome aromas of roast meat and baking plum cakes drifting out from the kitchen just added to the festive feel.

"Jean!" Brighde poked her head out of the kitchen. The cook's cheeks were flushed after hours of cooking, yet she was smiling. "The lasses have just brought in the roast geese from the spit ... the skin's nicely browned. I've got the birds resting, but supper will be ready soon."

Jean nodded. "Ye might as well send Fiona and Kenna out to call everyone in," she instructed. "We're almost done here too."

Brighde nodded before disappearing into the kitchen once more.

Leaving her decorated tables, Grace skipped across the fresh rushes to where Jean was untangling her last long vine of ivy. The ceiling was already adorned—Brian had climbed up a ladder to fix ivy to the smoke-blackened beams that stretched overhead—but she wanted to hang one last vine over the mantelpiece.

Dipping into the basket at Jean's feet, Grace withdrew a sprig of drualus—mistletoe—and held it up. "It's such a plain-looking plant compared to holly," she observed, her brow wrinkling. "Why do we use it at Yule?"

Jean observed the sprig of mistletoe that dangled from Grace's hand. She supposed the silvery-green leaves and white berries weren't as vibrant as the dark, glossy green and bright red of holly sprigs. Nonetheless, she'd always loved drualus. "When most other trees drop their leaves during the bitter months, drualus remains green and vibrant," she replied, recalling the explanation her mother had once given her. "It's a reminder to us all that even in the depths of winter, there is still life and vitality."

Grace smiled, evidently pleased by her explanation. "Can I put up some on the walls and over the doorways?"

"Of course, lass ... hurry though. This hall will be filled with hungry men soon enough."

Taking her own advice, Jean bustled across to the great hearth, where a huge oaken log burned, and trailed her last ivy vine over the mantelpiece. As she did so, nervousness fluttered up under her ribcage.

Mackay had warned her not to festoon his broch with decorations—yet she'd gone ahead anyway.

He won't even notice, she assured herself, stepping back to admire her handiwork. *The man never strays from his solar when he's indoors.*

12

DANGEROUS GAMES

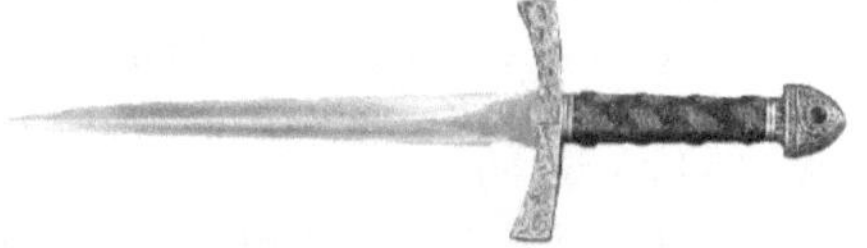

"WHAT HAVE YE done to my hall?"

Jean halted abruptly in the doorway, causing Grace to run into her. They'd been in the kitchen, helping Brighde with the final touches for the Long Night supper. The cook had just laid out smoked fish to be served with loaves of crusty bread. Kenna was whipping up cream to serve with the plum cakes and honey, while Fiona was busy carving the goose.

Everything had come together perfectly.

Until now.

Robin Mackay blocked Jean's path. He stood there, legs planted wide, arms folded across his broad chest. And he didn't look happy.

Jean's heart bucked against her breastbone. God's rood, what's he doing down here?

In her time at Melness, the laird hadn't ventured into the hall *once* for supper. Jean usually took her meals with the servants, or increasingly often, with Grace in the library.

Unfortunately, they weren't alone in the hall. Mackay's men and their families filled the circular space. Danny MacVane was among them, enjoying a cup of mulled wine near the hearth. Like the others present, MacVane's gaze settled upon the irate laird and the woman who'd vexed him.

The rumble of conversation died away, and Jean's palms turned sweaty. She hated being the center of attention in crowds.

Just brazen this out, she counseled herself. The tactic had worked for her in the past when she'd done something that had annoyed her father. She just hoped that Robin Mackay wasn't in such a sour mood that he couldn't be won over.

Glancing back at Grace, Jean forced a bright smile. "Go and take a seat next to Captain MacVane, lass ... supper's about to be served."

With a nod—and a worried look at her father—Grace moved away.

Jean then drew herself up and turned back to the chieftain, forcing herself to look him square in the eye, even as her heart started to pound. "It's just a few trimmings," she replied, keeping her voice low and firm. "See how lovely the hall looks."

Mackay grunted before moving closer, his gaze never leaving hers. "I told ye I didn't want a fuss made for Yule," he growled, his hazel eyes narrowed. "And ye deliberately ignored me."

"I did not," she replied with a definite shake of her head. "Ye shall see I have restricted my decorations to this hall."

"And ye have put on a feast for my retainers ... without my permission."

"It's just a supper," she countered, a quaver to her voice now. "I didn't want to bother ye ... and if ye wish to retire to yer solar, I will ensure yer meal is brought up to ye."

A deep groove appeared between Robin Mackay's brows. "So I'm supposed to hide away, am I? In my own broch?"

Jean swallowed. "Of course not, Mackay. Yer presence would be welcomed ... but I didn't want to—"

"Bother me, I know," he cut her off, stepping closer still. Robin Mackay wasn't as tall as some men, yet he still towered over Jean, for she was the shortest of all her sisters, standing at only two inches above five feet. "Ye deliberately disobeyed me, Jean."

She stared up at him, even if it took everything she had not to drop her gaze to her feet. "I never meant to give offense," she murmured.

"No, ye just thought ye'd do as ye pleased."

A brittle silence settled between them. Jean's cheeks started to burn—and she was painfully aware all eyes in the now silent hall were upon them. Panic gripped her chest then. Surely, he wouldn't stop the festivities?

"Enough grumbling, laird." A hearty voice carried across the hall. Jean tore her gaze from Robin's face to see that one of the older men-at-arms, a heavy-set, grizzled warrior called Evan Pollard, had spoken. His bearded cheeks were flushed with drink, and he clearly didn't wish for his evening to be ruined. "Come … join us for some mulled wine."

Jean swallowed, glancing back at Mackay. His expression still hadn't softened. "Aye," she said softly. "The meal is about to be served … will ye join us?"

Robin Mackay's mouth pursed, and she tensed, anticipating his blunt refusal.

However, Evan called out again, forestalling him. "It's Yuletide, Mackay. Let us all make merry." He paused then before nudging the man next to him with his elbow. "Have ye seen where they're standing?"

Jean tensed. A few feet from Evan, MacVane was grinning. "Well spotted … someone's hung drualus above the doorway."

"That was me," Grace chirped from where she sat next to the captain. However, the lass now wore an anxious expression. "Shouldn't I have?"

Skin prickling, Jean glanced up. Curse it, she'd forgotten Grace had placed a sprig of mistletoe over the kitchen doorway. The leaves and berries gleamed in the light of a nearby burning cresset, silently mocking her.

"Kiss her then," Evan boomed, holding his cup of mulled wine aloft. "Let's get the celebrations off to a start."

Cheeks burning like two hot coals, Jean looked wildly about the hall. Mother Mary, she wished she could disappear. Organizing a supper for the Long Night had seemed a bonny idea at the time, but now she wished she'd left well alone.

"Go on," MacVane added, still grinning. "It's tradition."

Next to the captain, Grace was watching the unfolding scene with wide-eyed fascination.

"Aye, so it is, Danny," Mackay murmured. "Thank ye for the reminder."

Something in his voice made Jean's attention snap back to the chieftain.

Robin Mackay was still staring down at her; however, there was a glint in his eye now and a grim look upon his face.

In an instant, Jean knew how he planned to punish her for her transgression.

Public humiliation.

The heckling of the surrounding warriors continued, and some of them had even started to bang their cups on the table in a steady rhythm, demanding action.

Heart galloping like a bolting pony, Jean took a hasty step back.

It was time for her to return to the kitchen—she'd planned on eating with Grace and Captain MacVane this evening, but she wouldn't do so now. She wouldn't show her face in this hall again tonight.

"No, ye don't, lass," Robin Mackay growled.

Reaching out, he caught her by the shoulders, pinning her to the spot. A heartbeat later, he released his hold, his hands rising to cup her cheeks. Wordlessly, he raised her face to his. The roughness of the callouses on his palms chafed against her skin, and the warmth and strength of his hands made Jean catch her breath.

Suddenly, she was keenly aware of him.

And then he kissed her.

Jean hadn't time to anticipate what his embrace would be like—whether it would be the merest brush of the lips or a hard peck—but it was neither.

Robin Mackay's kiss was firm—and hot. Jean gasped as his tongue delved between her lips, forcing them apart. His hands slid to the back of her head, cradling it as he kissed her deeply, thoroughly.

Jean was so shocked by his bold act that she didn't fight him, didn't try to push him away.

Instead, she surprised herself by melting into his kiss.

He tasted faintly of wine, but at the same time cool and fresh, like the scent of pine and the salt-tang of the sea. The chafe of his stubble against her smooth skin made heat ignite in the cradle of her hips.

Suddenly, she forgot where they were.

It was only when Robin broke off the kiss, and slowly drew back, that the roar of approval from the onlookers intruded.

Jean's hand flew to her mouth, tingling from his thorough treatment.

Robin's gaze was hooded as he watched her, his expression frustratingly inscrutable. In contrast, Jean was sure every emotion that roiled within her was as plain as day upon her face.

"That's how ye do it, laird!" Evan shouted.

A chorus of 'ayes' followed, and Jean's face burned hotter still.

"I shall check to see if the kitchen is ready to serve," she muttered, cursing her lack of composure. She couldn't look Grace's way; she couldn't believe the laird had taken such liberties, in front of his daughter too.

"Aye, lass," Mackay replied. Jean turned to go, and the laird landed a slap upon her backside. "Fetch me a horn of mead while ye are in there."

Laughter boomed through the hall. Mackay's men were thoroughly enjoying the show they were putting on for them.

Jean gasped. Skidding to a halt, she cast an outraged look over her shoulder.

How dare ye?

Of course, this was all part of her punishment for defying him. She'd thought Robin Mackay a shy, retiring man—yet he wasn't so this evening. She glimpsed the challenge in his eye: he was daring her to reprimand him.

When she didn't, he cocked an eyebrow. "Get yerself a drink too, Jean," he ordered. "Ye shall be joining us for supper at my table."

Seated at the long trestle table before the roaring fire, Jean stabbed her eating knife into the slice of goose upon her trencher.

Jaw clenched, she ignored the man sitting next to her.

Curse him, she'd been looking forward to this supper, but Mackay had ruined her appetite.

Oblivious to her upset, the others at the table dug into their meals. Across from her, Grace was talking animatedly to MacVane between mouthfuls of roast goose and chestnut, sage, and pork stuffing. The captain was attentive to the lass, listening to her eager chatter with a smile before asking her questions.

Under usual circumstances, it would have warmed Jean to see Grace happy. The lass had led such a lonely existence before her arrival here, and she rarely had the opportunity to dine with others. However, Jean's insides were in knots, embarrassment pulsing through her.

Robin Mackay's behavior had been churlish.

She was chatelaine to this broch, yet he'd treated her like some tavern wench to be kissed and then groped, in full view of his retainers.

And to her further chagrin, she'd *let* him kiss her, had enjoyed it—she'd actually been disappointed when the embrace had ended.

What had come over her?

Jean took a bite of goose. As she'd expected, it was delicious. Beth would have been impressed by Brighde's cooking skills; her sister was a talented cook herself, and the residents of Castle Varrich had certainly eaten better since Beth had wed Niel.

Thinking about her elder sister made Jean's chest ache. It made her dwell upon Eilidh too. They would all be sitting in the great hall of Castle Varrich this eve, making merry and eating and drinking to excess. Wee Angus would be sitting upon Beth's lap, while Niel tickled his son under the chin. It was the bairn's first Yule, a special time.

I could be there too, she reminded herself. *If I wasn't so willful and foolish.*

Longing for her sisters rose, so hard and swift that Jean froze as she reached for her cup of wine. She would have done anything to see them right now.

Jean's vision blurred, and she blinked rapidly. Lord, she didn't want to start weeping, not now. She had to keep control of herself until she was alone.

"This feast is a fine one, Jean," a low male voice intruded then. "Ye have done well."

Straightening up, Jean forced herself to look at the laird, at her tormentor.

"I only gave a few instructions," she replied tightly, unsmiling. "It is Brighde and her assistants who did all the real work."

Robin Mackay looked back at her, his expression also serious. "Ye angered me earlier, lass," he replied, his voice lowering further. They sat close, with their elbows nearly touching. Around them, the table was getting rowdy as more wine, mead, and ale was consumed. No one could likely overhear them, yet Mackay clearly wanted to make sure. "However, I acted rashly, and I apologize."

Jean picked up her cup of wine and took a gulp, welcoming the heat. Robin Mackay's closeness, as well as the intensity in his hazel eyes, made her uncomfortable— as did her conflicting reactions to him.

She wished to be as far from him as possible, and yet the heat of his body, which reached out to embrace her, and the low timbre of his voice, drew her in.

"I, too, apologize," she replied, still stiff. "For I disobeyed ye."

Robin Mackay helped himself to more goose and took a bite.

It really was delicious. And despite the tense start to the Long Night, he was enjoying this meal more than he had any in a long while. It felt good to just relax and let himself be part of the festivities for once.

Outside, snow was silently falling, and the air was cold enough to freeze one's breath, yet the roaring hearth filled the hall with radiant warmth.

Chewing slowly, Robin leaned back, letting his gaze travel around the interior of the space. It had also been a long time since he'd joined his retainers for a meal in here—not since Liosa and Gordon's departure. He'd almost forgotten how much he used to enjoy the sense of fellowship, the roar of voices that rose and fell, punctuated by laughter.

"Do ye like the decorations, Da?"

Robin glanced his daughter's way. Grace had noted his surveillance of his surroundings and was now watching him closely, worry etched upon her heart-shaped face.

Guilt constricted his chest then; he hoped his altercation with Jean hadn't upset Grace. "It's bonny, lass," he replied, smiling. "Ye have a fine eye for detail."

Indeed, the hall had never looked lovelier. He'd marked the candles lining all the tables, and the pretty wreaths. The ivy vines hanging from the rafters added a nice touch too—as did the drualus.

The drualus.

Robin shifted his attention from Grace and glanced once more at the silent woman beside him.

Jean was pale and tense, as she had been ever since he'd shamed her in front of his retainers. He could tell she was still upset. After their brief exchange, she'd focused once more upon her meal. She ate with little enjoyment, her spine stiff.

However, when she licked some grease off her fingers, Robin's gaze strayed to her lips.

They were full and soft—deliciously soft.

Robin wasn't sure what madness had possessed him to kiss her like that, especially with his men, and his daughter, all looking on. He could have just given her a perfunctory peck on the lips, yet it was as if there had been a devil on his shoulder.

Jean had defied him, and he would teach her a lesson.

Slapping her backside had been a mistake too—for the moment his palm connected with her rounded bottom, his groin had stirred, hardening painfully. And then, to make things worse, he'd ordered the lass to eat with him.

It's a dangerous game ye play, Mackay.

Indeed, he'd woken something within himself tonight—something that had long lain dormant.

Desire.

"I've been a cantankerous bastard of late," he murmured then, more to himself than to anyone else. However, his candid words made Jean glance his way.

Her grey-green eyes were guarded, and he didn't blame her. Ever since her arrival, he'd gone out of his way to be unfriendly—when he wasn't actively avoiding her. He'd known the lass had carried a candle for him, although these days, he doubted she felt the same way.

Especially after his rude behavior tonight.

Nonetheless, surrounded by revelry and joy, he found himself lowering his defenses, just a little. He was tired of his own company these days; the evenings were long, and the nights longer still. The only people he spoke to were MacVane and one or two of his men. The rest of the time, he spent alone.

Suddenly uncomfortable, Robin cleared his throat. "Jean ... I've noted what a fine job ye are doing as chatelaine. The broch has never been cleaner or so well organized ... I should have told ye a while ago."

Jean's full lips parted in surprise, her cheeks flushing the same charming shade of pink they had after he'd kissed her.

Robin tried not to stare at her lips. He'd enjoyed that kiss too much.

"MacVane tells me that the store houses and granary are well-stocked for winter," he continued, trying to focus, "and I haven't seen Brian idling since yer arrival."

Jean lowered her gaze, and he noted she had long, curling lashes that fluttered like butterfly wings against her lightly freckled cheeks. There was nothing seductive about that look—she was merely embarrassed—yet Robin's breathing quickened.

He shifted awkwardly on the bench seat. "Shall we make a pact, Jean?"

"A pact?" she asked, her voice wary.

"Aye, I shall stop behaving like an arse ... and in turn, ye shall start heeding me in future."

Jean lifted her chin, and they looked at each other once more.

After a heartbeat, his chatelaine's mouth curved into a slight smile. "Very well."

13

AS BONNY AS A FAERY MAID

"DA KISSED YE."

Glancing up from where she'd been checking the passage Grace had just written, Jean inwardly groaned. She'd been expecting her charge to mention that incident. Surprisingly, Grace had waited till Saint Stephen's, the twenty-sixth day of December. The pair had recently returned from an early-morning visit to Melness village, where they'd distributed bread and currant buns to the poorest folk among the inhabitants.

It was a tradition for the laird's household to deliver food to the less fortunate on Saint Stephen's, although doing so had brought another poignant reminder of Jean's sisters—it was something Jean had always done with them.

She missed Eilidh sorely these days—especially their spirited banter, and even their squabbles. They wrote frequently to each other but reading her younger sister's lively missives was no substitute for hearing her voice. Life at Melness had settled into a routine—albeit a busy one—and she no longer lived in fear of failure. Yet Yuletide made her reflect on what she'd left behind. Sometimes she missed her sisters with a force that made her chest ache.

"Aye, he did," Jean replied, not sure how else to respond. "Ye know it's tradition to steal a kiss under a sprig of drualus."

"But he was angry with ye." Grace's smooth brow furrowed as she clearly tried to make sense of the scene she'd witnessed. "Why would he kiss ye?"

"To make a point," Jean muttered, pushing the sheet of parchment back to Grace. "This is good. Yer writing has improved immensely, of late."

However, Grace wasn't so easily steered off the topic. "What do ye mean?"

Jean stifled a sigh. "He didn't want me to decorate the hall or put on a special feast for the Long Night ... in fact, he'd ordered me not to." She paused then, pulling a face. "Yet I went ahead and did so."

Grace's features tensed. "But our decorations were so bonny!"

"Aye, they were ... and yer Da thought so too," Jean assured her. She didn't want Grace to think Robin was upset with his daughter.

The lass nodded, accepting the chatelaine's words. She then inclined her head. "Ye seemed to like the kiss ... ye *both* did."

Feeling her cheeks warm, Jean cleared her throat. She heartily wished Grace would let the subject drop. "Aye, well ... he took me by surprise."

"What's it like to kiss a man?" Grace's face was a picture of innocence.

Mother Mary! "Ah ... well ... it's difficult to explain," she replied, stumbling over her words. Since this had been her first kiss ever, she was hardly an expert on the subject. "It depends ... on the man ... and on the situation."

Silence fell in the library. "I never saw Da kiss Ma, ye know?" Grace said softly after a lengthy pause. "Not once."

Jean tensed, unbalanced by the abrupt turn the conversation had taken. She'd heeded Mackay and never brought up his wife with Grace. But the lass often mentioned her. "Aye, well, some couples are private about such things," she murmured. "They prefer to not show affection in public."

Grace nodded, as if that made sense. "I watched ye and Da during the feast," she admitted then, her expression veiling. "He looks at ye strangely."

Jean swallowed. God's teeth, she needed to stop this conversation. Yet Grace Mackay was like a dog with a bone this morning. The lass wanted answers. "Does he?" she replied, keeping her voice light. "I hadn't noticed."

The laird had held her gaze a few times during the feast, but that was only because he'd been apologizing for his behavior.

"Aye," Grace affirmed with a nod. "Ma was as bonny as a faery maid, yet he never looked at her like that."

Jean stiffened. Grace hadn't meant to slight her, and yet she'd done so.

Unlike Liosa, she wasn't a beauty. No doubt the lass was bemused at why her father would favor such a plain woman with attention, when she'd never seen him behave that way with her own mother.

"Ma always liked to look pretty," Grace went on, her tone earnest. "She asked Da for a special looking glass, and he had one made especially for her in Inverness ... big enough to be able to view herself from head to foot. Ma told me that a woman's face and figure are her greatest assets." Grace's brow furrowed. "I don't know what she meant."

Jean's mouth compressed. She wasn't surprised Grace had been bemused by the comment, although it revealed much about the woman who'd betrayed Robin with his own brother. Liosa Mackay might have been lovely to look upon, but she sounded vain.

"Beauty isn't everything, Grace," Jean said after a pause. Yet as she said the words, her chest constricted; she spoke the truth, but there was a part of her that denied it. "Aye, a bonny face attracts attention ... but a person's true worth is what lies here." Fisting her hand, she pressed it against her own heart. "Looks don't last forever, yet goodness does."

Grace took this in, her young face creasing in thought.

"Right," Jean said briskly, retrieving a book from a neat stack upon the table. It really was time to speak of something else. "How about we read Tristan and Isolde again?"

Grace's eyes illuminated like two bright embers, and she clapped her hands together. "Oh, aye!"

Smiling, Jean opened the small leather-bound book. It had been a gift from her mother upon her thirteenth birthday. She'd read it countless times, and yet never tired of it. Likewise, the tale was now one of Grace's favorites.

It was a story of forbidden, yet irresistible, love.

"I wish the tale ended happily," Grace said with a sigh. "Tristan and Isolde were perfect for each other."

"They were," Jean agreed. Indeed, the ending, in which Tristan perished of a poisoned wound before Isolde died of a broken heart in his arms, was tragic. "But there were forces at work against them from the very beginning." She paused then. "They had little control over their destiny."

Grace's eyes grew wide. "Is life really like that?"

Jean favored her with a smile. "Fortunately not ... for one thing, there are no potions that will make ye fall in love as they did."

"There aren't?" Grace looked deflated. "Kenna told me there's a cunning woman in the village who makes love potions."

Jean harrumphed. "Aye, but I doubt they actually work ... in reality, life is what ye make of it, Grace."

She glanced away then, focusing distractedly on the bookshelf opposite. It was sage advice to be sure—but easier said than done. When she shifted her attention back to the chieftain's daughter, she saw the lass was frowning.

"But what about when bad things happen?" Grace asked softly. "Is that our doing?"

Jean tensed. She had to tread carefully now, for she knew Grace was referring to her mother's departure and the rupture of her parents' marriage. She wondered then if Grace was entirely ignorant of the events that had unfolded. The shadow that had just fallen across her soft hazel eyes hinted that she wasn't.

"Sometimes it is," Jean sighed, reaching out and placing a hand over Grace's, squeezing gently, "and sometimes it isn't. The stories in books are easy enough to explain, lass ... but life is a bit more complicated."

Brighde was brandishing a rolling pin at Danny MacVane when Jean entered the kitchen.

"Out with ye, man," she snapped. "Touch those tarts, and I shall club ye!"

"Oh, go on, Bri," the captain said with a grin, dodging the sweep of the rolling pin as he helped himself to one of the apple tartlets. "Don't be such a scold ... I'm starving."

Thud. The rolling pin connected with the side of his head.

MacVane let out a yelp and jumped back, although he still managed to keep hold of his prize. "Ye hit me!"

"Good morning, Captain ... making friends, I see." Jean stopped in the doorway and folded her arms across her chest. "I suggest ye let the cook get on with her chores."

MacVane swiveled to face her, rubbing his skull. He then gave a lopsided smile. "Good morning, Jean ... I'm just getting something to eat."

Jean pursed her lips in an effort not to smile back. MacVane was incorrigible. In her time at Melness, she'd grown fond of him; however, Brighde still barely tolerated the man.

"Those tarts are for the noon meal," the cook muttered, returning to the table, where she'd been rolling out pastry.

"Behave yerself, MacVane." Jean approached the captain and plucked the tart from his hand before returning it to the table. "Ye can just wait like the rest of us."

MacVane gave the cook a mock-wounded look. "I thought Bri might favor me with special treatment,"

In return, Brighde cut him a glare. "Ye are the last man on earth I'd favor," she muttered. "Get out!"

MacVane went, but not without flashing Brighde a grin.

When he'd departed, the cook went back to rolling out pastry, although her movements were jerky, her cheeks flushed. That pastry would be as tough as leather if she continued to bash it around so roughly.

Jean pulled up a stool next to the fire. It was another gelid morning. Damp and cold had drilled deep into her bones. "I think he likes ye."

Brighde pulled a face. "He's wasting his time."

Jean watched the cook as she began cutting the pastry into rounds for the next batch of small tarts. Brighde's cheeks were still pink, something that made her even prettier than usual; it was hardly surprising that MacVane couldn't keep away.

"Danny MacVane is a bit full of himself," Jean admitted after a pause, "but he seems a decent man. Why do ye shun his attentions?"

"I'm not interested in him," Brighde replied crisply, "or *anyone*."

Indeed, Brighde attracted a lot of male attention, yet she ignored it all. The cook repelled any advances and refused to dance with anyone at Yuletide. No one had asked Jean to dance, yet they'd pestered Brighde.

Jean inclined her head. "Why?"

Brighde glanced up, meeting Jean's eye for an instant. "My father was a violent man ... he terrorized us all. As soon as I was old enough, I escaped, marrying the baker's son." Brighde's features tightened then. She glanced away and started pushing the rounds of pastry into a tin. "Unfortunately, my husband turned out to be an even worse bully than my Da." She spooned cooked apple into the tin. "He beat me regularly ... once so badly that he dislocated my jaw, broke my arm, and cracked three of my ribs. When he died of the flux on the second winter of our marriage, I rejoiced."

Jean tensed, taking a moment to absorb Brighde's words. They were brutal—a reminder that the loving, safe environment Jean had grown up in wasn't the reality for many women. "So that's how ye became a cook here?"

Brighde nodded. Straightening up, she met Jean's eye once more. "I'm safe within the walls of this broch. No one lifts a hand to me. The laird is a kind man." She paused then, her features tightening. "I won't take another husband."

14

THE CRONE'S CAVE

JEAN ENCOUNTERED THE laird on the narrow stairwell.

Halting, on her way down, she looked around frantically for a place to step into so that he could pass. However, the stairs were narrow; there was nowhere to go.

"Good afternoon, Mackay," she greeted him, plastering herself against the rough wall. A week had passed since Yule, and she'd barely seen Robin.

"Greetings, Jean," he replied, mounting the stairs toward her. Robin Mackay's gaze slid over her heavy winter mantle. "Where are ye off to?"

"I'm taking Dusty out for a ride ... it's a while since I exercised him."

His brow furrowed. "Alone?"

"Aye."

"Take two of my men out when ye go riding ... ye shouldn't go unescorted."

"I'm not going far," she assured him. "The tide's out, so I shall take a ride along the beach."

Robin nodded, although his brow still hadn't smoothed. Nonetheless, he could hardly complain about her taking a ride on the beach. It was but a stone's throw from the broch. Reaching Jean, he shifted sideways to pass her.

She inhaled the smell of him. Robin had used a cologne of some kind on his jaw after shaving. The spicy scent, mixed with the smell of leather and man, made her feel a little lightheaded. Hastily, she pushed the reaction aside. She couldn't let the infatuation she'd once had for this man resurface. The last few months had matured her, had given her clarity.

Not all women were destined for marriage. Instead of pining for a man who wouldn't return her affections, she had to keep focused on making a success of something she could control: her role as chatelaine.

"I've been thinking … we need to go over the accounts together," Robin said, halting. This close, she could see that his hazel eyes were a blend of gold, oak, and moss green. "I haven't checked them since yer arrival."

Jean held his gaze before nodding. "Shall I bring the ledger up to yer solar after supper?"

"Aye." Robin moved past her. "See ye then … enjoy yer ride, Jean."

Watching him go, Jean exhaled slowly. His amiable manner had caught her off guard. She wasn't sure what to make of it.

Dusty was eager to see her, nuzzling Jean's arm as she saddled him for their ride.

"Greedy lad," she admonished him. "No treats for ye today." She patted his barrel-like stomach. "Ye get fed too well as it is."

In truth, the garron lacked exercise. The weather had been so cold of late that she'd barely taken him out.

Leading Dusty from the stables, Jean caught sight of MacVane taking his men through swordplay drills at the far end of the barmkin. Spying her, he waved.

Jean waved back. She then mounted Dusty, urging the pony toward the gates.

Beyond the walls of the broch, a chill breeze snagged at Jean's fur mantle. But at least the wind wasn't howling today. The sun had also shown its face, although there was no heat in it.

Riding through the village, Jean greeted the locals she passed.

Most of them responded in kind, for she'd become a familiar face these days.

Warmth suffused her chest then, a welcome sensation. Her first months away from Varrich and her sisters had been challenging indeed, but Melness was starting to feel like home. She no longer awoke every morning expecting Eilidh to chatter in her ear.

Smiling, Jean urged Dusty into a jolting trot, across the bare hills beyond the village and down onto the broad swathe of pale-gold sand. The tide was far out this afternoon, and the sun glistened on furlongs of flats. The beach was a wide pristine crescent that just begged to be galloped upon.

Dusty wasn't a leggy courser built for speed. Nonetheless, the garron was eager to stretch his legs after being stabled for days. He tore along the strand in a fast, choppy canter. Jean leaned forward, one hand gripping the reins, while holding onto his bushy mane with the other. She'd never been the ablest of riders, yet the exhilaration of taking off down an empty beach, while gulls wheeled above her, was hard to beat.

She felt brave today, ready to take the world on.

The hollow tattoo of Dusty's hooves on the hard-packed sand pounded in time with her heart. Urging her gelding on faster still, Jean felt the garron's gait change from a canter to a gallop. It wasn't wise to let the pony have his head on the beach, for he'd likely remember next time she brought him down here—yet the temptation to let go was too great.

By the time she pulled him up at the far end of the beach, both pony and rider were out of breath.

A rocky headland rose before Jean, tumbling down to a collection of huge boulders—and near to the foot of the cliffs, she spied the opening to a cave.

"The Crone's Cave," she murmured, reaching forward and stroking Dusty's sweaty neck. Kenna had told her about the cavern just two days earlier at supper. A witch was said to have dwelt in the cave many years ago, and the place was now cursed.

"No one's set foot there in years," Kenna had informed her with wide eyes. "They're too afraid."

Brighde had snorted at the maid's hushed tone. "It's only an old wives' tale, lass."

Like the cook, Jean was too practical in nature to believe the cave was cursed. Instead, her racing pulse quickened once more at the sight of it.

"Let's see just how brave ye are, Jean Munro," she murmured.

Aye, she'd done herself proud of late, but she was in the mood to test herself further: she was going to climb up and explore that cave.

Swinging down from Dusty's broad back, Jean tethered him to a rock, not far from the first of the boulders sitting at the foot of the headland. Then, glancing up at her destination, Jean began to climb.

It wasn't easy to reach the top; the rocks were slippery with sea spray, bird droppings, and kelp, yet Jean was determined. A thrill went through her when she reached the flat stone ledge before the entrance to the cave. Halting to catch her breath, she turned and looked down at the beach.

Dusty looked like a child's toy from this height. The ledge gave an uninterrupted view east, along the arching curve of the beach. From here, she gazed across the rolling green hills studded with boulders and a few wind-stunted pines, to where Melness broch rose against the sky.

Another smile stretched across Jean's face, happiness stealing through her. Aye, she really felt part of this place now.

Jean sucked in a lungful of briny air. Turning, she then peered inside the opening of the cave.

It was much bigger than it appeared from below: the entrance was at least six yards across, and the ceiling was nearly seven feet high, making it easy for her to walk inside without ducking her head.

She did just that, scanning the walls.

Jean wasn't sure what she was looking for exactly, maybe some sign of the fabled 'crone' who'd once dwelt in this cold, damp cave.

And when her attention shifted to the dark recesses within, and her eyes adjusted to the dimness, she spotted the remnants of a hearth. Intrigued, she moved forward, her boots scuffing on damp stone, before crouching down in front of the fire. She then reached out and touched one of the charred stones ringing it.

It's warm.

The crone was long gone, but it appeared that not all the locals heeded superstition. Someone lived here.

The fine hairs on the back of Jean's neck prickled then.

She'd just intruded upon someone's home, and the inhabitant of this cave could return at any moment.

Straightening up, she took a step back from the hearth. It was time to go.

"What's this then?" A man's gruff voice echoed through the cave.

Jean's heart kicked hard. She raised a hand to her chest and took another rapid step back.

Curse it, the resident of the Crone's Cave was at home.

An instant later, a big figure emerged from the shadows at the back of the cavern. Dressed in rags, the man was hunched and dirty, his features obscured by a knotted mane of black hair and a wild beard.

Jean's breathing hitched. He was a frightening sight.

He peered out at her. She would be backlit against the sky; it wouldn't be easy to make out her features.

And yet, somehow, he did.

"Jean Munro." He gave a wheezing laugh, his heavy features creasing. "I don't believe it."

Jean froze, her heart racing now. "How do ye know my name?"

The man barked another laugh. "I'd know a Munro sister anywhere," he rasped. "Although, ye are a drab wee thing—no match for Neave."

He shuffled farther forward then so that they stood barely four yards apart. His movements were stiff, pained, as if he was nursing an injury.

However, when Jean saw his iron-grey eyes, alarm slammed into her.

"Roy Gunn," she whispered.

God's bones, she was in trouble here. She'd have thought the man, who'd tried to rape Neave and kill John Mackay, was either dead or far from Mackay territory.

Instead, here he was, living just a day's ride from Castle Varrich—and a stone's throw from Melness broch.

Gunn grinned. "Aye, that's right, lass. In the flesh." His gaze raked over her. "This is a boon indeed. I might have been denied yer sister, but I shall have ye instead."

And with that, he lunged.

The shock that had frozen Jean to the spot dissolved.

She hadn't realized she could move so fast, and yet she did.

Jean flew backward, rushing out of the cave onto the ledge beyond. Under normal circumstances, she would have hesitated then, carefully climbing down the slippery rocks. But now there was no time for hesitation.

She knew what Roy Gunn was capable of. He might think her a poor substitute for her sister, yet he'd rape her all the same. She knew it with terrifying clarity.

Fear robbed her of any trepidation.

His grasping hand caught her cloak, yet when she threw herself off the ledge, she ripped herself free.

Roy Gunn's curses followed her.

Jean slid, tumbled, and fell to the glistening sand below. Her journey down scraped her elbows and knees. Sharp edges dug into soft flesh, yet she couldn't halt her path. She hit hard sand with a slap before scrambling to her feet.

Glancing up, Jean's heart leaped into her throat to see that Gunn had followed her.

Despite that he was clearly still suffering from the wounds John Mackay had dealt him months earlier, he slithered down the rocks on his back, his face a hard mask of determination.

Jean stumbled over to where Dusty waited, blissfully unaware of her panic.

Untethering the gelding from the rock, she scrambled onto his back and kicked him into a jolting canter. Together, they tore away from her pursuer.

Jean did not look back.

15

A DRAB WEE THING

ROBIN WAS EXAMINING an abscess on one of his horse's hooves when a panicked woman rode a lathered pony into the barmkin. Jean's face was flushed, her eyes wild. Her hair, usually drawn back into a tidy bun, had come half-undone, and sand and a bit of seaweed dirtied her clothing.

Frowning, Robin lowered the horse's fetlock and straightened up, his gaze alighting upon his chatelaine. "Jean, what's wrong?"

"Roy Gunn's been living on yer lands!" she gasped. "I rode down to the end of the beach and went up to explore the Crone's Cave ... and he was in there!"

Robin stilled. A heartbeat later, heat kindled in the pit of his belly.

He couldn't believe that treacherous wretch had dared take refuge in that cave, within the shadow of his own keep. Stepping forward, he helped Jean from her garron. She was trembling.

Robin's chest tightened. "Did he hurt ye?"

She shook her head, even as her eyes now shone with unshed tears. "He tried to grab me, but I ran." Her throat bobbed. "I took a few knocks on the rocks as I escaped though."

Robin took one of her hands, turning it over to see that her palm was scraped and bleeding. The hot coal in his gut started to pulse. "Go and see Brighde," he said, his voice roughening. "I'll deal with Gunn."

Releasing Jean, Robin swiveled, his gaze alighting upon MacVane, who'd come down from the wall upon seeing Jean's rushed return to the broch. "Saddle our horses, Danny ... we're going after him."

With a nod, MacVane made for the stables, calling to one of the other men-at-arms to ready the chieftain's mount.

Robin turned back to Jean. She was blinking furiously as the shock of her narrow escape settled in. Gunn had nearly caught her. The whoreson had tried to rape Neave the Beltaine previous, but John Mackay had thwarted him; the man was still out for revenge. He must have been delighted when Jean Munro wandered unwittingly into his hideout.

Robin hadn't been up to the Crone's Cave in years. He and Gordon had often explored it as bairns, heedless of the superstitions surrounding the cavern. However, they'd always found it empty.

It had been a bold, yet clever, place for Gunn to take refuge.

Robin clenched his jaw hard, sending darts of pain through his ears. *Not any longer*.

Jean watched Robin and his captain thunder from the broch upon two fast coursers, their faces grim.

As the laird had mounted his horse, she'd spied the banked rage in his hazel eyes. He'd retrieved his axe from the armory and wore the weapon strapped across his back. Jean had no doubt he planned to take Roy Gunn's head off with it.

"Here, Jean," one of the stable lads took Dusty from her. "I'll see to yer pony. Ye go inside and get cleaned up."

Numbly, Jean nodded, too shaken to dredge up a smile. "Thank ye," she croaked. "Please rub him down well ... I pushed him hard."

The lad flashed her a smile. "Aye ... Dusty did well to keep ye safe." He led the garron away, toward the stables.

Turning, Jean limped her way across the barmkin. She'd been so terrified during her flight from Gunn that she barely felt her injuries. Yet now that she was safe, her elbows and hands stung, and her knees throbbed. She could feel blood trickling down the front of her leg.

Inside the kitchen, the servants gathered around her, peppering her with questions.

Already, news of what had happened was circulating in the broch. Everyone wanted to know the details.

"Out ye go, all of ye!" Brighde shooed Fiona, Kenna, and Brian out of the kitchen. "Jean's clearly upset ... and none of ye are helping."

Grumbling, Fiona and the others retreated.

As soon as they were alone, Brighde sat Jean down upon a stool in front of the fire before retrieving a flask of vinegar. "Let's have a look at yer knees," she murmured.

Wincing, Jean drew up her skirts. As she'd thought, both her knees were badly skinned.

Brighde pulled a face. "Och, ye really did take a tumble."

"In truth, I was so scared, I'd have rolled down the cliff-face to escape him," Jean admitted shakily.

Brighde's gaze shadowed. Of course, she knew what it was like to be afraid of men. "I heard what Roy Gunn did last year," she admitted. "What a nasty man. I can't believe he's been sheltering right on our doorstep. How long do ye think he's been living there?"

Jean shrugged. She had no idea.

"How badly was he injured?"

"It was hard to tell. John Mackay dealt him a serious wound last year ... it could still be troubling him."

"Ye must have gotten a real scare ... coming across him in that dark cave. Will ye send word to yer sister ... to let her know Gunn's still alive?"

Jean sighed, her brow furrowing. "I doubt I'll need to ... word will spread soon enough."

She was tiring of this interrogation. Brighde had sent the others away for being nosey—only to fire questions like crossbow quarrels herself.

As if realizing this, Brighde flushed. "Fear not," she murmured. "The laird will see to the brute."

Unstoppering the flask, she poured vinegar onto a clean

strip of linen. She then dabbed gently at Jean's bloody knees.

It stung, and Jean's breath hissed through her teeth. Nonetheless, she didn't utter a sound as Brighde cleaned her scrapes. Once her knees were dealt with, Jean rolled up her sleeves so that the cook could treat her elbows and the backs of her hands.

"Scrapes always hurt," Brighde said as she finished her task. "Ye'll be a bit sore for the next few days."

Jean nodded. Now that she was safe, exhaustion settled over her in a heavy mantle—the after-effects of shock, she supposed. Thankfully, Brighde had ceased her questions for the moment at least.

Her eyelids suddenly felt as if they had weights attached to them, and despite that it was warm by the fire, she shivered.

Marking Jean's reaction, Brighde frowned. "Why don't ye retire to yer chamber for an hour or two? Ye should rest."

Jean rubbed at her eyes. "I can't really ... I promised Grace I'd—"

"Nonsense." The cook's tone turned brisk. "I'll send Kenna up to fetch ye when the men return. Off ye go."

"Let's try that again, shall we?" Jean said with a smile. "Don't rush it this time."

Grace nodded before clearing her throat. She then began to read from the poetry book she held, enunciating each word carefully in French.

Once the lass finished, Brighde heaved a sigh. "That sounded beautiful." "Although I have no idea what it means."

Jean smiled. "It's a passage about courtly love ... from *Le Roman de la Rose*." She then turned her attention to Grace. "That was much better."

Grace grinned. "Do ye want me to continue?"

"No, that's enough for today." Jean motioned to the small stack of books they'd been studying. Five days had passed since her encounter with Gunn, and it was freezing this morning, hence why they'd moved their lessons to the kitchen. Outdoors, a blizzard swept over the Highlands, carpeting the land in a thick white crust. A deep chill had settled, one that not even the roaring hearths could keep at bay. "Take these back to the library, and Kenna will bring yer noon meal up shortly."

The lass did as bid, calling out a cheery greeting to Fiona who was scrubbing down tables in the hall beyond as she headed toward the stairwell.

After Grace had gone, Brighde huffed another sigh. "I wish I was able to read one of those beautiful poems."

Jean inclined her head. "If ye enjoy the poetry, I can read to ye sometimes in the evenings, if ye like?"

Brighde's cheeks dimpled as she grinned. "Aye ... I'd like that very much."

The cook turned back to the stew she'd been tending all morning, while Jean opened a wooden box and the ledger she'd brought downstairs with her. The box contained all the chits from their various suppliers. There were a few new ones to add to the ledger.

Dipping her quill into the ink pot at her elbow, she began to carefully copy out the amounts.

However, it was difficult to concentrate on her task. Her thoughts kept straying to other matters.

"It's been a week," she muttered as she worked. "What's happened to Mackay and his men?"

"No doubt still out hunting Gunn," Brighde replied. "I can't believe he got away."

Jean's mouth pursed. She couldn't either. It was after dusk when Robin had returned to the broch. He'd been in a black mood, for the fugitive had eluded them. Gunn fled south on a fast horse. The following morning, Robin had gathered his men and set out for Varrich to inform the clan-chief.

Days had passed, and Jean spent far too much time reliving the incident with Roy Gunn—and her narrow escape. She broke into a cold sweat every time she recalled the wild look in the man's eyes and the way he'd lunged for her.

"Ye are so clever, Jean." Glancing up, Jean saw that Brighde had turned from the hearth. The cook's gaze fell upon the open ledger. "Brighter than most men, I'd wager."

Jean smiled at the compliment, even if a part of her withered.

Practical, capable Jean.

A drab wee thing.

Roy Gunn's carelessly cruel words whispered to her then, as they had numerous times over the past days. She'd been too frightened to pay them much heed at the time, but now that she was no longer in peril, they returned regularly to torment her.

Aye, she'd done her best to keep focused on her role, and took a lot of satisfaction from it, but her longing for Robin was still there. She'd felt his absence from Melness over the past week.

Curse her, she wanted him to notice her. But if the world saw her as a plain creature, maybe he did too?

"Perhaps," she replied cautiously, "although men generally don't like women who are cleverer than they are."

Brighde harrumphed. "Aye, well, that's because most of them are fools."

Jean went silent, her gaze dropping to the numbers she'd just entered. Then, with a sigh, she replaced her quill in its pot. "Am I ugly?"

Brighde's eyes flew wide. "No ... why would ye think such a thing?"

Jean splayed a hand upon the table, next to the ledger, her fingertips digging into the scarred surface. "Men never look at me," she murmured. "It's as if I'm invisible."

Silence fell in the kitchen, and when Brighde finally replied, her tone was surprised. "Do ye wish to be *noticed*, Jean?"

Heaving in a deep breath and gathering her courage, Jean lifted her chin to meet Brighde's eye. "Aye," she admitted softly.

16

HIDING AWAY

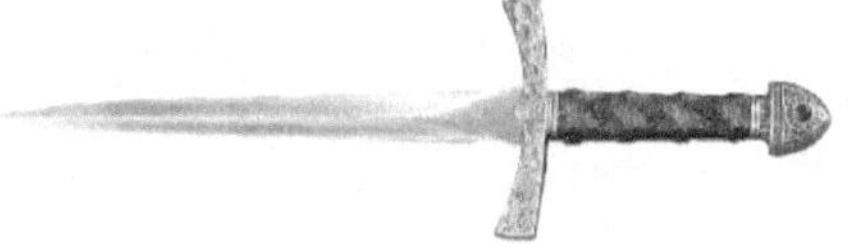

"IT'S THE LAIRD, isn't it?"

Brighde's observation made Jean's breathing hitch, and her pulse took flight.

Mother Mary, how had Brighde guessed?

"Aye," she whispered, the truth tumbling out of her before she could stop herself. "But please ... don't tell a soul."

Brighde huffed. "Of course I won't."

"I thought I was hiding it well ... I'd almost managed to convince myself I was cured of this foolish obsession."

Her friend cocked an eyebrow. "Ye conceal it well enough ... but ye sometimes blush when Mackay is mentioned ... and we all know that he kissed ye at Yuletide. When ye came back into the kitchen afterward, ye were as red as an ember."

Jean murmured an oath under her breath and reached up, covering her hot cheeks with her hands.

Silence fell in the kitchen, and when Brighde broke it, her voice was subdued. "Mackay's not the best choice, Jean ... he may never look at ye in the way ye desire."

"Of course he won't," Jean replied bitterly. "I'm not beautiful ... not like ye."

She glanced back at the cook to see that a groove had formed between her finely arched black brows. "Ye *are* bonny." Holding her gaze, the cook then approached Jean and lowered herself down onto the bench seat next to her. "But ye hide yer loveliness away."

Jean tensed. "What do ye mean?"

Brighde sighed. "Ye cover yerself in sack-like garments that do ye no favors whatsoever."

Jean glanced down at the light-brown, high-necked kirtle she wore today and stifled a wince. "But they're comfortable."

"Aye, and if they were black and white, ye'd resemble a nun!"

Jean stiffened. "My sisters dress in beautiful kirtles that show off their figures ... but I've always been embarrassed."

"Of what, exactly?"

Jean glanced down at her bosom. "These."

Brighde snorted a laugh. "Many women would wish to be so endowed." She paused then, her eyes glinting. "Ye and I have similar figures ... but if I wore loose kirtles as ye do, it would look as if my bosom were the prow of a ship. Bustier women need to wear lower necklines, or we look matronly."

Jean pursed her lips at this, although she didn't argue. Brighde did have a point.

Her friend's mouth quirked then. "Ye were blessed with curves ... wishing otherwise is pointless." Brighde paused, running a critical eye over Jean. "Ye also need to do something about yer hair."

"What about it?" Jean reached up, patting her tight bun. "I like wearing it out of the way ... it's frizzy and impossible to manage otherwise."

"It gives ye a spinsterish air, Jean. Take it out a moment so I can see what we're dealing with."

Jean didn't want to, yet the determined look upon Brighde's face warned her the cook would merely insist. With a sigh, she reached up and loosed the bun, letting her long hair tumble down over her shoulders. "I've never been able to do anything with it," she muttered.

Leaning forward, Brighde touched it, her brow furrowing. "It's a bit wild, to be sure, but ye could wear it as I do ... with the sides pulled back so it's off yer face."

"Aye ... but yer hair isn't as wiry as hog bristle."

"A touch of perfumed oil will deal with that," Brighde assured her. "Do ye have any?"

"Aye ... some lavender oil."

Brighde nodded. "Good. Ye need to smooth a drop or two through yer hair in the mornings and evenings." She sat back, fixing Jean with a level look. "Ye are a lovely lass, Jean ... but if ye are going to make changes, do it for yerself ... no one else. Forget about men for the moment."

Jean stared back at her, a little taken aback. Brighde provided a perspective that hadn't occurred to her before. "Where do I start?" she murmured.

"After the noon meal, we shall take a look at the kirtles ye own," Brighde replied, with a rueful smile. "There has to be at least one that doesn't hang off ye like a sack."

"I was wrong," Brighde muttered as she looked over the selection of kirtles spread across the bed. "None of these will do."

Jean stiffened before folding her arms across her chest defensively. "What? Not one?"

Brighde shook her head. She then turned and retrieved the garment she'd carried into Jean's bed-chamber with her from a nearby chair. "Just as well I brought one of mine for ye to try on."

Panic fluttered under Jean's ribcage. "It won't fit me," she squeaked.

"Aye, it will." Brighde made an impatient gesture at Jean. "Go on, take that awful brown thing off."

Bristling with indignance and embarrassment, Jean complied.

Clad in nothing but a thin, ankle-length lèine, Jean shivered. It was freezing in her bed-chamber, despite the lump of peat that smoldered in the hearth behind her—not surprising really, for snow covered the world outdoors. She took the pine-green kirtle Brighde passed her and carefully wriggled into it.

She didn't want to damage the garment, for the cook wouldn't possess many fine dresses.

"Pull it up a bit," Brighde instructed, stepping forward and yanking up the bodice. "Ye don't want yer paps bursting free." She snorted then. "That'll get ye some attention ... although not the kind ye want."

Mortification rose within Jean. "Mother Mary," she muttered.

Grinning, Brighde took a step back and surveyed her. "I knew it," she crowed.

Jean glanced down, her gaze widening at the sight of her cleavage peeking up at her, and the milky expanse of skin between her throat and bosom the kirtle exposed. It was a winter garment, woven from wool with fur trim at the neck and sleeves. "I don't believe it," she murmured, genuinely surprised. "It fits."

Brighde cast her an arch look. "Aye, like a glove." The cook moved over to the bed once more, her gaze sweeping over the kirtles. "We shall need to adjust these ... it shouldn't take us more than a few evenings if we work together." She glanced over at Jean. "In the meantime, ye can borrow that kirtle."

"I can't wear this," Jean gasped. "It's yer best dress."

"Aye ... and I'm sure ye will look after it." Brighde moved behind Jean then and, reaching up, loosed her hair. "Now, let's see what we can do here," she murmured. "Hand me the lavender oil then ... just or drop or two on yer hair works wonders."

Jean did as bid, and an instant later, a popping sound of the stopper releasing filled the chamber. She inhaled the floral yet woodsy scent of lavender while Brighde used her hands to work it through Jean's unruly mane. The cook then pulled the sides back, securing them. "There, that's more like it," Brighde murmured. "Do ye have a looking glass?"

"Aye." Jean moved to the bedside table and picked up her looking glass, gazing at her reflection. The oil had indeed smoothed her frizzy hair, taming its wiriness into heavy curls. Jean stared at the lass looking back at her. *I look pretty.*

"What do ye think?" Brighde asked.

Jean lowered the looking glass and glanced over at her friend, her mouth curving into a smile. "I think ye can work miracles, Bri."

"Of course, I can't," Brighde replied, making a frustrated noise in the back of her throat. "Ye *are* bonny, Jean. Ye have a natural, earthy beauty many women would give their eye teeth for. Don't talk as if ye are the Bean Nighe!"

Jean laughed. The stories her mother told her as a bairn described the Bean Nighe—an omen of death—as a small and hideous woman with a hooked nose who had one large nostril, a protruding tooth, webbed feet, and long, hanging breasts. "Even *I* wouldn't go that far."

17

RETURNING HOME

WHEN ROBIN FINALLY spied Melness broch in the distance, a sigh gusted out of him. It was so cold that his breath formed a cloud of steam. A bone-numbing chill bit through the layers of plaid, leather, and fur he wore. During the journey home, the sun had glinted off the surrounding snow with a brilliance that made his eyes water. However, the light was fading now, leeching what little warmth the pale winter sun had brought from the world.

"At last," MacVane rode up next to him. "A roaring fire and a cup of warm mead beckons."

Robin gave a grunt in reply.

"Gunn's disappearance isn't yer fault, Robin," the captain said eventually, when it became clear the laird had nothing to say. "The weasel is adept at hiding himself ... the Mackay certainly doesn't blame ye."

Robin's mouth thinned.

Day after day of hunting ... and nothing.

Over the past fortnight, he and his men had joined Niel's in a full-scale search for Roy Gunn. And just like months earlier, the fugitive eluded them. It was frustrating beyond belief.

And to make matters worse, their search for Gunn had led to the discovery that the Sutherlands had taken to making opportunistic winter raids along the Mackay's southern borders. On the way home, Robin and his men had stopped off at the village of Strathan, within his own lands, only to learn that sheep had been going missing. It was an odd time of year for rustling, and instinct told him this was just more Sutherland mischief.

"He should," Robin muttered. "Gunn was on my lands, and I failed to catch him." He drew in a deep breath then, to settle the anger that still pulsed within him. His failure was a reminder of another search, over three years earlier, that had yielded nothing. Once he'd recovered from the injuries they'd dealt him, he'd hunted his wife and brother for months. But Gordon, curse him, was clever. The pair had disappeared without a trace.

"Gunn will be found eventually," MacVane assured him, unaware of the direction of his laird's thoughts. "It's out of yer hands now."

"Aye … but it's one thing after the other at the moment." He cast the captain a rueful look. "The sheep rustling concerns me."

MacVane grimaced, making it clear that he, too, wasn't happy about their discovery at Strathan. "Shall I take some men south on patrol tomorrow?"

Robin nodded. "I'll join ye."

They rode through the village, where locals ventured out to greet them.

Robin's mood lightened at the sight of their ruddy faces and warm smiles. It was the first time in a while that coming home had brought a sense of relief; usually, a lingering dread crept upon him as the last furlongs to Melness approached.

But of late, something had shifted within Robin. Over the past fortnight, he'd found himself missing home.

Maybe Jean Munro was right—perhaps time was what he needed.

Jean.

Did she have something to do with his change in attitude? He'd found himself thinking of her often while he'd been away, wondering how she was faring. Jean had taken to her duties as chatelaine with her usual determination and energy. She was dependable, and she'd brought a sense of 'home' into his broch, one that had been lacking for a long while. He'd fought her efforts, at times, and was sorry for it now.

It occurred to him then that he'd missed her too.

It's gratitude, that's all, he told himself. *Jean has made yer life easier ... and she's giving Grace the attention ye won't.*

Considering this, he urged his gelding up the last incline and rode under the archway into the barmkin. The snow had turned to muddy slush in here. Stable lads hurried out to greet him, and Robin dismounted, inhaling the aroma of what smelled like venison stew, drifting out from the kitchen.

"Brighde must have known we were on our way back," MacVane announced with a grin. "The lass will have been missing me."

Robin pulled a face. "She'll have been enjoying the peace, Danny." Although Robin largely kept to himself, he wasn't oblivious to the goings-on in his broch.

Once their horses were seen to, the men left the stables and made their way indoors, kicking snow and mud off their boots on the stone steps outside the broch, and tramping into the hall.

A wall of heat buffeted Robin, followed by the nutty scent of baking bread and the rich aroma of venison. Supper wasn't far off. Pleasure rushed through him as he surveyed his surroundings. The hall looked inviting: the rushes that covered the floor appeared to have been changed, and the great hearth glowed.

Fiona and Kenna were laying the tables for supper, and Brian had perched on a stool near the fire, where he played a jaunty tune upon a bone whistle.

Robin's shoulders lowered, the day's tension draining from him.

Roy Gunn and the sheep rustling be damned. They couldn't take this away from him.

Maybe he'd eat down here this evening, with his men for once. The thought of ensconcing himself in his solar didn't appeal. He didn't want to be alone.

He started to remove his heavy fur mantle.

A familiar female voice hailed him then. "Good eve, Mackay ... I hope ye had a good journey home?"

Robin Mackay's gaze swept over her. His expression was difficult to read, although his hazel eyes widened. "Aye, thank ye, Jean," he replied finally, a slight huskiness to his voice.

Jean's breathing quickened as she fought shyness. Brighde had assured her that the green, fur-trimmed kirtle suited her, and that wearing her hair down was a feminine touch. But she hoped she hadn't gone too far.

"However, we return with ill-tidings," he continued, his expression sobering. "Roy Gunn still hasn't been found."

Jean tensed at this news, and she forgot her embarrassment. "He's slippery indeed," she muttered.

"Aye," Robin agreed, his brow furrowing. He shifted his attention from her, surveying the hall that was starting to fill up. "Where's Grace, this eve?"

"She's in her chamber, as always," Jean replied. "Kenna's about to take her supper up to her."

Their gazes met once more, and then Robin smiled.

Jean's breathing caught. The saints preserve her, it lit up his face.

"Fetch Grace and bring her downstairs." He stepped forward to take a cup of warmed mead that Fiona was ladling out to the men. The servant had brought an iron pot out from the kitchen, and Robin's warriors were gathered around her. However, they parted for their chieftain. "I wish to see my daughter."

"Of course."

Jean was moving toward the stairwell when Robin called out to her. "I'd like ye to join me for supper as well, Jean."

Taking a mouthful of stew, Jean tried to focus on her meal.

Yet she was far too aware of the man seated next to her.

She was pleased that the laird wished to eat in the hall, and that he'd invited her and Grace to join him. Yet she was also flustered. His proximity was doing strange things to her pulse. Her stomach had tied itself in knots.

In truth, her borrowed kirtle and different hairstyle made her feel self-conscious.

Over the past days, she'd marked the stares she'd attracted from men. Indeed, she was no longer invisible, but she wasn't sure she liked the attention. Just this morning, she'd caught Brian staring at her breasts when she reached for a wedge of bannock. She'd shot him a narrow-eyed look, and the lad had hurriedly glanced away, yet the incident had made Jean want to rush upstairs and change clothes.

Do it for yerself ... no one else. Brighde's advice made sense. Nonetheless, Jean was used to fading into the background, and there was part of her that *preferred* anonymity. A new look was all well and good, but it didn't change who she was on the inside.

Grace's laughter drew her attention then. The lass sat opposite her father and was regaling him with her favorite French phrases. Grace was an eager pupil, and her language skills had improved enormously over the winter.

Robin's mouth curved as he responded to her in the same tongue.

"Ye speak French well," Jean noted.

The chieftain glanced her way and favored her with another disarming smile. "My mother was French."

"Really?"

"Aye ... she was a merchant's daughter from Cherbourg in Normandy ... my father met her on one of his many travels. They fell in love, and he brought her back to the Highlands."

His tale intrigued Jean. How little she knew about the man she served. During their conversations at Varrich, Robin had always been careful to talk of things outside himself.

"Did she enjoy living here?" Jean asked. She imagined it must have been quite a shock for the lass to move from a bustling French port to an isolated corner of the Scottish Highlands.

Robin nodded, still smiling. "Ma loved Melness."

"Aye, she did," Evan spoke up from farther down the table. Jean glanced the man-at-arm's way to see that he'd been listening in on their conversation. "But then Elodie was a woman who always made the best of things." His weathered features softened as he spoke her name, and Jean wondered if he'd carried a candle for her. "She learned our tongue within months of her arrival. The lass had a smile that warmed a room."

Robin's smile widened at Evan's description, even if Jean marked the trace of sadness in his eyes.

"When did ye lose her?" she asked quietly.

"Nearly ten years ago now," he replied, his expression sobering. "My father died suddenly, of a convulsion ... and in the months following, Ma sickened."

"Aye, she wasted away before our eyes," Evan murmured.

"Did she die of a broken heart?" Grace asked, speaking up for the first time since they'd started discussing her grandmother. "Like the maidens in the songs?"

"She did, lass," the warrior replied. "It happens in real life too ... sometimes."

Grace's expression turned thoughtful. "I wish I could have met her."

"So do I," Robin answered softly.

Silence fell, while Grace toyed with her stew. When she glanced up once more, her hazel eyes were curious. "Do ye think I look like my Ma?"

Robin's throat bobbed. "Aye, lass ... ye are her image."

The meal resumed, although there was a subdued edge to it now.

Jean searched for something to say. She was rarely at a loss for words. Her father had often lamented that all four of his daughters could talk the hind legs off a mule. But that wasn't so this evening. After talking about Robin's mother and Liosa, trivial subjects like the weather didn't seem appropriate. Neither did comments about the day-to-day running of the broch. However, after a short spell, conversation around the table resumed.

"We never did go over the accounts together, Jean," Robin said finally. Across the table, MacVane was laughing as Grace recounted one of the fables Jean had recently taught her; the chatelaine and his laird had a moment of relative privacy. "Would ye like to do so this eve, after supper?"

Surprise fluttered through Jean. She was sure he'd forgotten, what with everything that had happened. "Are ye sure? Ye must be tired after yer journey?"

"Not overly," he replied, his mouth lifting into another half-smile that did strange things to her insides.

Quashing her sudden nervousness, Jean smiled back. "Very well ... it shouldn't take too long."

18

BEFORE THE FIRE

ROBIN SAT BEFORE the fire, the ledger perched on his knee. Holding a candle above the page, he ran his eye down the inked columns.

Jean watched him, shifting nervously upon the high-backed chair.

It was deliciously warm inside the solar, cozy enough to chase away the cold drafts that pushed in through the cracks around the windows and doorways. Under normal circumstances, she'd have basked in the heat and even dozed off.

However, with Robin seated just a few feet away, she was wide awake.

She was good with numbers—a skill Beth had found useful at Varrich—but even so, she worried that she'd made a mistake.

She wanted Robin to be confident in her ability to manage the accounts. Any foolish errors in her counting would damage the respect she'd earned thus far.

Eventually, the laird glanced up. "Heavens, don't look so nervous, lass," he said, his mouth quirking. "I'm no ogre."

Jean gave a nervous laugh. "No ... but I want ye to be pleased with me."

Their gazes fused, and Robin's expression grew serious. "I am." His gaze dropped to the ledger once more. "I see ye have ordered twenty extra sacks of oats ... why's that?"

"Brighde told me that the granary supplies ran perilously low last winter," Jean replied without hesitation. "I didn't want that to happen again this year."

Robin nodded. "Makes sense … I like that ye look ahead." He put aside the candle and closed the heavy ledger with a thud, before setting it down on the low table next to his chair. "Ye weren't boasting when ye told me ye were capable. I always thought Lachlan did a fine job of managing this broch … but ye bring a much-needed woman's touch that's been lacking since my mother died."

"But what about yer wife?" The moment the question slipped from Jean's lips, she wished she could call it back. Curse her, she was too nosey by half.

The chieftain's gaze shadowed before he shook his head. "Liosa had little interest in the daily running of my household … or in managing the servants. She left all of that to Lachlan."

Moments passed, and then Robin got to his feet.

Disappointment tightened Jean's throat. Had she offended him? Was their meeting already over? Standing up, she was about to move toward the door, when he asked, "Would ye like a cup of wine?"

Jean abruptly sat back down. "Aye," she murmured. "Thank ye."

Robin moved across to the sideboard and poured them both a drink. He then returned to the fireside and handed Jean her cup. Their fingers brushed as he did so, and her breathing quickened at the warmth of his touch.

And when she glanced up at his face, she noted he'd felt it too—for his pupils had dilated, and he was looking at her with an intensity that made heat prickle across her skin.

Lord, she found it difficult to concentrate in this man's presence.

Get ahold of yerself, Jean Munro, she told herself sternly. *Ye are his chatelaine, not a giddy lass. And the man is wedded anyhow.*

Struggling not to let her discomfort show, Jean took a sip of wine.

"Ye are certainly keeping the accounts in better order than I did," Robin said, settling himself down once more in the chair opposite. He stretched his legs out then and crossed them at the ankle. Jean noted how his well-worn leather boots molded his muscular calves.

Distracted, she took another sip of wine, larger this time. "Thank ye."

"And ye are doing a wonderful job of tutoring Grace," Robin went on, seemingly oblivious to the effect his nearness was having on her. "The lass loves ye."

Jean's mouth curved. "She's a delightful bairn ... and a quick study too."

A shadow flitted across Robin's eyes. "Aye ... ye have been a positive influence on her." He cleared his throat then. "On *all* of us. I've noted how the servants respect ye ... Evan tells me ye put one of the men-at-arms in his place last week."

"Aye," Jean replied, suddenly wary. She wasn't sure how Robin would react to discovering she'd taken a broom to the man. She'd been outdoors, returning from taking stock of their supplies of oats and barley in the granary, when a terrible din had erupted at the east end of the barmkin. Taking care not to slip in the slush of mud and snow that covered the yard, she'd picked up her skirts and hurried across to see what the matter was. The guard was viciously kicking one of the laird's wolfhounds as the poor creature whimpered and howled against the wall. A red-hot wave of rage had swept across her at the sight, and, without thinking, she'd grabbed a broom and smacked the man hard around the head with it. Evan had arrived moments later as her curses rang against the stone.

"I can't abide cruelty," Jean admitted then. "The dog had stolen food ... but it didn't deserve such a beating ... he could have killed it."

Robin nodded, his features hardening. "Ye did well."

Relieved, Jean wrapped her fingers about her cup. Meanwhile, the laird picked up a poker, leaned forward, and stabbed at the lump of peat burning in the hearth.

While they'd been speaking, the flames had died, although the fire now flared to life once more.

"Ye have a good character, Jean," Robin said softly. "Common decency was something I once took for granted, yet I value it highly in folk these days."

Jean's cheeks warmed under his praise. Yet at the same time, nervousness fluttered up within her. While she appreciated all the compliments he was giving her, a part of her was waiting for the criticism that was sure to follow.

However, none seemed forthcoming.

Leaning back in his chair, Robin lifted his cup to his lips and took a sip of wine. "I've made many mistakes over the years."

Jean cleared her throat. "Aye, well, find me a person who hasn't."

He looked her way once more, his mouth quirking. "Ye are fine company, do ye know that?"

Once again, discomfort wreathed up within Jean. She wasn't used to Robin Mackay treating her like this. "I hope I am," she replied uncertainly.

"Aye ... right from the day we met at Castle Varrich, I sensed yer warmth." He paused then, looking a little embarrassed at the admission. "I feel at ease when I'm with ye."

Jean gave a wry smile. "Even when I let my tongue run away with me? I do tend to prattle. It runs in the family, I'm afraid."

He laughed. "Ye don't 'prattle', Jean. Ye are completely yerself ... something I find refreshing."

She inclined her head. "I take it, Liosa didn't put ye at ease then?"

Robin's face stiffened, his gaze guttering—and Jean gave herself a hard mental slap. *Goose!*

"Sorry," she muttered. "I did warn ye about my tongue."

"It's all right," he replied. "I'm not used to talking about her ... that's all."

"Just forget I said anything."

A brittle silence fell then. Setting down her half-finished cup of wine next to the hearth, Jean rose to her feet. "I should leave ye be," she said, avoiding his eye. She'd been enjoying his compliments, yet her rash tongue had unwittingly ruined things. "Ye will be tired."

Robin set his own wine aside and stood up. "Ye don't have to rush off, Jean," he murmured. "I'm not going to shatter if ye bring up my past."

"No, but ye warned me when I first arrived at Melness that—"

"I behaved like a boor." And then, to her shock, he reached out, taking gentle hold of her chin. "Look at me, Jean."

Swallowing, she forced herself to raise her gaze. Her heart started to kick against her ribs when she saw he was smiling. "Liosa is nothing like ye," he said firmly. "She's cold and haughty ... and thinks herself better than others. But ye light up the world with yer warmth, yer generosity. Never change."

Her breathing caught. "There's no risk of that," she whispered back. Indeed, despite her pretty kirtle and unbound hair, she felt as gauche as ever in this man's presence. The promise she'd made herself to keep her thoughts focused on her chatelaine duties and away from Robin now lay in tatters at her feet.

She couldn't think straight standing this close to him, breathing in the scent of leather, clove, and musky male. Suddenly, the fire wasn't the only source of heat in the solar: the warmth of his body reached out and embraced her.

They both fell silent then, and the moment drew out.

Carefully, as if she were made of glass, Robin removed his fingers from under her chin and caressed her cheek instead. His touch was breathtakingly gentle, but Jean forgot to breathe, all the same. He had strong, calloused hands, and yet he touched her with reverence.

She couldn't believe they were standing here like this, so close. She'd told herself this day would never come.

And yet, an instant later, he kissed her.

Like his hand upon her cheek, his lips were gentle—the merest brush against her mouth—at first. But then a sigh escaped Jean; she couldn't help it. And with a sound low in his throat, Robin cupped her face with his hands and kissed her more firmly. His mouth against hers was yielding, yet firm. Without realizing what she was even doing, Jean's lips parted.

His tongue slid into her mouth, and the kiss changed. In a heartbeat, it turned from gentle to hot. Still cupping her cheeks, he explored her mouth with languorous determination. His tongue slid against hers, and his teeth grazed her lips. Then one hand slid around to cup the back of her head, and he deepened the kiss further.

Jean was lost.

She swayed against him and gave herself up entirely to his embrace. She had no idea what to do. But instinct overrode all else, and excitement thrilled through Jean when her untutored response—her tongue delving into his mouth—drew a groan from him.

Robin hauled her into his arms, his hands sliding down to her back. Until now, Jean hadn't touched him, yet his reaction made her bold. Reaching up, she let her hands splay across his broad chest.

Excitement spiked through her once more when she felt the thunder of his heart under her right palm.

The saints preserve her, she'd never expected a kiss to feel like this. The kiss he'd given her at Yuletide had been a punishment, yet this was something else. It was just two mouths fusing, but the act made her body catch fire. Every sense sharpened, and wildness arched up within her.

The rasp of Robin's chin against her own, the taste of his mouth, the feel of his hands as they cupped her backside and pulled her to him made the world recede. Their bodies were flush now, and she could feel the hard muscles of his legs and torso pressed against hers.

And when he drew her closer still, she felt something else: a thick, rigid shaft pressing against the softness of her belly.

A wave of dizzying lust crashed over Jean.

Robin drew back then, breathing hard as if he'd been running. His gaze was hooded, his expression hungry.

Jean swayed toward him, her hands sliding up so that her fingers caressed his neck. He couldn't just stop there—she wanted more. She wanted him to kiss her again.

But he didn't.

Instead, Robin placed his hands upon her shoulders, his touch firmer now, and stepped back from her. "Sorry, Jean," he rasped, his chest rising and falling sharply. "I forgot myself."

"Don't apologize," Jean breathed. "I enjoyed it."

His mouth kicked into a half-smile that made her breathing hitch. "Ye are lovely indeed." He reached up, his fingers threading through her unruly curls. "I like yer hair down … it's golden-brown, the color of oak."

"It's frizzy … difficult to manage."

"It's bonny." His hand left her hair then, his fingertips trailing down her jaw to her neck. "Yer skin is like milk."

Jean went still. She wanted him to continue touching her; maybe if he did so, he'd forget himself again.

But Robin withdrew his hand and stepped back from her. "Go on," he said, his voice roughening once more, his gaze hot. "Ye should return to yer chamber, lass … before I do something I shouldn't."

Robin listened to his chatelaine's soft footfalls as she left his solar.

When the door whispered shut behind her, he exhaled sharply.

What had come over him tonight?

There was no ulterior motive in inviting her up to his solar after supper. He really had wanted to look at the accounts and discuss her role as chatelaine. But, somehow, the conversation had gotten away from him.

Jean Munro was disarming—in every sense. And when he'd kissed her, desire—stronger than any he'd ever experienced—had barreled into him. Her mouth was so soft, and tasted so sweet, and her body was pliant and willing against his.

God forgive him, he'd wanted nothing more than to tear that kirtle off her, lay her down on the sheepskin before the hearth, and worship her. He'd come close to letting lust override good sense.

But luckily, his wits had returned to him, just in time.

He couldn't swive his chatelaine. As laird, he was in a position of power; and he'd been on the verge of exploiting it.

Jean wanted him—he'd known that since before she'd come to live at Melness. In truth, he'd thought his churlish behavior had made her feelings toward him cool.

Yet tonight had proved differently.

There was an innocence to her response that had sobered him, had made him pull away. He couldn't take advantage of her.

He'd been open with Jean this evening, far more so than he'd intended to be. However, there was something about her—a calmness and strength—that made him feel safe with her. As if he could pour out the most wretched, ugliest things in his soul, and she wouldn't judge him. Jean Munro was as beguiling as a kelpie's song, yet he couldn't succumb to her. He couldn't let himself trust her.

Raking a hand through his hair, Robin turned to the fire and stared at the flickering flames.

Bitter experience had taught him that trust was a poison chalice.

It would only lead to pain.

19

I'LL THINK ON IT

Two months later ...

"CAN I BUY a meat pie?" Grace's face was flushed with cold, her blue eyes gleaming, as she turned to Jean. "I'm starving!"

Jean smiled back. "Well, we can't have ye going hungry, lass." She dug into the purse at her waist and extracted a penny, passing it to the woman selling mutton pies in the market.

"Be careful, Lady Grace," the vendor warned, handing over the pie. "It's fresh out of the oven, so it'll be hot."

Grace nodded, taking the pie and nibbling at the crust.

Watching her, Jean's mouth curved once more. Like her name, Grace was neat and graceful in all that she did. In the past months, she'd grown truly fond of the lass. Grace was a warm-hearted, vivacious girl, although her energy and enthusiasm masked an underlying melancholy and loneliness. These days, the lass seemed less troubled. However, Grace still saw little of her father.

Jean's smile faded. Over the past two moons, since he'd returned from hunting Roy Gunn, Robin had retreated from his daughter, and his chatelaine, once more. Robin's mood wasn't taciturn these days—he was always pleasant when Jean encountered him—but the intimacy they'd shared that evening in the solar hadn't been repeated.

There had been no more kisses.

"Come on," Jean murmured, moving away from the pie stall. "Let's walk to the beach."

As she walked, memories of that encounter returned to torture Jean, as they often did. She tried not to relive the feel of his lips on hers, the languorous way he'd explored her mouth with his tongue, how his touch had made her melt into him—but she couldn't help it. She'd gone to bed feeling as if she were floating three feet above the floor. Excitement danced within her the following morning when she'd awoken. She'd been impatient to see him again, for them to talk openly once more. But she hadn't seen Robin all that day—for he'd ridden out on patrol—and not the next one either.

Grace had been excited too. After the three of them had taken supper together, she'd expected him to start asking her to join him in his solar in the evenings, for him to poke his head into the library in the mornings and chat to her in French. Every morning, she asked Jean if he was planning to join them.

Yet he didn't.

Jean and Grace wove through the dense crowd—it was the busiest she'd seen in Melness in months—taking their time to browse a cloth merchant's stall. The sight of the colorful bolts of fabric reminded Jean of all the hard work she and Brighde had put in to alter her gowns. They all now fitted properly, showing off her figure. But none of the gowns were colorful: they were all muted earth tones. Now it was early spring, it would have been nice to wear brighter colors.

She was getting used to dressing differently these days, to taking more care with her appearance. It was just as well she'd taken Brighde's advice about doing this for her own benefit and no one else's—since Robin had taken to treating her like his grandmother. He was polite, warm, yet behaved as if they hadn't ever kissed.

It was hard not to feel slighted.

Leaving the village behind, chatelaine and lass walked over green hills where spring bulbs poked out of the soil, and down to the wide beach.

Jean glanced left, toward the far end of the strand—to the cliffs and the Crone's Cave. She then suppressed a shudder. Hopefully, Roy Gunn had fled the Highlands now, never to return.

Banishing thoughts of that brute—for she didn't want him to cast a shadow over the day—Jean then linked her arm through Grace's as the lass finished her pie.

It was a rare windless morning, and the tide was rolling in, giving them only a narrow strip of sand to walk upon.

"This is such a beautiful spot," Jean murmured, her tone wistful. "Whenever I need cheering up, I bring my pony down here."

Grace glanced up at her, and Jean realized she'd inadvertently let slip something she hadn't intended.

"Do ye get sad sometimes?" the lass asked.

Jean flashed her a reassuring smile, inwardly kicking herself for being so candid. Grace might have been young, yet she missed little. "Only occasionally ... when I miss my sisters." That wasn't a falsehood—she did. "I received a missive from my elder sister Neave yesterday ... she's with bairn."

Grace grinned. "So ye shall be an aunt?"

"Aye ... for the second time. Wee Angus will have a cousin."

"When will ye see yer sisters next?"

"I don't know. I'd like to visit Castle Varrich at Easter ... if the laird allows it."

In truth, she'd hoped Robin would have organized another visit to Varrich—for she hadn't seen her sisters over the winter as she'd expected. Yet the weeks were passing, and there had been no word from the laird of a planned trip.

"I'm sure he will." Grace dropped her gaze then to the scattering of crescent-shaped shells along the tideline, where they walked. "I so want to visit Castle Varrich, but Da never takes me with him."

Jean's brow furrowed. Ever since their initial conversation about the seat of the Mackay clan, Grace had questioned her often about Varrich. Indeed, the lass was desperate to see it for herself.

"Perhaps he will let me take ye if I go for Easter," Jean replied after a pause. She shouldn't make such an offer without checking with Robin first, yet the joy that flared across Grace's face made her smile. Why shouldn't the lass make a trip away from Melness? She was surely old enough now, and Beth and Eilidh would be delighted to meet her.

"Will ye ask him?" Grace asked eagerly.

Jean smiled back. "Aye. He's out on a hunt this afternoon ... but as soon as he returns, I shall seek him out."

Men, horses, and dogs filled the barmkin when Jean emerged from the broch.

Dusk wasn't far off. The sun had slipped beyond the western walls, and the warmth it had brought with it disappeared. Jean was glad of the woolen wrap she wore around her shoulders.

Spying Robin amid his men, she straightened her spine, descended the steps, and made her way purposefully across to him.

In truth, she was feeling a trifle nervous. Ever since making her impulsive invitation to Grace, she'd regretted not thinking it through first. She could have waited until this evening to ask him but was wary about disturbing him in his solar.

"Good eve, Jean," MacVane greeted her with a grin as she approached. "Did ye see the boar we caught?"

Jean eyed the huge beast slung over the back of a pony. It was a grizzled male with a wiry black coat and long yellow tusks. "My word," she murmured, intimidated by the size of it. She then glanced over at where Robin Mackay had turned, upon hearing his captain greet her. "Ye already have a boar's head hanging over the hearth in yer solar ... will this one grace yer hall?"

"Perhaps," Robin replied, his mouth quirking. Once again, he was cordial but with a reserve that frustrated her.

"His father brought down the one in the solar," Evan piped up, winking at Jean. "Nearly gored him too."

Jean glanced around, noting the long spears the warriors all bore. Robin's one was blood-stained. "Did *ye* kill it?"

He nodded before inclining his head. "Did ye want something, Jean?"

"Aye." She stepped closer to him, wishing MacVane and the others would give them some privacy. However, she could feel their curious gazes upon her. "I'd like to visit Varrich at Easter. Neave is going to be there … and I've just learned she's with bairn."

Robin smiled, although his gaze was veiled. "Of course … be sure to pass on my congratulations."

Forcing down her discomfort, Jean moved nearer still, meeting his eye. "Grace would like to accompany me … can she?"

Robin's smile faded. "I'd prefer Grace stayed here."

"Why? Grace is eager to see the castle. We shall travel with an escort … and my sisters would be delighted to meet her."

"She's too young."

"She's eight … old enough to behave herself and appreciate such a trip."

A groove etched between Robin's brows, while Jean's pulse quickened. This wasn't going to be straightforward after all.

Pretending not to notice his reluctance, she favored him with a reassuring smile. "No harm will come to her, I promise."

A tense pause followed, and the rumble of conversation in the yard around them died. Jean could feel the weight of many curious gazes upon them now, yet she didn't look away from the laird.

"I'll think on it," Robin replied finally. His manner had turned aloof; nonetheless, a thrill of victory spiked through Jean. At least he hadn't refused her outright. He'd likely come around to the idea soon enough.

Turning, she headed back through the crowd toward the broch. Men parted to let her pass, and as she alighted the stairs, a grin split her face.

A trip to Castle Varrich was exactly what she and Grace needed. Jean longed to see her sisters again. Easter was a fortnight away, and she would write to Beth and Eilidh this evening and tell them she would be visiting.

Strathnaver—near the Mackay-Sutherland border

"Damn the Mackays to hell," Roy Gunn muttered, "and curse those Munro bitches too."

Roy jabbed the embers of his dying fire. His feet ached with cold, and the chilblains on his fingers pained him constantly. Spring was upon the Highlands, yet the evenings were still bitterly cold. His enemies had hunted him for months now. He wasn't sure how much more of this he could endure.

Grabbing a coarse blanket, Roy wrapped it about himself and shuffled as close as he dared to his hearth. Around him stretched bleak moorland, overshadowed by the looming bulk of Ben Hope. He'd lived out here for a while, eluding those who hunted him, and surviving off the birds he caught on the fringes of pools. His fires at night were pitiful, for although he was surrounded by peat bogs here, he didn't have any dry bricks of fuel. Instead, he scoured the moors, gathering spindly branches of broom and gorse to burn.

It was a bleak landscape out here—but at least he was the only one desperate enough to live in such inhospitable terrain.

Roy's mouth thinned, heat igniting in the pit of his belly. He could have run—could have left the Highlands for good—but hatred bound him to these lands. If he departed, it would be on his terms. And he would have his vengeance first.

On the Mackays. On his own kin.

A snort behind him roused Roy from his brooding. Glancing over his shoulder, he peered into the gloaming at where his horse stood. He'd hobbled the beast to stop it from wandering off. However, his gaze didn't alight on the courser he'd stolen from a traveler he'd killed—but on the burly figures on horseback that flanked it.

Roy lurched to his feet.

Satan's cods, where had the bastards sprung from? The last time he'd looked around, the surrounding moorland had been empty. But this group of riders had materialized like wraiths.

Snarling a curse, Roy whipped out his dirk and lowered himself to a crouch.

A dull ache twisted in his side, as it did whenever he made any sudden movements. John Mackay's blade still made itself felt, even now, nearly a year after their altercation.

"Easy." A huge man with wild brown hair dismounted and stepped forward. "We aren't looking for a fight."

"Ye'll get nothing from robbing me," Roy growled, his gaze scanning the stranger. The man was roughly dressed in frayed wool and worn leather. Roy looked for a clan sash—for the tell-tale flash of green and blue that would warn him he was facing a group of Mackays—yet none of the band before him wore anything that identified them.

The leader flashed Roy a toothy grin. "That's a nice horse ye have though."

Roy clenched his jaw. His stolen courser had been a boon over the past few months. The gelding ran like the wind. Without it, the Mackays would have caught him. He couldn't lose it.

The man moved closer. He walked with the arrogant, rolling stride of a warrior. "Do ye have a name, stranger?"

Roy bared his teeth. "No."

Sharp blue eyes assessed him. "I hear that the Mackays are hunting a fugitive." The man paused, his mouth curving. "Ye have a hefty price on yer head ... Roy Gunn."

Roy's pulse quickened. He rounded his shoulders, his grip on the dirk tightening. "Ye won't take me alive," he rasped.

The man snorted. "I'm no friend of the Mackays, Gunn ... they can keep their silver."

Roy scowled, his gaze surveying the band once more. *Warriors deliberately dressed like peasants upon Mackay lands.* Realization dawned. "Ye are Sutherlands."

The leader of the band gave a mocking bow. "Keiran Sutherland, nephew to the clan-chief at yer service." His gaze then flicked to the smoldering remains of his fire. "We have fuel ... can we join ye?"

Roy hesitated, his gaze narrowing. "Do ye have food?"

"Aye ... cold mutton. We shall share it with ye."

Roy's mouth watered. He hadn't eaten today—not since the grouse he'd caught the day before. His gut ached with hunger. These men might steal his horse, or slit his throat, but at least they weren't Mackays. He was surrounded anyway. There was nothing to be gained by trying to fight them off. He would take their food and deal with the consequences later.

Sheathing his dagger, Roy nodded.

A short while later, the fire was roaring, and Roy was wolfing down his second slice of mutton. He was stuffing food into his mouth like a beast, yet he was too hungry to care. Across the fire, Keiran Sutherland watched him.

The man might have given him food, but Roy didn't trust him. After everything he'd been through, he didn't trust anyone. Not anymore.

Swallowing, Roy met his eye. "So ... what are ye doing on the Strathnaver?"

Sutherland grinned. "Stirring up trouble." He motioned to Roy's supper. "That's Mackay mutton."

A feral smile stretched Roy's mouth. "Is it?" He took another bite and chewed vigorously. It tasted even better now. "So, ye are rustling sheep?"

"Aye ... my uncle has a score to settle with the Mackays." Sutherland's gaze turned speculative then. "He could do with men like ye at his side ... tough and full of spite for our enemies."

Roy snorted.

"An outlaw's life is a harsh one, Gunn. How long do ye think ye'll survive out here in the wild?" Sutherland paused then. "Don't ye want reckoning?"

Roy swallowed another mouthful. "Why do ye think I'm still here?"

Sutherland held Roy's eye. "Ye'll never get it on yer own. Join us, Gunn. We all want the same thing."

Roy scowled. Did they?

"If I were ye, instead of lurking on the fringes of Mackay lands, I'd head south, into Sutherland territory." Keiran leaned forward then and flashed Roy another toothy grin. "Make for Dunrobin Castle ... and tell the clan-chief I sent ye."

20

BETRAYALS

"YE'RE SUBDUED THIS eve, Jean ... is something amiss?"

Jean glanced up from her mending to find Brighde observing her. The two women sat in the kitchen. It was easily the warmest spot in the broch, and Jean enjoyed the evenings she spent in Brighde's company. At this hour, the other servants had all retired, and a rare silence settled over the kitchen. Chatelaine and cook both worked on sewing projects, their feet up on settles, before the glow of the hearth.

Pulling a face, Jean glanced away and stabbed her needle into her lèine. "It's a week since I asked the laird if Grace could join me on my visit to Varrich at Easter ... and he still hasn't answered me."

"Well ... he has been busy," Brighde replied. "What with the sheep rustling."

"I know ... but it only takes a moment to say 'aye' or 'nay'."

Brighde's brow furrowed. "Are ye sure this is about ye and Grace ... and not ye and the laird?"

Jean's breathing hitched, heat flowering across her chest. "No—it's about Grace."

The cook inclined her head. "Aye, well, she's never been away from Melness before ... maybe he's worried about her."

Jean snorted. "He spends no time with his daughter. Don't tell me he cares about her well-being."

Brighde set her own sewing aside. "He wasn't always like this, ye know," she said, her voice lowering as if she were afraid of being overheard. There wasn't much chance of that though. The kitchen door was closed, and the warriors sleeping in the hall beyond the kitchen annex wouldn't be able to hear them. "Before Lady Liosa left, he was a doting father."

"Well, he's not anymore." Jean scowled then. "It's not fair on her."

"No, it's not."

Silence fell between them for a few moments before Jean cast her friend a probing look. "No one ever speaks of what happened that day?"

Brighde cleared her throat and picked up her sewing once more. "Aye, and for good reason."

"Were ye here when it happened?"

Brighde nodded.

"Can ye tell me of it?" Brighde's features tightened, and Jean thought she might refuse her. "As chatelaine, I should know," she added. It was a gentle reminder that although the two of them had enjoyed a companionable relationship over the past months, Jean was in charge. It was a dirty trick, but Jean had to know what had transpired.

"I didn't see the events unfold," the cook admitted after a pause, her gaze shifting to the fire. "But I recall hearing the laird return from Varrich. His arrival was unexpected, for we'd all thought he'd be away for another day at least. I got to work, preparing more food for supper, while Mackay left his men to see to his horse and went straight inside. Shortly after, I heard shouting." Brigdhe's green eyes shadowed then, while Jean's pulse quickened.

"From upstairs?"

"Aye ... the din was coming from the top floor of the broch, yet I could hear it, even down here. Then a woman's shriek followed. I rushed out into the hall to see Lady Liosa and Gordon hurrying down the stairwell. They were both scantily dressed and barefoot. 'My brother tried to kill me!' Gordon shouted. 'I struck him down in self-defense!'"

Jean gasped. "What? Surely, no one believed him?"

"Indeed, it seemed improbable," the cook replied, "But Gordon might have been able to convince us if auld Lachlan hadn't appeared on the stairs behind him. 'Murderer!' he yelled, pointing a bony finger straight at the laird's brother and wife. 'I saw it all. She hit Mackay over the head with a lantern while he stabbed the laird with his dirk!'"

Jean's gaze widened as she imagined the scene. "Lord," she breathed. "How vicious."

"Fortunately for Gordon and Liosa, Danny MacVane and his men hadn't yet ventured indoors," the cook continued. "Nonetheless, their ruse had been exposed before the servants. Gordon went after Lachlan and knocked him out with one punch. He and the laird's wife then ran from the broch. Kenna saw to Lachlan while Fiona and I hurried upstairs." Brighde paused then, her gaze shadowing. "We found Mackay lying in the open doorway to his chamber, insensible, bleeding all over the flagstones from a deep wound to the side of his chest."

Jean muttered a curse. "Poor Robin!"

Brighde nodded. "I left Fiona with the laird and went downstairs to raise the alarm."

"Did anyone try to stop Gordon and Liosa?"

Brighde pulled a face. "Aye, MacVane attempted to bar their way out of the barmkin, but Gordon, who'd managed to fetch two horses by then, ran him down. The laird's brother and wife rode bareback out of the broch and haven't been seen since."

Silence fell in the kitchen, broken only by the gentle crackle of the fire and the whisper of the wind beyond the stone walls of the annex.

Queasiness stole over Jean. Of course, she'd known that Gordon and Liosa had tried to kill Robin—yet hearing the details made it clear just how vile those two were. "Mackay caught them coupling then?" she asked eventually.

"Aye ... the marital bed was untidy. It wasn't difficult to guess what they'd been up to. Like the rest of us, they hadn't expected the laird back so soon." Brighde gave a pained look then. "The laird was bed-ridden for nearly a

fortnight with the wound his brother dealt him ... and
when he rose from it, Robin Mackay was a changed man.
So grim ... so withdrawn. The sense of betrayal has eaten
him up inside ever since."

Murmuring an oath, Jean met Brighde's eye. "I know
he's been through much ... but he shouldn't punish Grace
for what his brother and wife did. I promised the lass she
could visit Varrich with me. I can't let her down." She put
her mending aside, her resolve firming. "I shall go up
and speak to him about it now."

Robin was seated by the hearth in his solar, nursing a
cup of wine, when a brisk knock sounded at his door.

Roused from worries about the mobs of sheep that
kept disappearing from his lands, he glanced toward the
door. Kenna had already been up to clear the supper
dishes, and he wasn't expecting any visitors. "Come in,"
he called out.

The door opened, and a small, comely figure wearing
a fur-trimmed, fawn-colored kirtle entered.

Robin tensed. He wasn't in the mood to talk to his
chatelaine this eve. Indeed, he'd been avoiding her ever
since she'd asked about taking Grace to Castle Varrich
for Easter.

Jean's hair was unbound, as it often was these days,
tumbling over her shoulders in that wild fashion that
made him want to tangle his fingers in it. When he'd
kissed her, he'd detected the scent of lavender. He
caught the scent once more now as she drew near, and
desire clawed at his gut.

Resolutely ignoring his body's traitorous reaction,
Robin frowned. "What is it, Jean?"

His chatelaine halted before folding her hands
together in front of her. "Apologies for disturbing ye,
Mackay," she murmured. "But Easter approaches, and ye
haven't yet told me if Grace can accompany me to
Varrich."

Robin pursed his lips. He should have known Jean
wouldn't let the matter drop. "I've been busy," he replied
gruffly.

"I know the sheep rustling has been a worry," Jean replied. "But Grace is eager to know yer answer."

Shifting in his chair, Robin fought a scowl. Her insistence vexed him, as did her presence in his solar. She was distracting; it was difficult to remain focused on her face when the light of the cresset on the wall next to her flickered across the milky swell of her cleavage.

He deliberately looked away, focusing on the fire once more. "Tell her she can't go," he said curtly before lifting his cup to his lips and taking a draft.

Long moments passed, and when Robin glanced back at his chatelaine, he saw that a faint flush had risen to her cheeks. Her jaw was set, and her hands, which now hung at her sides, were balled into fists.

She looked like she wanted to blacken his eye.

"Ye have my answer, Jean," Robin said after a heavy pause. "Ye can leave now."

Her finely arched brows snapped together. "I'll go when ye remember yer manners."

The laird's response was almost comical: Robin's hazel eyes snapped wide, his lips parting. "Excuse me?"

"Ye heard me," she snapped, even as her pulse raced. "Don't pretend ye have cloth in yer ears, man."

The chieftain set his cup of wine down on the mantelpiece with a thud before rising to his feet. "Do ye forget whom ye are speaking to, Jean?"

She hadn't. However, her temper had gotten the best of her, turning her reckless. Staring him down, Jean folded her arms across her breasts. "Ye hide yer daughter away as if ye are ashamed of her. Why won't ye let Grace go to Varrich?"

"My reasons are my own."

"But it's not Grace's fault!" Jean burst out, unable to contain herself any longer. "God's blood, ye are a mulish bastard!"

Jean's mouth clamped shut as soon as the words left her lips. Lord, what had come over her?

A deathly silence settled over the solar then.

Robin approached Jean, in stalking footsteps that made fear curl through her. Until now, she'd known the chieftain of Melness as a gentle man, but had she pushed him over the edge?

Halting before her, Robin's narrowed gaze fused with hers. "Ye have a lot to say for yerself, this eve, Jean Munro," he growled.

Heart slamming against her ribs, Jean forced herself to hold his gaze. "Only because I care about Grace. Yer aloofness wounds her. I don't want to have to tell her tomorrow that she can't go to Varrich ... to see the disappointment on her face, and not even be able to give her a good reason."

"It isn't yer place to worry about such things."

"No, but since ye refuse to talk to the lass, these tasks fall on me."

He flinched then as if she'd just slapped him. "Ye blunder into things ye don't understand," he ground out.

"Well then, help me to understand." Her own boldness both thrilled and appalled her. She couldn't believe she was standing toe-to-toe with the man she served, questioning him like this—but stubbornness refused to let the matter drop. There was something amiss here, something that perplexed her, like the line of a riddle she couldn't solve.

She didn't understand why he retreated behind that aloof mask whenever they spoke about Grace. He knew his daughter wasn't to blame for his wife's betrayal, and yet it was as if he was trying to punish the lass.

Robin Mackay's face hardened. "Go to bed, Jean ... there's nothing more to speak of."

Jean stared back at him. "There's an ocean of things unsaid, Mackay," she replied, her pulse thundering in her ears. "And if ye continue like this, all the things ye keep locked inside will poison ye."

She took a step back. Enough. She wouldn't push further. She'd been reckless this eve, but not so foolish as to ignore the anger smoldering in his eyes.

Stiff-backed, she turned and made for the door, grabbing the handle.

"Grace isn't mine."

Hand clenching around the iron knob, Jean looked back over her shoulder, frowning. "Excuse me?"

Robin stood, his body frozen, in the midst of his solar. His expression was grim, his voice raw with pain. "She isn't my daughter."

"But she has yer hazel eyes?"

Robin's face twisted. "She has *Gordon's* eyes."

Jean's breathing hitched. "But ... how do ye know?"

Reaching up, Robin raked his hands through his hair. Even standing a few feet away from him, Jean could sense his turmoil. "Liosa told me," he replied, his voice hoarse now. "When I opened the door to our bed-chamber that day ... I found my wife riding my brother." He halted then, a muscle in his jaw feathering. "Liosa didn't cover herself up, didn't even have the decency to look ashamed. She just stared me in the eye and said: 'Grace is Gordon's daughter, not yers.'"

Jean raised a hand to her chest, nausea rolling over her. How could anyone be so cruel? "She could have been lying," she pointed out, desperately wanting that to be the case.

Robin shook his head. "Liosa didn't stop there. As she got up from the bed and eventually covered her nakedness, she went on to tell me that whenever we lay together, she'd inserted a herbal pessary beforehand to prevent her womb from quickening. It was my brother's child she wanted, not mine. They'd lain together frequently from the early days of our marriage ... enjoying their freedom while I was out campaigning with Angus and John Mackay."

Jean stared at him, struck speechless by this admission. She didn't need to hear any more, but now that Robin had begun his tale, he would finish it. "Liosa told me that Gordon was everything I'm not ... and that *he* should have been laird."

Outrage, on his behalf, grabbed Jean by the throat, and she went rigid.

Noting her reaction, Robin gave a humorless laugh. "Ye wished to know why I keep my distance from Grace

... and now ye do." He raked a hand through his short brown hair. "I love that wee lass with every part of me ... but every time I look at her, it's as if my brother has just stabbed me afresh. I remember that she's his, and I'm filled with such darkness, such rage toward my wife and brother that it scares me."

"Oh, Robin." Jean moved toward him then, instinctively taking his hand and squeezing hard. "I'm so sorry ... I had no idea." She felt like a complete fool. She'd barged in here, full of self-righteousness, completely ignorant of the awful pain he'd been carrying.

"Aye, well ... apart from Liosa, Gordon, and myself, no one else knows. So I'd appreciate it if ye kept this a secret."

"I swear." Jean's vision blurred, guilt crushing her chest. How she'd pushed him, shamed him. No wonder he'd retreated from the world. The betrayal he'd suffered was worse than she'd thought.

"I know it's not right that I ignore Grace as I do," he admitted softly. "It's not her fault."

Jean could almost taste the rawness of his pain. Scrubbing away a tear that had escaped and was now running down her cheek, she tried to pull herself together. "Grace loves ye," she whispered.

And so do I.

Her heart kicked hard against her ribs.

Mother Mary, when had that happened?

Aye, she'd been drawn to Robin from the first, but she'd spent most of her months at Melness frustrated by the man's intractability. She'd buried her yearning deep and instead focused on proving herself as chatelaine. And she'd been successful too—until that night he'd kissed her in this solar. Ever since, she hadn't been able to look upon him the same way.

Love had stolen upon her—but there was no denying the sensation that felt as if a hand were squeezing her heart, mingled with a tenderness that robbed her of breath.

Indeed, she was madly, hopelessly, in love with him.

21

LET'S FORGET ABOUT THE RULES

ROBIN WATCHED JEAN try to wipe away her tears. "Why are ye weeping?"

"I can't help it." She hiccoughed the words. "I'm just so sad ... for both ye and Grace."

Robin swallowed hard, to dislodge the lump that had formed in his throat as he'd poured out his story to Jean. He couldn't believe he'd told her, for he hadn't whispered a word to a soul, not even to God. Instead, he'd carried his secret with him for the past three years.

There's an ocean of things unsaid, Mackay ... and if ye continue like this, all the things ye keep locked inside will poison ye.

Jean's words had caused the dyke to burst within him, allowed the hurt to come gushing free. She was right of course: bitterness was like a tumor growing in his gut. Now, strangely, although his insides felt tied in knots, and his pulse hammered in his ears, he felt unburdened for the first time in a long while.

"Soft-hearted Jean," he said huskily, reaching up and brushing away her tears with the back of his hand. "Always worrying about the happiness of others."

She sniffed, favoring him with a tremulous smile. "Some folk ... ye included ... would call it meddling."

"Aye, but it's done with good intentions," he replied. Staring down at her face, Robin's breathing quickened. Tears glittered off her long lashes and turned her eyes luminous. Her expression was so vulnerable he couldn't bear it. "Don't cry, lass," he whispered. "Or ye shall see a grown man weep as well."

She swallowed, although her tears didn't stop—and without thinking about what he was doing, Robin leaned down and kissed them away.

The act was supposed to be a soothing one, yet as he tasted the salt of her tears, and felt her tremble under his touch, the last of the restraints binding Robin Mackay loosed. It was no good. Over the past moons, he'd tried to forget how this woman tasted, how she felt in his arms, but he couldn't.

His need for her was stronger than his fear of being hurt again.

He captured her mouth with his and kissed her deeply.

Their last kiss had started gently, but this one didn't. His mouth moved over hers hungrily before his tongue swept her lips apart. Jean gasped, and she melted into him, her arms coming up to link around his neck.

Robin stifled a deep groan. How he'd missed this, how he'd longed for this. She tasted so sweet, and her body against his was so yielding and lush. Before he knew what he was doing, he'd walked her back against the door.

There, he pressed himself up against Jean, slowly grinding his hips against hers as the kiss deepened.

Jean responded to him with a hunger that equaled his own. She writhed against him, her body trembling.

Robin ripped his mouth from hers and whispered her name, his lips trailing across her cheek so that the tip of his tongue could explore the shell of her ear. Her soft cry of pleasure made his already hammering heart slam against his ribs. Murmuring endearments, he trailed his lips down her neck, feasting on the sweetness of her skin.

God's teeth, she tasted better than cream and honey or the first strawberries of summer. He longed to kiss every inch of her, to strip her bare right here.

The thought sobered him, reason spiking through the haze of lust that had turned him witless. Raising his head, Robin met her gaze. Jean's eyes were glazed with desire. "I want ye, Jean," he rasped. His voice, raw and rough, didn't sound like his own. "But we can't take this any further. I don't wish to ruin ye."

"I don't care if ye ruin me," she gasped back.

Her recklessness was both heady and alarming. "Ye should," Robin ground out. "Ye are a clan-chief's daughter."

"That doesn't matter," she replied, staring up at him with such naked desire that he nearly forgot himself once more. "Let's forget about the rules, Robin."

Her words were heady; indeed, they made him want to throw caution aside and take her in a wild storm of passion. But Robin Mackay wasn't a man who despoiled virgins. And Jean had reminded him that she was his responsibility.

No, he couldn't ruin her.

Reaching up, he cupped her cheek with his hand before running the pad of his thumb along her plump lower lip. "Ye are enchanting," he said, his voice tight with longing. "But I can't rob ye of yer maidenhead." He paused then, drowning in the limpid depths of her eyes. "We can kiss ... and touch, but it can go no further."

She nodded slowly, understanding rippling over her face. She reached out then, her hands plucking at where his lèine was loosely tucked into his braies. "So, we can explore each other?"

Her boldness excited him, even as the tightening under his ribcage warned him this was a bad idea. They were playing with fire, and although Jean didn't seem to care if she got burned, Robin had been scarred enough by life to be more cautious.

What are ye doing, man? The voice of reason surfaced then. *Ye know where this leads.*

To pain. Betrayal.

Nonetheless, he found himself nodding, allowing her to slide her hands under his lèine to explore the skin beneath. Her fingers traveled over his belly and up to his chest, and then she stood on tiptoes, her eyes fluttering shut as she invited him to kiss her again.

God's blood, he couldn't resist her.

Leaning down, Robin's mouth covered Jean's. They kissed slowly, languorously. This time, he kept his lust leashed. Instead, he would focus on Jean, on giving her pleasure. His own roaring need would be set aside.

Jean gave a grunt of frustration then, tugging at his lèine. Clearly, she wanted him to take it off. Mouth curving, he broke off the kiss and did as she wished. Fortunately, the weather had started to warm, and the evenings were no longer icy. The glowing hearth warmed the solar and his naked torso.

Murmuring words of appreciation, Jean explored his chest with her hands before leaning forward and tasting the skin at the hollow of his throat.

She slid downward, her lips and tongue tracing his chest to his nipples.

Robin started to breathe hard, his senses sharpening. His groin was now throbbing. He couldn't let go, couldn't give in to the wildness building within him. Instead, he had to turn the focus back to Jean.

Gently, he pushed her back against the door, his mouth claiming hers once more as he loosed the ties upon the bodice of her kirtle. Both the over-dress, and the lèine she wore underneath, were low-cut. As such, it was easy to push them down over her shoulders, exposing her chest and torso to him.

Robin stared at her breasts, transfixed. They were large and proud, with translucent skin and rose-colored nipples that strained toward him. Of course, he'd imagined what Jean Munro's tits looked like over the past few months—especially since she'd started wearing dresses that showed off her shape. But her breasts were even more delicious than he'd envisaged.

Murmuring an oath, he took hold of them, marveling at the softness of her skin, pushing them up to meet his eager mouth. Suckling her breasts, he tried to ignore his throbbing shaft. However, when Jean let out a low, sensual groan, he struggled not to give in to the desire to hike up her skirts, loose his rod from his braies, and plunge into her.

She was a virgin. He couldn't treat her so roughly.

Indeed, he couldn't penetrate her at all.

But he could give her pleasure.

Releasing her breasts, he straightened up. Jean's eyes were closed, her face a picture of desire. Leaning in, Robin kissed her again, exploring the sweetness of her mouth, while his hands delved under her skirts. Gently, he pushed her thighs apart with his knee, while his fingers slid up the smooth skin of her inner thigh.

And when the pad of his thumb found the tender spot between her legs, Jean let out a startled gasp against his mouth. Her eyes had flown wide, her pupils dilated.

"Aye, lass," he murmured, excited by her reaction. "Let me show ye."

He started to stroke and rub her.

Jean's head fell back, and she moaned. A moment later, she began to move against his hand, her breasts rising and falling sharply as her breathing quickened.

"Do ye like that, Jean?"

"Aye," she gasped, her eyes glazed.

Robin leaned in, teasing her lips with his teeth and tongue. "Would ye like more?"

"Oh, aye."

Gently, he slid a finger deep inside her, and the wet, tight heat of her core made his rod twitch hard in his braies. If he wasn't careful, he'd spill like an over-eager lad.

Jean's eyes were huge now, her lips parted in wonder. "Robin," she breathed. Her hips bucked against his hand then, demanded more still.

Watching her face, Robin withdrew his hand for just an instant before sliding into her once more with two fingers.

Jean went rigid against him, her breath hitching.

Robin froze too, realizing his mistake. "Have I hurt ye?" he rasped.

A heartbeat passed, and then Jean shook her head. "No ... it pinched for a moment that's all ... but I'm fine now."

Robin silently cursed himself. In his eagerness to please her, he'd just taken her maidenhead with his hand.

He was about to remove his fingers and apologize when Jean gave a breathy sigh and rotated her hips against him. And then she groaned his name.

Lust roared in his ears, drowning out the voice of good sense. Slowly he began to move his fingers inside her once more, curling them up slightly with each stroke.

Jean came alive in his arms.

Gasping his name now, she writhed against him. The wetness and heat of her against his hand nearly undid him. Robin hadn't been with a woman in a long while, not since Liosa—and before his wife, he'd been able to count the number of lovers he'd had on one hand. Unlike his brash younger brother, he'd been a shy lad. Nonetheless, he was experienced enough to know when a woman truly wanted him.

Liosa had never responded to him like this.

Jean Munro was fire, and she consumed him. He could feel his self-restraint unraveling—and there was a part of him that longed to give in. Life had been joyless for so long, and Jean brought him alive. But this had gone far enough.

Tremors rippled through her body then, and she arched against his hand, before she collapsed, shaking, against the door.

Robin stepped close, cradling Jean's small, soft body against his while she recovered. "That was ... incredible," she breathed into his ear.

He huffed a soft laugh. "I'm glad ye enjoyed it."

And he was—even if his nerves were now stretched taut like a bowstring and his groin was in agony.

"I want more, Robin ... and so do ye," she whispered. An instant later, her small hand slid over the bulge in his braies. She stroked him eagerly, from root to tip, through the thick material, and Robin's shaft swelled harder still.

Lord help him, he was going to explode.

He buried his face in her neck and bit back a deep groan. "Ye had better stop that, Jean," he rasped.

"Why?" she whispered as her other hand fumbled with the laces on his braies. "Ye have pleasured me, and I wish to do the same for ye."

22

GIVING IN

JEAN'S FINGERS WERE deft, for she unlaced his braies fast. And then, before he could say anything else, his rod jutted out to meet her hands.

Lowering herself before him, she stroked him again, staring down at his manhood with unabashed fascination.

Sweat beaded upon Robin's skin, heat gathering at the base of his spine.

What are ye doing? They were taking things too far, and yet he yearned just to give himself over to this woman.

"The skin is so soft," she murmured. "Yet yer rod is so hard."

Robin made a strangled sound.

Jean glanced up, her eyes widening. "Am I hurting ye?"

"No." He bit out the word. "But if ye continue touching me like that, I'm going to spill."

To her surprise, Jean released him and straightened up. Then she wriggled out of her lèine and kirtle, letting them pool around her ankles. Kicking them, and her slippers, aside, she faced him.

Naked, her skin bathed in firelight, she looked like a beautiful wood nymph: all curves and pale skin, her thick hair tumbling in wild curls over her bare shoulders. However, her eyes glinted when their gazes fused once more, and her chin lifted in a gesture he'd come to know well. "I want ye, Robin," she said firmly. "All of ye."

Panic spiked through Robin, even as his belly muscles clenched with desire. "Ye don't know what ye are asking," he replied, his voice hoarse now. "What if—"

"Leave thinking about the future until dawn," she cut him off. "Let tonight be about us." Her confident expression wavered then, color rising upon her cheeks. "Unless ... ye don't want me?"

Robin's breath gusted out of him. "I want ye with everything that I am," he growled. "I'm nearly insane with wanting ye."

"Then ... give in to the want," she whispered back, placing the palm of her hand over his heart. "I shall never reproach ye for it."

Silence fell between them then, the moment stretching out.

Robin made his decision.

Without another word, he heeled off his boots, before pushing down his braies, and kicking them aside. He wasn't thinking now—only acting. And then he scooped Jean up in his arms and carried her across to the fire. There, he set her down upon the soft sheepskin and lowered himself down before her.

On their knees, they faced each other, their mouths fusing with hunger.

And this time, Robin didn't hold himself back. All thought fled his mind as instinct took over. His hands slid over her nakedness, exploring every curve. Jean kissed him back with a savage hunger that merely inflamed his own.

For the first time in his life, Robin Mackay truly forgot himself. He'd never let go like this with Liosa. He'd never given all of himself to a woman, yet he wanted to with Jean Munro. She made him want to trust.

Lying back on the sheepskin, he pulled Jean astride him.

Breathing hard, she rubbed herself against the thick column of his erection, moving her hips in sinuous rolls.

Robin groaned an oath. It was too much. He had to be inside her.

Gripping hold of Jean's hips, he lifted her up, settling her upon his engorged length. She slid easily down his rod. Robin watched her face, yet unlike earlier, there was no pain. Instead, pleasure tightened her features, her lips parting in a sigh as she lowered herself upon him.

God's blood, where has this woman been all my life?

Robin stopped breathing for a few instants. Being buried to the hilt inside her was incredible. Nothing had ever felt so right.

"Ride me, Jean," he ground out, guiding her with his hands on her hips.

Jean started to rock, back and forth, in a timeless rhythm, gasping each time he slid home. "Robin!" Her voice was high and tight. She was close to peaking; he could feel the fluttering of her muscles against his shaft.

"Aye," he growled. "Don't stop."

She didn't. Instead, Jean increased her tempo, riding him hard, her breasts bouncing, her head thrown back.

Robin stared up at her, transfixed.

He loved how she let go, but he wanted to see her unravel completely—just as he was about to.

Reaching up, his fingertips brushed through the damp curls between her thighs, his thumb caressing the sensitive spot he'd found earlier.

With a ragged cry, Jean shattered.

Her shoulders rounded, and she clutched at him, tremors convulsing her. An instant later, she arched hard against him, sweat glistening off her skin.

Robin's release barreled into him then. It swept over him, utterly consuming. For a few instants, he forgot himself. The past didn't matter, or the future. He wanted to remain buried deep inside this woman forever. Gasping her name, he lifted his pelvis off the sheepskin, his fingers digging into the soft flesh of her hips. He then drove her down on him one last time and chased Jean over the edge.

Lying sprawled atop her lover, listening to the wild beat of his heart against her ear, Jean struggled to form any coherent thought.

No wonder Beth and Neave look so pleased with themselves, she thought dazedly. She and Eilidh had been a trifle puzzled, and envious of the powerful attraction their elder sisters had with their husbands.

In truth, Jean had never thought to find passion like this.

There had been moments, as she'd ridden Robin, when her want for him had almost frightened her, as had the climax that had broken over her. It was as if her body took over, as if she had no will of her own. Pleasure had rolled over her in wild waves, and her body still hummed from it.

Sliding her hand up Robin's sweat-slicked torso, she raised her head to look at his face.

Her lover's eyes were closed, his lips parted slightly as he recovered his breath. Jean hungrily took him in, viewing the chieftain of Melness with fresh eyes. She'd wanted Robin for a while yet had no experience to draw from to imagine what it would be like to couple with him. The withdrawn man who'd retreated from her company at Samhuinn seemed a distant memory now.

For she'd never seen Robin like this. With the fire's glow highlighting the flush upon his cheekbones, he looked much younger. The harsh lines that once bracketed his mouth and nose were gone. And when he opened his eyes, his gaze meeting hers, Jean's chest constricted with love.

She wanted to tell him what lay in her heart, to pour out her feelings for him, yet something—perhaps a latent sense of self-preservation—halted her. This was all so new, so raw, for them both.

To speak of love might shatter the moment, might scare him away.

"Ye are a vision of loveliness, Jean Munro," Robin said then, his voice husky.

Jean's cheeks warmed with pleasure. "I had no idea"—she whispered back, suddenly shy— "that coupling was like that."

He stared up at her before his mouth lifted at the corners. "It isn't ... well not in my experience. Not until tonight."

Jean's breathing hitched. What was he saying? Was he admitting that he'd never let go like that when he'd lain with Liosa?

Liosa.

A chill feathered down Jean's spine, and she lowered her head to Robin's chest once more so that he wouldn't see her face. He was still married, and while his wife lived, he would continue to be.

They could be lovers, but he could never take her as his wife.

Jean bit the inside of her cheek then, to quell such thoughts. She'd urged him to let go—there was no point in regretting it now. She was also getting ahead of herself. Hadn't she told Robin to leave thinking about the future until dawn? She needed to take her own advice.

Glancing back up, she saw that he was watching her, a furrow between his brows. Had his thoughts slid in the same direction?

Jean reached out, her fingertips tracing the lines of his face. Although not handsome in a classical way, Robin's face was a blend of strength and sensitivity that she found irresistible.

"I want tonight to last forever," she whispered, her throat thickening then.

His hazel eyes gleamed, and he reached up, placing his hand over hers. "If only it could."

Bolting the doors to the granary, Jean pushed a wayward curl out of her face. Dust devils chased each other across the barmkin, although the wind today gusted in from the south, bringing the sweet scent of spring.

Merchants had just delivered a load of oats and barley. The broch had almost exhausted its stores, but the granary was full once more; she could relax.

A smile creased Jean's face. However, it wasn't just the satisfaction of a full grain store that made joy dance within her.

It was thoughts of her lover.

Every night for the last week, she'd gone to the chieftain's solar after supper. There, she and Robin had shared a cup of wine and talked for a while, before they'd undressed each other and coupled on the sheepskin before the fire. Last eve, he'd been so impatient to be inside her that the wine and conversation had been left until afterward. Instead, he'd lifted her up onto the table that dominated the solar, pushed her skirts around her waist, and taken her with a fierceness that had left her limp and gasping in his arms. Later, he'd wrapped them both in a thick plaid blanket before the fire, and they'd dozed together.

Still smiling as she relived the scene, Jean made her way toward the kitchen. She was late for the noon meal, as she had been often over the past days. Even when she should have been concentrating on her duties, she caught herself daydreaming.

Quickening her pace, Jean entered the kitchen annex and took her place at the table.

"Ye look cheerful today, Jean," Brighde commented as she ladled out some stew into bowls for the noon meal. "Ye must be looking forward to seeing yer sisters?"

"Aye." Jean's smile faded then as guilt stabbed her. Of course she couldn't wait to see Beth and Eilidh—and Neave too, who'd be visiting from Achness—but over the past few days, she'd barely thought about them.

Robin had consumed her.

"Ye are leaving tomorrow then?" Fiona asked.

Jean nodded. "I wish to be there for Good Friday."

"Grace is beside herself with excitement," Kenna said, envy flitting across her face.

"Aye," Brighde agreed. "I don't know how ye managed to convince the laird to let her go, Jean ... but Grace certainly is grateful."

Jean dipped her head, hoping that a telltale blush wasn't blooming across her cheeks. It was hard to act normally these days.

Not when everything had changed.

Aye, the past week would remain etched forever in Jean's mind. It had been perfect. The moments they'd shared had been wonderful—the only blight being that they didn't talk about what lay ahead. Neither of them wished to shatter the fragile cocoon of happiness they'd woven about themselves by speaking of the reality of matters.

Jean wasn't Robin's wife, and never could be.

He'd taken her maidenhead, and she'd given it willingly.

A bairn could take seed in her womb—if it hadn't done so already.

All three of those things should have worried Jean, and yet she found herself floating through her days, counting down the hours until she and Robin could be alone together again.

Jean focused on her stew then, taking a mouthful as the conversation around the table moved to other subjects.

The future doesn't matter, she told herself, even as unease fluttered up within her. *The present is all any of us have anyway.*

Maybe if she repeated that to herself enough times, it would become the truth.

23

A CHANGE OF PLAN

"ARE THERE ANY bairns my age at Castle Varrich?" Grace asked, glancing up from eating her dish of braised mutton and cabbage.

Jean paused while tearing off a piece of bread, her brow wrinkling. "I think not ... wee Angus is under a year old. However, there will be plenty of people who'll want to spend time with ye." She favored the lass with a warm smile, knowing that she yearned for the company of other children. "And Eilidh is a bairn at heart ... she won't leave ye be."

Grace grinned back. "I can't wait to meet her."

"All the Munro sisters are charming and warm-hearted, Grace," Robin Mackay spoke up then. "Ye will feel very welcome at Castle Varrich ... I always have done."

Grace shifted her attention to her father before she dropped her gaze in sudden shyness. When she was with Jean, Grace wasn't a bashful girl. However, she spent such little time with her father that she was a bit in awe of him. In all the months Jean had resided at Melness, this was the first time the three of them had taken a meal together in the chieftain's solar.

Grace was clearly delighted, as was Jean. Just that morning, he'd visited them while they'd been reading 'The Nine Maidens of Dundee' aloud in the library. The laird had pulled up a seat at the table and listened while his daughter recounted the tale.

"Why don't ye come with us to Varrich, Da?" Grace favored her father with a hopeful look.

"I'm needed here, lass," Robin replied, picking up his goblet of wine and taking a sip. "But I wish to hear all about yer visit upon yer return."

Grace flushed with pleasure at these words, and Jean smiled too. Nonetheless, she wished Robin could have joined them. Aye, he was busy, but there were always things to do at Melness. Surely, he could be spared for a few days at Easter?

"Can I ride Blossom to Varrich?" Grace asked then.

Robin's expression shadowed just for an instant before he smiled once more. Yet, this time, there was a brittle edge to the expression. "Of course, lass," he murmured. "The pony is yers."

Grace glanced over at Jean, grinning. "Ma gave me Blossom for my fifth birthday."

"Ye were too young to ride the mare at the time," Robin replied. His voice was even, although Jean marked the tension around his mouth. "Although, ye are tall enough now."

He took another gulp of wine and turned back to his meal. The convivial atmosphere at the table ebbed slightly. For the first time, Grace noted her father's altered mood. Her smooth brow furrowed as she realized that, in bringing up her mother in conversation, she had discomforted her Da.

Initially, Jean had thought Robin's reaction to any mention of his wife was because he didn't want to be reminded of her infidelity. Now she knew it was more than that. His wife's betrayal went far deeper than she'd realized. It was little surprise Robin didn't want to be reminded about Liosa.

"Dusty will be pleased," Jean said, attempting to brighten things up again. "I swear my garron is in love with Blossom. Every time I visit them in the stables, the pair are snuggled up to each other. He follows her around like a puppy, desperate for attention."

Grace laughed at this, the light sound filtering through the solar.

Robin chuckled too. "Aye well, I've asked Evan to lead yer escort tomorrow. He will look after ye both."

Warmth suffused Jean's chest at these words. She looked across the table, her gaze fusing with Robin's. The moment drew out as Grace returned to her mutton. There was no mistaking the affection in his voice or the softness in his eyes. And as she and Robin continued to stare at each other, his mouth curved into a slow, sensual smile.

Jean's heart kicked against her ribs. It was a smile that promised much. Once supper ended and Grace retired to her chamber, they would be alone.

But it wasn't just the physical intimacy she craved; it was the emotional closeness. They got on so well, and never ran out of things to talk about. Every time he wrapped his arms around her, she felt as if she belonged there.

Pulse quickening, Jean smiled back.

Jean awoke with cramps in her lower belly. Pushing herself up in bed, she realized her courses had arrived. Her monthly bleed was a couple of days late, and she'd begun to worry that it wouldn't come.

She'd lain abed the night before, considering what falling pregnant would mean. The past week had flown by. She'd been walking on a cloud of pleasure. Yet a bairn would change all that.

Beneath the glow of happiness, she was concerned.

She wasn't Robin's wife. They could never be open about their relationship. A bairn would bring shame on them both. But now the tension had been released. For this month, at least, she had dodged having to deal with the consequences of the affair she and Robin had embarked on.

Ye'll need to face this, sooner or later, Jean, commonsense whispered to her as she rose from the bed.

Ye and Robin can't continue like this, or ye shall come to grief.

Ignoring the niggling voice, she padded across to the washbowl upon a table in the corner of her chamber. There, she washed herself, before placing a folded piece of linen between her thighs and pulling on a pair of woolen leggings to keep the rag in place.

Adjusting her leggings, Jean's brow furrowed. Despite that she couldn't wait to see her sisters, she felt tired and draggy this morning. Her monthly bleed wasn't great timing, for she'd be spending the day in the saddle. It would be uncomfortable, yet it couldn't be helped.

Robin Mackay watched his chatelaine and daughter ride out of Melness.

It was a fine spring morning, although windy, as it often was on this exposed stretch of coast. Standing on the wall, next to the guard tower, his gaze tracked the knot of riders as they made their way out of the village and joined the rutted road stretching south.

In the midst of them, he spied Grace's golden hair. Next to her, Jean wore a forest-green cloak. Her hair had been pulled back from her face and tumbled down her back in unruly curls.

Heat kindled in Robin's belly as he relived tangling his fingers in her hair, burying his face in it, and breathing in the scent of lavender. Jean had complained that her hair had a will of its own, but he loved how untamed it was—it was a reminder of the wildness that beat within her.

A brisk manner and serious nature hid a sensual heart.

The past week had been the happiest of Robin's life. For the first time ever, he'd truly let go. He'd thought his battered heart couldn't trust again—but maybe he was wrong. His soul was slowly thawing, like frozen ground after the last of the winter snows. He went through each day anticipating the time, after supper, when Jean would knock on his solar door.

They were discreet in their affair, although it wouldn't be long before someone noticed the chatelaine's evening visits to the laird's solar. Robin supposed he and Jean shouldn't see each other every evening. When Jean returned from her trip to Varrich, it would be wise to exercise more caution.

They hadn't spent a full night together though, for he hadn't yet invited her upstairs to his bed-chamber.

Robin's mouth thinned then. He hadn't been able to sleep in that room for months after Liosa and Gordon fled. He'd had the bed—a massive carven and canopied affair—taken out and burned. The village carpenter had fashioned him a new one of oak, although when he'd finally returned to his quarters on the top floor of the tower, he'd slept fitfully.

No, it was best he continued to spend time with Jean in the solar, where his memories hadn't been tainted.

A few furlongs west of Melness, two figures watched the company of riders depart the broch. Screened by a stand of wind-battered pines, the man and woman looked on as the party headed south.

Excitement quickened in Liosa Mackay's breast when she spied her daughter amongst the riders. She and Gordon had been visiting Melness for a few days now, hoping to see Grace venture out of the broch.

And now they had.

However, there was an unexpected complication: in addition to her maid, Grace had an escort of six warriors with her.

Liosa's excitement dimmed a little. Pushing her hair out of her eyes, for a brisk wind rushed in from the sea this morning, she glanced across at where Gordon stood beside her. "I was hoping Grace would go flower-picking with her maid," she admitted, her voice tight. "But she's too well-defended for us to approach."

"Aye," Gordon replied, glancing back at where the riders had just disappeared over the crest of a hill. "It's just as well we have a band of men at our disposal then, isn't it?"

Liosa's mouth curved into a smile. Her lover's confidence and capability were the things she liked best about him. Over the past three years, as they'd lived as fugitives, those traits had gotten them out of a few scrapes.

During recent months, he'd gathered a band of warriors loyal to him. They were waiting a few furlongs west of Melness. The men respected Gordon, but he'd also ensured their allegiance with silver. Fortunately, Liosa and her lover had taken a bag of coins upon leaving Melness—swiped from Robin's belt as he lay bleeding on the floor—which had saved them from destitution in the weeks afterward.

Gordon released the pine branch he'd been holding and turned to Liosa. "Come, mo ghràdh." He then flashed her a grin and walked to where their horses waited, tied to a stump behind them. "There's no time to lose."

"Why are ye still here?"

Robin glanced up from where he was sitting upon a stool before the armory, sharpening the blade of his axe with a whetstone. MacVane stood before him.

"Isn't it obvious, man?" Robin resumed his task, the scrape of stone against steel reverberating off the surrounding walls. It was sheltered in the barmkin, and he was enjoying the feel of the sun on his face.

"I'm sure ye like to keep that blade sharp, Mackay," the captain replied, a wry edge to his voice, "but I thought ye'd be off to Castle Varrich with yer daughter."

"There's too much to do here." Robin looked up once more to see MacVane had folded his arms across his chest and was looking down his nose at him. "*What?*"

The captain frowned. "That's a feeble excuse. Grace would be over the moon if ye joined her."

Robin stiffened, halting in his task. Danny had been with him a while and had watched Grace grow from a babe to lass. Robin had seen the way the pair of them had chatted together whenever Grace joined them in the hall: the captain treated her like his younger sister. It was obvious he was fond of her. However, Robin didn't appreciate the implied criticism.

"Grace has a pure heart," MacVane went on. "She's a credit to ye, Rob … and she worships ye. I know things have been difficult, but isn't it time ye put it all behind ye?"

The two men's gazes fused, the moment drawing out. A kernel of warmth germinated within Robin. He'd always considered Danny MacVane a friend. However, of late, he'd taken his captain for granted.

The truth was he *did* want to go with Jean and Grace. He'd just talked himself out of it. Things between him and Jean had gotten so intense of late that it would be hard to hide their attraction for each other at Varrich. It could get awkward indeed if the clan-chief or his wife suspected he'd been bedding his chatelaine.

All the same, he was now regretting his decision.

Moments passed, and then Robin sighed. "Maybe I *should* ride after Grace."

The captain nodded. He then flashed Robin a knowing smile. "They won't have gotten far … I wouldn't mind a few days at Varrich, enjoying Niel Mackay's hospitality either. Shall I saddle our horses?"

24

THEY TOOK THEM

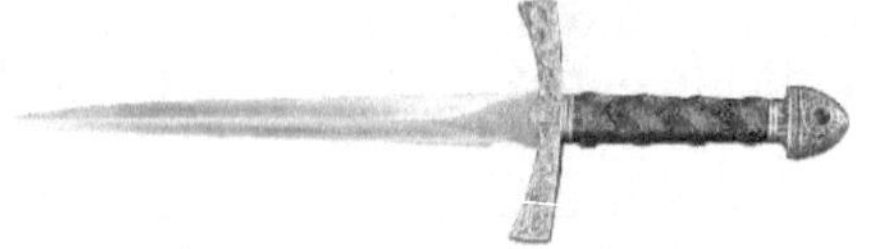

"WHEN WILL WE reach Varrich?"

Jean turned from where she'd been looking across the glittering water of the Kyle of Tongue. It was noon, and the party had halted to eat and rest their horses for a short spell. The road hugged the kyle all the way down to its southern edge before it would veer east, crossing the river at Kinloch. From there, they would head north again to where Castle Varrich perched like a sentinel over the eastern shore of the kyle.

"It's a full day's travel," Jean replied with a smile. The lass had already asked her that. Of course, Grace had never been away from Melness before. Although Castle Varrich didn't lie a great distance from home, it would seem so to her. "If we keep up a steady pace, we should reach it by late afternoon."

"Early evening more like," Evan piped up from behind them. "With those two fat ponies slowing us down."

Jean glanced over at where the guard leaned against a birch, finishing the last of his bread and cheese. To his left stood Dusty and Blossom. The two garrons cropped at grass greedily.

Jean sighed. Evan was right. Dusty was as broad as a barrel, and Blossom wasn't any slimmer. "I think we need to cut back on their feed," she admitted.

"Lady Grace will have to stop bringing them treats," Evan said, winking at the laird's daughter. "Don't think I haven't seen ye sneaking into the stables in the afternoons, lass."

Grace's cheeks flushed. "It's just a few apples and carrots."

His smile widened. "Those hardy garrons can survive on the scent of grass," he replied. "If they get much fatter, they'll be waddling."

Crestfallen, Grace finished the last of her meal and brushed the crumbs off her skirts. She then rose to her feet. "Well, if the ponies are going to slow us down, we'd better be on our way."

"Just a few more minutes, lass," Evan replied. "Duncan's gone off to take a piss in the bushes."

Grace giggled at this, while Jean flashed Evan a censorious look. Although she usually appreciated his direct manner, she'd prefer him to remember propriety when he spoke to the laird's daughter.

Catching her glare, Evan favored her with a contrite smile. His lips parted then as if he was going to apologize for his crudeness.

But Evan Pollard never replied.

The twang of a releasing bowstring cut through the air, and an instant later, a fletched arrow protruded from Evan's throat.

His eyes flew wide. Evan staggered forward, dropping the remains of his meal. His mouth gaped, and his hands flew to the arrow, his fingers fumbling with the shaft.

Thud. Thud. Two more arrows embedded in Evan's chest.

Jean watched in horror as Evan dropped to his knees and then toppled forward.

Grace's scream echoed across the kyle, lifting high into the windy sky.

Leaping to her feet, Jean grasped the lass, pushing Grace behind her. Together, they backed up, toward the shore of the kyle, while Jean's gaze darted around, trying to locate the bowman who'd killed Evan.

The scrape of steel against leather filled the air then, as the remaining members of the escort drew their dirks and formed a protective semi-circle around Jean and Grace.

More arrows flew, coming from a copse of birch on the other side of the road—and then Jean saw them: leather-clad figures closing in.

Terror grasped Jean by the throat and squeezed. *Outlaws!*

The warrior just in front of Jean grunted then and crumpled to the ground, a crossbow quarrel embedded in his eye.

Clutching Grace against her, Jean screamed.

Robin reined his courser in, his gaze sweeping over the bodies strewn by the roadside.

"God's bloody rood," MacVane growled from beside him. "What happened here?"

Robin didn't reply. Instead, he leaped from the saddle and drew his axe from where it was strapped to his back. Whoever had done this had likely fled, yet he wasn't taking any chances.

As he approached the fallen men, his heart started to pound in his ears. He recognized them: it was the escort he'd sent to accompany his daughter and chatelaine. But where were Grace and Jean?

Spying Evan, Robin went to his side and rolled the warrior over. His blue eyes stared back at Robin, wide and sightless. Wet blood dripped from his mouth, and his body was still warm.

"We just missed them," Robin announced hoarsely.

His gut twisted as he stared down at Evan's face. The warrior had been like an uncle to him. He'd been a good friend of Robin's and had trained him to fight.

Red-hot fury burned through the icy shroud of shock.

"I'll kill whoever did this to ye, Evan," he promised the warrior. "I swear it."

A groan made his chin kick up. One of the men was still alive.

MacVane moved across to the fallen warrior. Casting his dirk aside a moment, he rolled the man over. "Duncan!"

Robin rose to his feet and swiftly approached them. Kneeling before Duncan—a young warrior who'd just taken a wife the year before—he stared into his glassy eyes. The man's lips were stained with blood, and he had two arrows sticking out of his chest. It was a miracle he still breathed.

"Duncan." Robin leaned close, his gaze spearing the younger man's. "Where are Grace and Jean?"

"They took them," Duncan replied, his voice so low and breathy that Robin barely caught the words.

"Who?"

"Yer brother ... yer wife."

Robin reeled back as if struck. His heart was pounding like a battle drum now, panic clawing at his throat.

Danny MacVane swore viciously.

Robin leaned close to Duncan once more. "Where did they go, lad ... did ye see?"

But it was too late. The flickering light in Duncan's eyes had gone out. The warrior lay there, still and silent, his gaze fixed upon something neither the chieftain nor his captain could see.

"Ye won't get away with this. Robin Mackay will hunt ye down. He'll—"

Jean never finished speaking. The warrior reined his courser in close and belted her across the face—snapping her head back with such force that she nearly toppled from Dusty's broad back. "Shut yer mouth." Lanky, with greasy blond hair and a thin, mean mouth, the warrior then swiveled in the saddle, glancing back at the man riding behind him.

"Ye should let me plow her, Gordon," he growled. "That'll make her less mouthy." He leered at Jean then. "Ye just wait ... I shall have ye tonight."

Clutching her aching jaw, Jean cringed in the saddle. Her heart started to buck like a wild pony against her ribs, fear making her breathing come in jagged pants.

"Stop yapping, Kester," Gordon Mackay drawled. Big with brown hair and hazel eyes, he bore a startling resemblance to his older brother. "That one isn't for humping ... Liosa wants a maid."

"Aye," the blonde woman next to him replied with a frown. "Keep yer slug in yer braies."

Kester scowled, although around him some of his companions sniggered.

Not for the first time since the attack, Jean wondered who these men were. She'd have thought them hired blades, if not for the obvious camaraderie they shared with Gordon. They minded him, respected him.

The party left the Kyle of Tongue behind now, cantering southwest, toward Sutherland territory. Liosa, Gordon, and their two captives rode amidst the group of warriors. Three men took the lead while three others brought up the rear.

Relieved that she wasn't going to be raped, Jean relaxed her death grip on the reins. She then glanced over her shoulder at the man and woman who'd abducted them.

It hadn't taken her long to realize who was behind the attack. As soon as Grace recognized the woman who stepped out onto the road once their escort had fallen, Jean had known that Robin's wife and brother had returned.

Observing Gordon Mackay now, she noted he was handsome—taller and more striking in appearance than his brother—but there was a hard edge to his good looks.

Jean shifted her attention to Liosa Mackay, to find the woman already watching her. Their gazes met, and then Liosa raised her chin imperiously, a challenge in her stare. Aye, she was as bonny as Jean had imagined with hair like liquid gold, tumbling in curls down her back. But she was haughty too. Even the woman's worn kirtle and cloak couldn't diminish her queenly air.

They continued to stare at each other before Gordon's rough voice intruded. "What are ye staring at, woman?"

Swallowing, Jean turned away.

25

A CLAN-CHIEF'S DAUGHTER

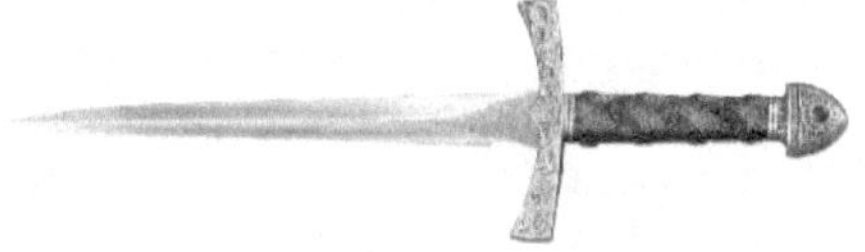

THEY RODE ALL afternoon, stopping only briefly to water their horses by a burn.

Jean remained silent, instead taking note of her surroundings. She needed to try to stay calm.

They traveled over a vast open area of hilly peatland. Ben Hope loomed in the distance, gradually marching closer as the day progressed. At first, the great mountain was nothing but a purple silhouette against the cloud-streaked sky. But after a while, the mountain became clear: a huge wedge with a great crag on the west side, and with two lower shoulders to the south and northeast.

Jean shifted uncomfortably in the saddle. She wasn't used to riding such long distances without resting. She'd be chafed, and as stiff as a crone, the following day.

The party made for the western foot of the mountain. The land gradually rose, purple heather blooming thick around them. Along the way, they passed burns and lochans—reed-fringed pools.

Although Jean had never ridden this way before, she instinctively knew that they were close to leaving Mackay lands behind them and entering Sutherland territory. Her pulse accelerated at the thought, panic constricting her chest.

Eventually, the sun settled to the west and the light started to fade. They halted under the shadow of Ben Hope. The mountain stood alone, the deep grooves upon its rocky sides making it look as if a great beast had clawed it.

The party made camp beside a river that cut through scree and pebbles before rushing down a narrow defile. It was a beautiful spot, with white alpine flowers growing amongst the rocks. The murmur of rushing water mingled with the whisper of the breeze.

Under other circumstances, Jean would have been captivated by the waterfall that tumbled down the rocks below, and the nearness to the great mountain that she'd only ever seen from a distance until now. But instead, her stomach was in knots, her throat tight.

She rubbed down her pony while Dusty, oblivious to what was happening, cropped at grass by the riverbank.

"The sky is clear, so it'll be a cold night," Gordon announced. "We need a fire."

There was little fuel here, for no trees grew up on the foothills. However, they'd come across a growth of gorse, which would burn well enough.

"There lass, don't weep."

Liosa's voice drew Jean's attention, and she glanced over at where mother and daughter sat.

"I'm scared," Grace whimpered. Her face was the color of milk, her large hazel eyes glistening with tears.

"Don't worry, sweetheart," Liosa replied, her tone soothing as she stroked Grace's hair. "Ye are safe with me."

Is that so? Biting her tongue, Jean seated herself on a lichen-covered rock. Meanwhile, the men got the fire going and set to plucking and gutting a brace of grouse they'd caught by one of the lochans.

Presently, Liosa stopped fussing over her daughter and turned her attention to Jean. She then gestured toward the rolls of bedding sitting with the saddlery a few yards away. "Go on ... make yerself useful."

Bristling at the woman's commanding tone, Jean rose to her feet. She was a clan-chief's daughter, not this woman's slave. Nonetheless, now wasn't the time to rebel. Jean walked stiffly over and unstrapped the sheepskins, rolling them out around the fire.

"Here." One of the men, a brawny individual with knotted dark hair and brown teeth, shoved the gutted grouse he'd been plucking at her. "This is woman's work," he growled, grinning at her.

"Hurry up … we're hungry," another man piped up, throwing the rest of the brace at her feet.

The other warriors laughed.

Swallowing a sharp retort, Jean got to work, viciously yanking feathers from the hapless birds.

"Today's success calls for a celebration," Liosa announced as she wrapped Grace in a warm blanket. "Do we have wine, Gordon?"

"Aye, my love," he rumbled, "although I'd prefer the men stayed sober tonight. We're not safe yet."

Liosa pulled a face. "Don't fret so. We're on Sutherland turf now."

"Aye, but not far enough away from my brother for my liking."

"Robin won't even know Grace is missing yet."

"Even so, there will be no wine," Gordon replied, his tone firm.

"Da will be worrying about me." Grace's plaintive voice interrupted them once more. "Ye can't take me away like this."

Liosa looked down at her daughter, her jaw tensing. "Hush now, angel," she murmured, patting Grace's golden head. "Yer place is with yer mother."

Grace tilted her chin back to meet Liosa's eyes. "Where have ye been, Ma?"

Liosa stroked her daughter's cheek, even if a nerve flickered under one eye. "Didn't yer father tell ye?"

Grace shook her head. "He said ye had to go away … but he wouldn't say why."

Surprise rippled over Liosa's face, while a few feet away, Gordon shifted uncomfortably.

Watching their reactions, Jean realized neither of them had expected that. Robin could have poisoned Grace against them, yet he hadn't.

Gordon leaned into Liosa then, his brow furrowing. "We should tell the lass the truth," he murmured. "About her … and us."

Jean froze, halting mid-way through plucking the second grouse. One of the warriors had grabbed the first one and impaled it upon a stick and was now roasting it above the glowing fire.

Mother Mary, no! Surely, they wouldn't reveal the secret Robin had worked so hard to keep from his daughter. It would rip Grace's heart out.

Liosa held her lover's gaze for a long moment—and then, to Jean's surprise, she shook her head. "Now isn't the right time," she murmured. "I'd prefer to wait until Grace is feeling stronger."

Gordon's mouth thinned, although after a few moments, he nodded.

Meanwhile, Grace's wide gaze flicked between them. "Tell me what about ye and me, Uncle Gordon?"

"Get back to work, wench!" Kester, the warrior who'd threatened to rape Jean, had noticed she'd stopped plucking the grouse to listen to Gordon and Liosa's conversation. "I don't want to eat at midnight."

Dipping her head, Jean complied. The warrior's insult washed off her—his interruption had been well-timed. Her heart pounded now, relief weakening her limbs. She had to get Grace away from these people—before they revealed Gordon was the lass's real father.

"Ye aren't going to let them hurt Jean, are ye?" Grace asked her mother, her voice wobbling as she struggled to stay brave.

Jean glanced up to see Liosa was smiling down at her daughter. "No, love. Yer maid will stay with us ... I promise."

"She's not my maid," Grace whispered. "Jean is chatelaine of our broch."

Liosa's eyes widened. She then glanced up, her gaze raking over Jean from head to toe as if taking her measure for the first time. "Chatelaine ... auld Lachlan died then?"

"Aye ... Da was so sad before Jean came to live with us ... but things are better now. Da smiles often these days, and everyone in the broch is happier for it."

Jean inwardly cringed. She appreciated Grace's affection for her, but this wasn't the right time to show it.

"Yer daughter is a credit to ye ... clever and kind," Jean murmured. "She is a delight to teach."

Grace managed a wobbly smile at her words, and Jean met the lass's eye, returning the smile. She was attempting to change the subject, yet her words were in earnest. She adored Grace and hated seeing her so frightened.

Jean shifted her attention back to Liosa then. "I know ye miss yer daughter ... but abducting her isn't the answer. She belongs at Melness."

Liosa pursed her mouth. "Don't tell me where she belongs." Her gaze narrowed then. "Are ye a Mackay?"

Jean shook her head, even as anger quickened within her. She was sick of this woman treating her like her inferior. "I'm Jean Munro ... daughter of George Munro of Foulis, and sister-by-marriage to Niel Mackay."

A beat followed, a heavy silence settling in the gloaming. A moment later, Kester muttered a filthy oath under his breath. "Satan's bollocks. We'll have both the Mackay *and* Munro clan-chiefs after us now."

Gordon snorted. "It makes no difference. Once Robin finds out Grace's missing, he was always going to send for help."

"But she's a—"

"She's *nothing*," Gordon cut the warrior off, his hazel eyes glinting.

Jaw clenched, Jean lowered her gaze once more. Ire now smoldered in her gut. *To ye maybe. Not to those who love me.*

26

TIME TO STRIKE

THE GLOW OF the fire was visible at least twenty furlongs distant.

Drawing his courser to a halt, Robin's mouth thinned.

"Fools," MacVane whispered next to him. "They might as well have lit a beacon."

"It's a cold night … and they clearly don't think they were followed today," Robin replied, his gaze never straying from the glow to the south. "Gordon's overconfident … and it will be his undoing."

It'll be his death.

Aye, they shared the same blood, but his brother would hang for this. If Robin didn't gut him first.

Drawing in a deep breath, and then another, Robin let the hammering rage that had howled in his ears all afternoon settle. He didn't want to go into this angry. Instead, he had to see this as battle. He needed a clear head.

"Duncan didn't have a chance to tell us how many men we're dealing with," MacVane murmured as if reading his thoughts. "We'll need to go in cautiously."

"Aye," Robin whispered back. "We'll leave the horses here and close in on foot."

They tethered their coursers to some lonely blackthorn, for there were no trees up here, in the foothills of Ben Hope. It was open country, but now that night had settled over the world—the sky above a purple-black curtain dusted with stars—they could approach the campsite without being seen.

Moving, silent as shadows in their hunting boots, the two men crept toward the fire. The silvery glow of the moon frosted the hills, aiding their journey.

Robin carried his axe strapped to his back. He'd likely need to use it later, but for now, his dirk would be more useful. He gripped it tightly, his gaze scanning their surroundings.

They were halfway up the hill toward the fire when Robin's hand shot out and grasped MacVane's forearm, bringing him to a halt. The captain obeyed the silent command.

Robin shifted close, whispering in his companion's ear, "There's someone up ahead, to the left … look."

He felt MacVane's arm tense under his grip.

Indeed, the figure hadn't been easy to spot, yet Robin had excellent eyesight. He'd caught the outline of the man seated upon a rock just a few yards distant. Gordon was taking precautions. His brother wasn't quite as foolish as he'd thought.

The sentry didn't hear Robin as he crept up behind him. And when a hand clamped across his mouth and cold steel touched his throat, it was too late.

Lowering the man's body to the ground, Robin moved close to MacVane and lightly squeezed his shoulder. It was the signal they'd agreed upon to continue. This close to the camp, they couldn't risk speaking.

It took Robin a while to draw near to the fire. He was aware of every intake of breath, every footstep. All it would take was the crunch of boots on pebbles or a stifled cough, and those gathered around the glowing hearth would be alerted to their presence.

Creeping steadily closer, Robin made out eight figures seated around the fire: Gordon, Liosa, Grace, and Jean—and four warriors. Robin's attention settled on the men that followed his brother. They were rough-looking brutes. He'd already killed the one guarding the northern approach, but Robin guessed there could be another sentry or two out there, lurking in the darkness.

Robin's jaw hardened. The odds weren't great. There were just the two of them against at least four warriors.

And then there was Gordon. His brother was an excellent fighter. They'd sparred often over the years, and Robin wasn't about to underestimate him.

He'd be even more dangerous when cornered.

Drawing in a deep breath, Robin's gaze slid over the women. Liosa was seated with Grace, while Jean knelt a few yards away. They'd clearly finished supper, although the greasy odor of roast grouse lingered.

Jean was pale and tense, the shadow of a bruise upon her jaw.

Robin's breathing quickened at the sight of her, while fury hammered in his ears at the thought that Gordon or one of his thugs had lifted a hand to her.

However, he stilled when his attention shifted to Liosa.

Grace was slumped in her arms, half-asleep. Liosa cradled the lass against her, an expression of contentment upon her face.

His wife was as lovely as he remembered, and the sight of her brought back many memories. Once, he'd been infatuated with her, taken in by her charm and beauty. But now, he saw those things for what they really were: guile and vanity. An unhappy marriage and a terrible betrayal had removed the scales from his eyes.

He couldn't believe Liosa and Gordon had returned to his lands, had abducted his daughter.

Yer daughter? A cruel voice whispered to him. *She's Gordon's, remember?*

Robin clenched his eyes shut for a few moments. He couldn't let old hurts resurface now. It didn't matter that Grace wasn't his; she *was* where it really mattered—in his heart.

Of course, Liosa had doted on Grace, which was one reason why her daughter pined so for her after she left. However, gazing upon the lass's face, he noted her cheeks were mottled from crying.

Grace had witnessed her escort cut down in cold blood, had likely seen Jean beaten. The lass would be traumatized.

Red-hot rage pulsed through Robin now. Resolve tightened every muscle and sharpened his senses. He didn't want Grace to witness any more violence and bloodshed today, but he didn't see how he could avoid it.

Jean shifted uncomfortably on the sheepskin before glancing over at Liosa. "I need to relieve myself," she murmured.

Stifling a yawn, Liosa motioned to the warrior seated a few feet away. "Clyde will escort ye."

Jean tensed, while Clyde, the warrior with knotted dark hair and stained teeth, leered at her.

Stiffly, she rose to her feet, suddenly wishing she didn't need to empty her bladder.

"Come on then, lass," Clyde said, licking his lips.

Jean's skin prickled. Like Kester, the warrior had been watching her all evening. Instinct told her he'd harass her the moment they were alone.

Perhaps sensing the same thing, Liosa scowled. "Ye are to keep yer hands to yerself, Clyde," she said, her tone commanding.

"Aye," Gordon rumbled. "Remember, she's Liosa's maid, not yer whore."

The other men seated around the fire snorted with laughter at this, before Kester muttered something crude.

Clyde scowled, making it clear that he had, indeed, intended to take liberties the moment he got Jean alone.

Rising to his feet, he led her away from the fire and down the steep hill to the south that led to the water. Shale slid under Jean's boots as she descended the slope.

Fortunately, the moon was out—and since it was almost full, it cast a silvery light over the world. Once Jean's eyes adjusted, she could see clearly.

Stopping by the banks of the river, below where water tumbled down the rocks, Clyde turned to her. "Go on then." His tone was goading. "Get it over with."

"Aye," Jean replied sharply. "Once ye back up a few yards."

The warrior stared back at her, his eyes glinting in the moonlight.

She thought he might deny her, but after a few moments, he muttered a curse under his breath and shifted away, to the foot of the defile. "Hurry up, woman," he growled. "And don't try anything daft ... or ye shall regret it."

Heeding his warning, Jean wasted no time. Keeping a wary eye on Clyde's shadowed figure, she pushed down her woolen leggings and crouched. Then she raised her skirts off the ground and emptied her bursting bladder.

She had just readjusted the folded cloth she used for her courses, and her leggings, when an angry shout splintered the stillness.

It was a windless night with a clear sky, and as such, the sudden sound made Jean jerk upright, her heart beating wildly.

A few yards away, Clyde cursed and took off up the slope, his boots crunching and sliding on the slippery shale.

Meanwhile, Jean stood there, frozen to the spot.

More cries echoed down the defile, followed by cursing and grunts.

This was her chance. Clyde had abandoned her—she could flee into the darkness.

But she didn't.

Jean had no idea who'd attacked the party, although her first thought was that outlaws had spotted their fire from afar.

Sweat beaded upon her skin. *Grace!*

No, she couldn't run off and abandon the lass.

Heart pounding, she reached down and picked up a river stone. It fitted neatly into her palm and was the only weapon she had.

Above, the sounds of fighting grew desperate.

And then Liosa started shrieking.

Jean scrambled up the bank, slowing her pace when she reached the crest. She stood back, just out of the light cast by the fire.

From here, she had an uninterrupted view of what had transpired, yet no one could see her.

Bodies lay scattered around the hearth.

Robin Mackay stood facing his brother, while behind him, Danny MacVane had just killed Clyde.

Jean dropped to a crouch, her gaze settling upon Robin. He held his axe, battle-ready, legs planted wide. Blood dripped from the sharp blade. His face was set in harsh lines as he glared at his brother.

"That was quick, Rob," Gordon murmured. He, too, stood, braced for a fight, a dirk clenched in his right hand. "Yer horses must be winged to have caught up with us so fast."

"Ye have a nerve," Robin growled, ignoring his brother's comment. "Returning to my lands."

Gordon's mouth twisted. "I'm a Mackay of Melness too, remember?"

"Not anymore. I no longer have a brother."

A groove formed between Gordon's eyebrows, and his expression turned appraising. "Ye've changed," he observed finally.

Robin's gaze narrowed. "Aye, thanks to ye and Liosa." His attention flicked to where the woman stood a few feet behind Gordon, clutching a struggling Grace against her. "Let Grace go." His voice softened then as if he were talking to a startled horse. "It's over now, Liosa."

"No, it isn't," Liosa snapped. Even so, her face had leached of color. "Gordon was always a better fighter than ye, Robin ... leave before he kills ye."

Robin's lips thinned, and he tossed his axe from one hand to the other. He then focused on Gordon once more. "All yer men are dead ... and MacVane stands behind me. Do ye really think ye can take us both on and win?"

Gordon didn't reply. Instead, he lunged forward, going in low and fast, his dirk-blade glinting in the firelight. Robin shifted sharply right, just narrowly missing being stabbed in the guts, and leaped out of reach. They were fighting with vastly different weapons.

Gordon's dirk required him to get in close, while Robin's axe was only of use to him if he had space to swing it.

Robin struck hard, his blade hissing through the air, and Gordon ducked. His brother dived low once more as he attempted to get under Robin's guard. The two of them continued their deadly dance for a short while longer—and then Grace's scream cut through the chill night air.

An instant later, Liosa's horrified cry joined it.

Gordon Mackay lay twitching at his brother's feet, an axe-blade embedded in his neck.

Jean blinked. God's bones, it had happened so fast. Gordon's last strike was vicious—but Robin had anticipated his brother's move, swiftly side-stepped, and brought his axe down in a lethal downward chop.

"The devil take ye, Robin Mackay!" Liosa backed away, tears streaming down her face. Meanwhile, Grace now fought her hard, arms and legs flailing.

Robin yanked the axe free of his brother's neck. "Release Grace," he said roughly.

"Never!"

Jean's heart leaped into her throat when she caught the glint of steel and realized that Liosa had drawn a knife and was pressing it to Grace's chest. The lass immediately stopped struggling. Liosa continued to edge away from Robin.

The laird's face was all sharp angles in the firelight. A muscle feathered in his clenched jaw. "What are ye planning to do, Liosa?" he rasped. "Kill yer own daughter."

"Ye're not having her," Liosa sobbed. "Ye've taken Gordon from me ... ye'll not have Grace too. I'll slit her throat before I'll hand her back to ye!"

"Let me go," Grace whimpered. "Please, Ma ... ye're frightening me!"

Robin's face had leached of color, and his gaze was hunted now. He hadn't moved, for he was clearly afraid Liosa might lose her wits entirely and hurt Grace. Jean understood his fear, for the desperation in Liosa's voice warned that she might do something unhinged. "Think about what ye are doing … ye shall hang if ye hurt yer daughter."

"I don't care … she's mine!"

"Aye, she is," Robin replied, his tone lowering, "but don't ye want her to live a full and happy life? Don't ye want her to be proud of her mother?"

Liosa stared back at him, the panicked rasp of her breathing cutting through the night.

For a moment, Jean thought Robin had managed to get through to her, but when he took a cautious step forward, Liosa jumped back, moving perilously close to the edge of the rocky defile. "Don't come any closer!" she shrieked.

Rising from a crouched position to her full height, Jean tightened her hold on the stone she still clutched in her right hand.

No, Robin couldn't do anything to stop his wife at present. But *she* could.

Breathing deeply, as the blood roared in her ears, she crept up behind Liosa.

It was time to strike.

27

A GRIM PROCESSION

JEAN LUNGED, HOLDING the stone aloft. She had to be careful, for she didn't want Grace to be injured. She needed to hit Liosa hard enough to distract her, hard enough for Robin to take advantage while her guard was lowered.

The stone hit the back of Liosa's head with a dull thud.

The woman gasped, staggering in surprise.

Robin moved, wresting the knife out of his wife's hand, and yanking Grace from her grasp.

Liosa let out a wail, clawing at Robin.

Dropping the stone, Jean flew at Liosa once again, wrapping an arm around her throat and yanking her back so that Robin could get Grace to safety.

The lass was weeping, arms linked around her father's neck as she buried her face in his chest.

Liosa cursed and drove an elbow back, catching Jean in the ribs.

Pain arced down one side, and Jean let go.

Liosa lurched away, her curses ringing through the night. And then the woman's arms cartwheeled, her mouth forming an 'O' of terror.

Without realizing, she'd stepped over the edge of the ravine—into nothing.

Jean jumped forward, reaching for her, but it was too late.

Liosa fell screaming until the sound eerily cut off.

Liosa Mackay didn't die from her fall.

Robin went down to the ravine below the campsite to search for her body and found her lying on her back upon the stones next to the small waterfall. She was groaning softly, her eyes tightly closed.

Hunkering down next to her, Robin touched her shoulder. "Liosa?" he murmured. "Can ye hear me?"

Her eyes flickered open. "My head hurts," she whispered, her voice slightly slurred.

"Can ye move yer arms ... and yer legs?"

A moment passed, and then she gave a soft sob. "No."

Robin's mouth thinned. It would have been a mercy if the fall had killed her. He'd seen similar injuries before, usually as the result of a fall from a horse. If she couldn't feel her hands and feet, it didn't bode well for her.

Rising to his feet, Robin looked down at Liosa's face.

She stared up at him, her eyes wide and startled in the frosted light of the moon. "Don't leave me here," she whispered. "Please, Robin."

God's blood. Did she think him a monster?

"I don't intend to," he replied curtly.

Robin climbed back up the defile and, with MacVane's help, fashioned a litter out of two staffs the warriors had with them, and sheepskins. Seated upon a rock, with Grace wrapped up in a blanket on her lap, Jean watched her companions.

In the aftermath of the fight, a deep cold had settled over Robin, numbing him to the marrow. He felt disconnected from his surroundings as he worked.

"Robin," she murmured eventually, breaking the brittle silence. They'd all barely spoken since the struggle had ended. "How *did* ye find us so quickly?"

Glancing up, Robin drew in a deep breath. The shadow in Jean's lovely eyes made his chest ache—but he couldn't let himself feel, couldn't let himself think.

If he let hurt in, it would shatter him.

"I decided to join ye and Grace on yer trip, after all," he said gruffly. "We left Melness a couple of hours after ye did."

"And it's just as well," MacVane added, his tone unusually flat.

A chill skated down Robin's spine. Aye, it was, although it was hard to feel any relief at present. Liosa and Gordon had returned to torment him. But they wouldn't any longer.

He'd been forced to kill his own brother.

And he'd watched the woman he'd once loved hold a blade to her daughter's … *his* daughter's chest.

Robin's pulse quickened then, queasiness stealing over him. Rising to his feet from tying the makeshift litter together, he glanced over at where MacVane was watching him. He sensed that, like Jean, the captain wanted to speak about what had just happened—but Robin didn't. Not now.

"Come on," he muttered, nodding to the litter. "Let's get this done."

Fortunately, MacVane sensed his mood. The captain refrained from commenting as they dragged the litter down the bank. They lifted Liosa onto it and hauled it back up the hill. Leaving Jean to watch over her, they then set about dragging the corpses of the warriors onto the fire.

They didn't burn Gordon with his men. Aye, Robin had disowned his brother, but now that the fury had leached from him, he found that he couldn't bear to throw Gordon upon the pyre. No, they'd bury him in the kirkyard outside Melness broch—and so, Robin and MacVane hauled him over the back of one of the horses.

All the while, Jean remained silent, holding Grace as she slept in her arms. Robin's chest ached as he observed the tender expression on Jean's face. She looked after his daughter, almost as if she were her own.

Jean glanced up then, and Robin hurriedly averted his gaze.

He continued in his task yet felt her watching him. However, he deliberately didn't look up.

None of this mess was Jean's fault, but the lass weakened him. The events of the past day had shown him how dangerous it was to lower his guard. Hadn't life already taught him that trust and vulnerability came at too high a price?

This is what happens when ye let people into yer heart.

He was a chieftain, and much responsibility sat upon his shoulders. He couldn't afford weakness—of any kind.

As the first rays of sun broke over the hills to the east, bathing the sculpted slopes of Ben Hope, Robin and his companions left a smoldering pyre behind them.

Dark smoke stained the pale dawn sky.

A grim procession rode into Melness.

Robin rode ahead upon his courser, Grace perched on the saddle before him. He led a horse with his brother's body slung across its back. Captain MacVane followed on his horse, dragging the litter bearing Liosa behind him.

Jean brought up the rear, riding Dusty and leading Grace's pony.

Villagers emerged from their cottages, their faces aghast as they watched Robin Mackay ride by. Murmurs followed them, yet the chieftain didn't speak, didn't acknowledge anyone.

He hadn't spoken all day. His silence was beginning to worry Jean, although she was wary of approaching him, of intruding. He was in shock and needed time to recover.

They'd stopped a couple of times on the journey north. Jean and MacVane had exchanged a few words in low voices, practicalities about food and water mostly, but Robin had remained mute, his expression stone hewn.

Jean's attention shifted from the laird's broad back to where Liosa slumped upon the litter. And when she looked upon the woman's pallid face, her breathing quickened. Liosa was seriously injured and hateful—but she was still Robin's wife.

And he was taking her home.

Goose, she chided herself. *He's doing what's right.*

Of course, she knew that. But Liosa's return to Melness reminded Jean that *she* didn't have any claim over Robin.

Liosa had drifted in and out of consciousness during the journey. The litter was rickety, and the trip would have been uncomfortable for her. Yet MacVane had whispered to Jean that the woman couldn't feel anything beneath her neck.

Jean was surprised Liosa was still alive when they returned to Melness, but when they halted inside the barmkin, her chest still rose and fell, albeit shallowly.

Robin finally spoke then, bidding two of his men to carry her litter into the broch, and put Liosa in one of the guest rooms. He then sent a lad off to fetch the village healer and ordered two men to take Gordon's body to the kirkyard and bury him. Finally, he instructed more warriors to ride south and retrieve the bodies of his daughter's escort. One of them was to ride swiftly to Castle Varrich, for Niel Mackay would be wondering why his visitors hadn't yet arrived.

Jean watched Robin closely as he spoke to his men. His voice was flat, his gaze shuttered. Unease rippled through her. His expression was so remote. It was as if a stranger stood before her. She, too, was still reeling from the events of the night before—but Robin appeared to have withdrawn to a place where no one could reach him.

Jean wanted to go to him, to put her arms around his waist and rest her head upon his chest. But she wouldn't do so—not with an audience. They'd talk later. Maybe then, the upset would have abated a little, and he'd connect with his surroundings once more.

"The saints preserve us … what happened?" Fiona's startled gasp echoed through the barmkin. Jean turned to see the older woman and her daughter huddled together on the steps before the entrance to the broch. Fiona murmured another oath then. "Is that Lady Liosa?"

Indeed, their arrival had brought all the residents of the broch outdoors. Men and women clustered around the fringes of the barmkin, whispering together.

"Ye shall find out what happened soon enough, Fiona," Jean replied curtly. Her tone was harsher than she intended, but now wasn't the time to pepper them with questions. "Go and light the hearth in the laird's chamber ... and his daughter's too."

Abashed, Fiona nodded. A moment later, she and Kenna hurried back indoors to do as bid.

Jean followed Robin and Grace into the broch. The laird carried his daughter upstairs to her bed-chamber.

Kenna was hurriedly stoking the fire when they entered. "Would ye like me to bring up some food for the lass?" she asked the chieftain.

"Aye," Robin replied. "And some warmed milk too."

Grace was worryingly silent as Jean moved forward and helped her remove her traveling clothes. Jean then wrapped her in a thick robe and tucked her up in bed. The lass watched her father with huge eyes as Robin propped extra pillows under her shoulders. "Are ye angry with me?" Grace whispered.

Jean's throat constricted at these words, and when Robin answered his voice was gruff, yet tender. "No, lass ... of course not."

"But ye are so quiet."

"Ye aren't the cause."

Relief weakened Jean's limbs when he lowered himself on the edge of the bed and took his daughter's hand.

"I'm sorry, Grace," he said, his voice roughening further. "Ye have seen things over the past day that no bairn ever should. I wish I could erase all of it from yer memory."

Grace stared back at him, her fingers tightening around his. "Why did they do it?" she murmured.

His throat bobbed. "I don't know ... yer mother missed ye, I suppose."

Grace started to blink rapidly, her eyes glistening now. "Da ... why did Ma run away with Uncle Gordon?"

A weighty silence followed. Jean swallowed hard, wishing Grace hadn't brought this subject up. Nonetheless, she could hardly blame her. It was a question that would have been burning within the lass for a long while.

Eventually, Robin cleared his throat. "Yer mother married me for my title ... and to escape her oppressive father." A nerve flickered on the laird's cheek as he continued. "But Liosa never loved me. Right from the first days of our marriage, she preferred Gordon."

Jean's breathing caught at the bluntness of his words and the rawness of his voice. Grace was still young, yet he wasn't making any effort to soften things. Her pulse accelerated; she hoped he wouldn't tell Grace that Gordon was her real father.

However, Robin halted then, bringing his brief yet brutal explanation to an end.

Grace now wore a bewildered expression. "I can't believe Ma loves Uncle Gordon and not ye," she replied, shaking her head. "His men were brutes ... one of them hit Jean."

Robin's features tensed, and he glanced across at his chatelaine—focusing on her for the first time since they'd entered the chamber. Their gazes fused and held for a long moment. "Ye acted bravely last night, Jean," he murmured. "Sorry I haven't yet thanked ye ... I haven't even asked if ye're injured."

Jean favored him with a weak smile. "I'm well." She still couldn't believe she'd had the audacity to launch herself at Liosa. She couldn't help but feel responsible for the woman's tumble. If she hadn't fought with her, she might not have staggered so close to the edge of the defile. "I didn't want to hurt anyone." Her voice caught then. "But I was afraid that Liosa was desperate enough to do something rash."

Robin's mouth thinned, and he nodded. Clearly, he agreed with her.

"Will Ma live?" Grace asked softly.

Robin tore his gaze from Jean and glanced back at his daughter. "She has been gravely injured ... but we have made her comfortable. Once the healer has seen her, we should know more.”

28

THINGS LOVE CAN'T HEAL

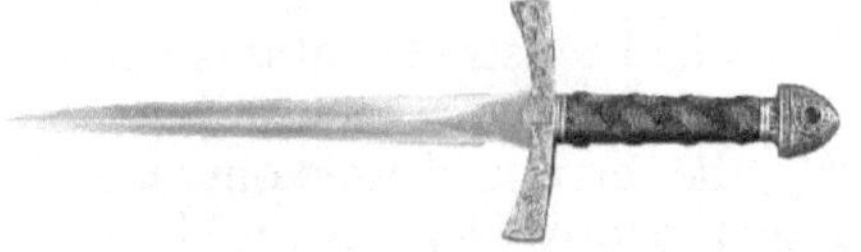

JEAN SHIVERED, MOVING closer to the kitchen hearth. It wasn't an overly cold evening, yet she felt chilled to the marrow.

It was the after-effect of shock, she supposed.

Now that she was safely back at Melness, the full impact of what she'd weathered over the past two days hit her.

To distract herself, Jean tried to focus on practicalities. "Kenna, have ye lit the hearths?" she asked.

"Aye, Jean."

She then turned to Fiona. "And have ye wiped down all the tables in the hall ready for supper?"

The older woman nodded.

"Stop fussing, Jean ... everything is under control." Brighde passed her a hot cup of meat broth. "Here ... ye look like ye could do with something comforting."

Managing a weak smile, Jean took the earthen cup from the cook, wrapping her fingers around it. Supper had come and gone, although Jean's appetite had been poor.

Of course, the servants had wanted to know what had happened—and so she told them, recounting the attack and the subsequent flight south. Her words were softly spoken, her voice faltering more than once when she described the harshest moments.

Fiona, Kenna, Brighde, and Brian had all watched her with strained faces—and when Jean was done, Fiona crossed herself. "Poor Evan," she murmured. "He served

Robin, and his father before him, loyally. He deserved a better end than that."

"All those men did," Kenna replied, scrubbing at the tears that trickled down her cheeks. "Duncan's wife is with bairn."

Jean's throat had constricted at this news—and it did now as she relived that brutal attack once more.

Eventually, the servants drifted out of the kitchen, returning to their chores—leaving the chatelaine and the cook alone. The cook resumed chopping vegetables for supper, while Jean stared sightlessly at the burning coals in the hearth.

"Don't think on it," Brighde murmured. "There was nothing ye could have done to prevent what happened."

Jean straightened up, glancing Brighde's way. The two women's gazes met. "Ever since last night, the laird's gone silent," Jean said huskily. "It's as if a wall has raised between us."

Something altered upon Brighde's face as she stared back at her, a flicker of understanding lighting in her green eyes. "Oh," she murmured.

Jean stiffened. "What?"

"I can't believe I didn't see it before ... ye and Mackay." Brighde's mouth lifted into a half-smile. "Ye've lain with him, haven't ye?"

Air gusted out of Jean's lungs. Curse her, she'd been too candid with Brighde. The cook was sharp-witted and had seen straight into Jean's heart.

Moments passed, and Jean considered lying to her. However, falsity had never been her way. She had an open nature and suddenly longed to confide in someone. With a sigh, she dropped her gaze to the rapidly cooling broth before nodding.

"Oh, Jean." There was no mistaking the edge to Brighde's voice. "Was that wise?"

Jean inhaled slowly before answering, "Probably not ... it just ... happened." She swallowed then. "I love him, Bri."

She glanced up, to see that Brighde's face was strained. "When ye first arrived here, I sensed ye carried a candle for the laird," she said softly, "but I thought ye'd put it behind ye." The cook sighed then. "His aloofness has nothing to do with ye, Jean ... although yer heart risks being broken because of it."

Jean stared back at Brighde. The woman was her friend. Nonetheless, Brighde's words now were a slap to the face.

"Ye make him sound like a hopeless case," she replied, cursing the wobble in her voice. "But there *is* a bond between us. Before this happened, he trusted me ... he will again."

Brighde sighed, her expression turning rueful. "Women always think they can mend what's broken in men," she murmured. "But there are some things love can't heal."

"Lady Liosa wishes to speak to ye, Mackay."

Robin set aside the pewter goblet of wine he'd been nursing and rose to his feet. Ian, the healer—a small bird-like man who lived in the village—stood in the doorway.

One look at Ian's face and Robin knew the end was near. However, the man's next words confirmed it. "She doesn't have long."

It was late. The rest of the broch slumbered, yet Robin hadn't been able to sleep. Instead, he'd sat staring at the glowing embers of his hearth, waiting.

Wordlessly, the two men made their way upstairs.

The guest bed-chamber was warm, for the servants had ensured the hearth was kept blazing. Yet the cheeks of the woman who lay upon the bed were ghostly. Looking upon Liosa, Robin thought she'd already passed away, for she was so still and pale. Whatever she wished to say to him would go with her to the grave. But then he spied the shallow rise and fall of her breast and realized that she still clung on to life.

"I shall leave ye for a few moments," Ian murmured. The healer then ducked outside, pulling the door closed behind him.

Robin moved over to the bed, lowering himself down onto a stool next to it.

"Liosa," he said softly. "Can ye hear me?"

Her eyes fluttered open, and she stared at him, her gaze unfocused. Her hands lay unmoving upon the coverlet. Robin stared back at Liosa, his chest constricting.

He bore no love for this woman now, yet it was difficult to see her in such a state. At least her suffering was drawing to a close.

Liosa's blue eyes cleared then, and she swallowed. "Ye came."

"Aye ... ye called for me."

She stared up at him. "I thought ye would ignore my request."

Robin clenched his jaw. Maybe he should have, yet it wasn't his way.

"Ye are good man, Robin Mackay," Liosa whispered, her voice reed thin. "Far better than I deserved."

Shifting uncomfortably on his stool, Robin cleared his throat. "Do ye wish me to fetch ye the priest?" If Liosa wished to make a confession, he couldn't absolve her. And if an apology was coming, he didn't want to hear it. Words couldn't change what Liosa had done—what Gordon had done.

"No." Her mouth lifted, just a touch, at the corners. "Father Malcolm would likely curse me to the devil."

Robin didn't contradict her.

Silence fell in the chamber, broken only by the crackling of the hearth behind Robin and the soft rasp of Liosa's breathing. Her eyes fluttered shut, for just that short exchange had drained her.

Robin waited patiently by her side. Perhaps that would be all. She would go now.

The moments drew out, and then Liosa's eyes opened once more. They were bright now, surprisingly lucid, as her gaze fixed upon him. "Tell Grace I love her."

He nodded. The words would stick in his craw, yet he couldn't deny a dying woman her last wish.

"Ye are right … I do want Grace to be proud of me … but it's too late." Liosa took a long, labored breath. "Let her know that I'm sorry … for everything."

Robin swallowed hard, forcing himself to reply, "I will."

"She doesn't know, does she … about Gordon?"

Robin's heart started to pound. God's blood, why did she have to bring this up? "No," he rasped.

Liosa sank deeper into the nest of pillows that propped her up then, her face sagging. Her eyes were sunken into their sockets, the brightness dimming now. "Good," she whispered. "Grace believes ye are her father … and it should remain that way."

"I *am* her father, Liosa." And he was—in the ways that truly mattered. He'd been a fool, allowing hurt and pride to blind him over the past years. He'd let that lass down. "Grace will never learn the truth," Robin promised, his hoarse voice echoing in the silent chamber. "I—"

His voice cut off then as he saw that Liosa's blue eyes had turned glassy. She stared up at him sightlessly.

Rising from his stool and moving close, Robin placed a hand upon her chest, confirming that she no longer breathed. He looked down at her waxy face. He'd seen death arrive many a time, yet the suddenness of it never failed to surprise him. Liosa was gone.

He reached out and gently closed her eyelids before straightening up. Staring down at the face of the woman he'd once adored, Robin drew in a deep, steadying breath. "Goodbye, Liosa," he said softly before finishing the sentence he'd begun moments earlier. "I swear Grace will grow up loved … and cherished. She will want for nothing."

With that, he turned and walked from the bedchamber.

29

THE HONORABLE THING

HEAVY GREY SKIES hung over the coast, and a stinging wind whipped in from the north, as the small group gathered by the graveside. They buried Liosa Mackay in the kirkyard, next to Gordon.

Robin stood with Grace as Father Malcolm recited a few words.

The priest hadn't been happy about burying either of the lovers in the kirkyard. "They're adulterers, sinners," he'd complained when the laird visited the kirk to inform him of the arrangements. "They shouldn't be buried on holy ground."

"They are both Mackays, and they shall be buried here," Robin had answered, his voice turning to steel. And that was that.

Jean and MacVane waited a few feet back from the laird and his daughter. As Mackay's two highest-ranking servants, they represented the rest of the household.

Grace sniffed, rubbing at the tears that stained her face. Robin's chest ached to see his daughter so upset. She'd been through too much in the past few days. He wanted to see her smile again and wished he could pull himself out of the mire of his own thoughts so he could ease her pain.

But in truth it was as if heavy hands pressed down upon his shoulders this morning. The fact he hadn't slept the night before didn't help. His eyes were gritty, and his temples throbbed.

After everything Liosa and Gordon had done to him, he thought he'd rejoice at their demise. However, their deaths pained him. Gordon was his brother, and he'd hacked him down with his axe. It had been in self-defense, yet it still weighed upon Robin.

And then there was Liosa. In the years since her departure, he'd hated her with a bile that felt as if it were burning a hole in his gut. Yet she was Grace's mother, and nothing could change that. She'd loved her daughter too, in her own twisted, selfish way—a love that had driven her back to Melness, and eventually to her doom.

Aye, this had been a nasty business—and it would be a relief to put it all behind them.

Father Malcolm finished speaking, leaving a judgmental silence behind him as he swept his dark robes around him and retreated into his kirk.

"Where did Ma go?" Grace asked then. "Is she really buried under all that earth?"

Robin stifled a sigh. Now that was a question.

Hunkering down, he turned his daughter to look at him. Their eyes were level now, and he could see the confusion, the pain, written clear upon Grace's face. At eight winters, she was still having difficulty understanding some things.

"Her body is under there, aye," he said, reaching out and stroking Grace's cheek. "But her soul is flying free now, untethered from the earth."

Grace's eyes widened. "Is she with the angels?"

After what Liosa had done, Robin doubted that. Nonetheless, he favored his daughter with a tender smile. "Aye, lass."

Rising to his feet, Robin took Grace's hand and led her from the kirkyard. Up ahead, he spied Jean and MacVane waiting for them. He'd been so lost in his own thoughts that he'd forgotten their presence.

Yet the sight of Jean standing there, her face solemn, her grey-green eyes filled with soulful understanding, made Robin's pulse quicken.

He'd been an idiot to bed his chatelaine. For a short while, he'd believed he could let another woman into his heart. He'd told himself that he could trust again.

But he couldn't.

Grace was his priority now. He had to focus on her—
had to ensure the lass never doubted his love again.

Approaching Jean, Robin tried to ignore the pain
twisting his chest. Aye, it had been a mistake to embark
on an affair with her, yet he couldn't undo what he'd
done.

He would need to take responsibility for his
recklessness.

He met his chatelaine's eye. "I wish to speak to ye,
Jean. Can ye come to my solar after the noon meal?"

Jean's stomach clenched as she mounted the steps to the
solar, the turnip and mutton stew she'd just eaten
churning.

Since their return to Melness, she'd been waiting for
this summons. During the funeral, she'd stood in silence
next to Captain MacVane, watching as the grumpy priest
rushed through the service, before hurrying away, and
leaving father and daughter at the graveside.

Her throat had constricted while she'd watched Robin
talk to Grace, observed the way he crouched down to his
daughter's level and met her eye as he explained
something.

Brighde's wrong, she'd told herself. *Aye, he's
hurting, and old wounds have been reopened, but he'll
heal. I'll make sure he does.*

And now he wanted to see her.

Halting on the landing before the heavy oaken door,
Jean smoothed her damp palms on her skirts. She didn't
know why she was so anxious.

This was Robin. The man who'd loved her body with
tenderness and passion. The man who'd revealed things
about himself, and his past, that he'd likely told no one
else. She shouldn't feel on edge about speaking with
him—and yet she did.

Jean ran her fingers through her hair, pushing the wayward curls off her face. She wore one of her own altered kirtles today, a grey-blue woolen garment that Brighde had given a daring neckline. In the first days after changing her appearance, Jean had felt like an imposter—as if her new clothes were nothing more than a guise she might wear at Samhuinn. Now though, she was comfortable in them. She couldn't imagine going back to wearing shapeless kirtles and dragging her hair back into a severe bun, as if femininity was just too much effort. These days, she walked taller, prouder.

However, she'd made a special effort with her appearance this afternoon. Robin had barely glanced her way since their return to Melness, but she wanted him to look upon her as he once had—with warmth and tenderness in his expressive hazel eyes.

Drawing in a brave breath, Jean knocked on the door. "Enter."

She pushed her way into the solar, her gaze sweeping over familiar surroundings. Memories of the intimate moments she and Robin had shared here came flooding back, and heat swept over Jean, awareness prickling her skin. Initially, she'd found the solar an austere, overly masculine space. And she'd never been fond of the terrifying boar's head that glared down at her from above the fireplace.

But the time she'd spent here with her lover had turned this chamber into the most welcoming space in the world.

The laird stood before the glowing hearth. Although spring was upon them, the day was grey and cold. They hadn't seen the sun at all.

Jean smiled at Robin. "Here I am ... as bid."

The chieftain nodded. "Take a seat, Jean."

Stomach pitching nervously, for his face looked so severe today, she complied.

"Would ye like some wine?" Robin asked.

"Aye, thank ye."

He fetched them two cups of bramble wine, and Jean took a grateful sip. She needed something to calm her nerves. Robin's stilted manner was unsettling her.

Meeting his eye, Jean smiled once more, although the expression was a little wary this time.

Robin didn't return her smile. "I apologize for ignoring ye since we got back," he said after a pause.

"Don't worry about that," Jean replied quickly. "Ye have been ... occupied."

He nodded, although the severity upon his face didn't soften. "I needed to see Liosa buried," he admitted, his voice lowering. "And to ensure Grace's well-being."

"The lass is understandably sad at present," Jean replied, "but she will rally ... especially with ye at her side."

Their gazes met then, and Robin swallowed. "No one can know that she isn't my daughter. Ye must swear to me ye will never tell a soul."

Jean stiffened, her fingers clenching around the cup of wine. "I already promised ye I wouldn't say anything," she said, her voice catching. "Do ye not remember?"

"I do," he answered, his tone firming. "But I must be sure. I will do everything I can to protect Grace from wagging tongues."

"Well, if tongues wag, it will not be my doing." Jean raised the cup to her lips and took another gulp of wine. Underneath her discomfort, irritation simmered. Did he really think her a gossip?

He nodded, taking a sip of his own wine. "Good."

Jean watched him, her gaze narrowing. "So, is that why ye asked to see me?"

He shook his head, a muscle feathering in his jaw. He was tense, she realized. His aloof, austere façade was hiding something. "We forgot ourselves, Jean," he said quietly after a pause. "*I* forgot myself. I compromised ye, ruined ye."

Jean's jaw clamped shut. "I lay with ye willingly, Robin," she replied finally, forcing her tone to remain calm, even if her heart was now pounding. "Ye didn't take anything that I wasn't willing to give up. I told ye that at the time."

"But ye could be with bairn now, after what we did."

Queasiness rolled over Jean. Was that what he was worried about?

"Ye need not concern yerself," she said stiffly. "My courses arrived on the morning we left to travel to Varrich. I'm not pregnant."

She'd expected relief to filter over his face at these words, yet his expression remained taut. "Even so, I took yer maidenhead … and I must do the honorable thing." He broke off there, draining the remnants of his cup of wine as if fortifying himself to continue. "Now that I'm officially a widower, I can take another wife. As soon as we can arrange things, I shall ask Father Malcolm to wed us."

Jean stared back at him, her lips parting in shock.

How she'd dreamed of Robin Mackay proposing to her. In her fantasies, Liosa had died of a fever on the streets of Edinburgh and news had been carried back to Melness that Robin was a widower. He'd swept her into his arms, his face suffused with joy, and they'd wed on the steps of Melness kirk. In her visions, she'd worn a beautiful pale-green kirtle and Eilidh had woven spring flowers into her hair.

But these blunt words weren't what she'd dreamed of. Nor had she envisaged his face to appear so grim. He looked as if he were about to have a rotten tooth extracted.

Cold sweat beaded upon Jean's skin, and she swallowed hard to try and keep a rein on her reaction to his brutal proposal.

The honorable thing? Was it even an offer of marriage? It had sounded more like an obligation. He was trying to fix a problem.

Her.

Jean's belly hardened. She loved Robin Mackay with everything that she was—but she wouldn't be treated thus. He'd retreated from her and now viewed her as an encumbrance. She couldn't stand it.

Slowly, deliberately, she set her wine down next to the hearth and rose to her feet. "As flattered as I am that ye wish to make me yer wife," she said, her voice low and clipped. "I must decline yer offer."

30

TIME TO GO

ROBIN STARED BACK at Jean, his lips parting in surprise. He clearly hadn't expected such a response.

But Jean wasn't yet finished.

Fire roared in her veins now, filling her with reckless fury. She'd had enough of minding this man, of tiptoeing around his feelings, when he clearly had no consideration for hers.

"I also inform ye that I won't be remaining at Melness … ye will need to find yerself another chatelaine." With that, she untied the heavy set of keys from her belt and thrust them out to him. "Here … I'm stepping down, as of now, and will be departing at first light tomorrow."

"Jean." Robin stood up. Yet he made no move to take the keys from her. "What are ye doing?"

"I think it's clear, Mackay," she growled back, jangling the keys at him. "Here."

Still, the laird didn't move. "I don't understand."

"Ye don't?" Frustration exploded within Jean, and she tossed the keys down onto the chair she'd just vacated. "Well then, let me spell it out to ye." She took a step forward, closer to him, her fists balling at her sides. "I understand ye have been through much in the past few days—we all have—but I'm not some inconvenience to be swept aside."

"I'm not sweeping ye aside, Jean," he countered, his voice roughening. "I wish to wed ye."

"Aye, out of some misguided sense of *honor*." Her throat clenched tight as she spoke, and the back of her eyes burned. What a fool she'd been. She'd believed he cared for her, as she did him. But she should have heeded Brighde after all. Robin Mackay had shut off the part of him she wanted. It was like interacting with the shell of a man. "But not because ye *love* me ... as I love ye."

His hazel eyes guttered, his body going rigid as if she'd just struck him. A heavy silence filled the solar then. "I can't give ye that, Jean," he croaked finally. "I'm sorry."

Jean's breathing hitched. She'd admitted her feelings for him, and he'd thrown them back in her face. Her throat started to ache then, her chest burning.

"Ye love Grace," she said, her voice catching.

"Aye ... but that's different." A shutter came down over his features then. "After Liosa, I can never trust a woman again."

Jean swallowed hard. He didn't love her—he didn't even trust her. The knowledge made her want to dig a deep hole and bury herself in it. What a fool she'd made of herself.

"And yet, ye treated me as if ye cared." She hadn't meant to throw that in his face, yet the pain tearing at her chest made her lash out.

Robin Mackay had a strong sense of decency, and indeed, her accusation made him flinch. "For a short while, I thought I could let ye in ... but I can't," he admitted roughly. "But I still wish to—"

"Wed me," Jean finished his sentence for him. "Aye ... ye'd wed a woman ye do not love to save her reputation." Trembling from the force of the anger and hurt that writhed through her, Jean moved away from the hearth, backing toward the door. "I don't need yer charity, Robin Mackay."

And with that, she turned and fled the solar.

Robin stood before the hearth, listening to the slam of the door and the patter of Jean's slippered feet as she climbed the stairs.

He should have gone after her, should have apologized for making her feel like an inconvenience that had to be dealt with—but he didn't.

He couldn't move.

He'd been dreading this exchange. It hadn't gone as he'd expected, yet he was still shocked she'd rejected his offer.

Cursing, Robin turned to the hearth and slammed his empty cup down on the mantelpiece. He then gripped the ledge, his fingernails biting into the wood as he lowered his head.

It's for the best.

Jean Munro deserved a man who wasn't broken, who could love her like the queen she was.

Robin squeezed his eyes shut. "I'm a reckless fool," he whispered to the dancing flames.

He should never have let Jean come to live at Melness. His initial instinct had been right. He was weak where she was concerned, drawn helplessly to her. Even since their return to Melness, he'd fought the urge to go to her chamber at night, to climb into her bed, wrap his arms around her warmth and softness, and let her tenderness soothe his bruised soul.

But he hadn't. Instead, he'd walled himself off, readying himself to 'deal' with her.

Jean had been right to spurn him. He'd offered her marriage, but he wasn't offering love. While he'd waited for her after the noon meal, he'd prepared a speech in his head. He'd planned to inform her that they would continue to have separate chambers, and that he would resume his old habit of eating alone. As his wife, she'd continue her duties as chatelaine. Things would go on as they had before he'd let his shields down.

Yet Jean hadn't let him get that far.

She'd seen right through him, and now she was leaving.

Robin's fingernails dug deeper into the wood. Aye, it *was* for the best. He should have been relieved.

Why then, did he feel as if the walls were closing in on him?

Jean packed the last of her things into her saddlebag and buckled it up. Then, stepping back from the bed, she glanced around the chamber.

Upon arriving at Melness months earlier, she'd found this room a damp, depressing place—but now it felt like home. She'd lime-washed the walls, and a small wooden chair with colorful cushions sat by the hearth.

Yet it wasn't her home any longer, and as Jean surveyed the chamber for the last time, her throat thickened.

God's bones, did she have any more tears left?

After leaving Robin, she'd returned to her chamber and wept for the remainder of the day. Kenna, and then Brighde, had come up to check on her, yet she'd sent them both away. Brighde's face had been bereft, and Jean felt bad about shutting the door on her.

However, she couldn't bear anyone's company right at present. She'd only sob on Brighde's shoulder, and although the cook was too kind-hearted to say, 'I told ye so', her presence would be a galling reminder of Jean's mistakes.

Right from the beginning, she'd forced things.

Her sisters had warned her, Brighde had cautioned her, but she wouldn't be told. She'd always believed that persistence had its rewards—that if she tried hard enough, things would work out as she wished.

Instead, she rushed blindly into a situation she couldn't control, and had ended up with her heart in tatters. No, it was better she remained alone in her chamber, to think on the part she'd played in this mess. Aye, Robin's callous behavior hurt her, yet she couldn't say she hadn't been warned.

Heaving a sigh and blinking rapidly, she reached for her woolen cloak, slinging it about her shoulders.

It was time to go.

The sun was rising over the eastern walls when Jean led Dusty from the stables. The garron was laden down with saddlebags, yet he was sturdy enough to bear the additional weight.

Around her, four of the chieftain's men were saddling their horses. Of course, Jean wouldn't travel alone.

"A safe journey to ye, Jean." Glancing up, from where she was tightening Dusty's girth, Jean spied Danny MacVane approaching. He flashed her a smile, although his brown eyes were shadowed. "We're all sorry to see ye leave."

"Aye, we are." A woman's voice intruded then, and Jean shifted her gaze to behind the captain, where Brighde neared. Fiona and Kenna followed at her heel.

Jean forced a smile, even if she felt fragile inside. "I shall miss ye all," she admitted, cursing the sudden huskiness of her voice.

"Why are ye leaving?" A small figure flew across the barmkin. Grace dodged past where Fiona tried to catch her and launched herself into Jean's arms. Jean's chest constricted when she realized the lass was weeping.

Hugging Grace tight, she fought back tears of her own.

God's blood, she'd hoped to leave quietly—but now it seemed as if every servant and man-at-arms within the broch had come outdoors to see her off.

Only the laird was absent.

Jean was grateful that Robin had stayed away. What was there left to be said? It would only be awkward and embarrassing to bid him farewell—especially with his household looking on.

Grace clung to her like a limpet, and eventually, Jean was forced to extricate herself. Lowering herself down to the lass's level, she met Grace's gaze. The lass's face was mottled from crying, her eyes swollen. The ache under Jean's breastbone knotted tighter at the sight. Wounding Grace was the last thing she wanted, yet Robin's daughter wouldn't understand the complexity of adult relationships.

"I must go, lass," she murmured, forcing a brave smile. "But fear not, we will see each other again. Next time yer father goes to Castle Varrich, make sure he takes ye with him."

Grace nodded, her eyes filling with fresh tears. "But *why* must ye go?"

Jean drew in a deep breath. Of course, bairns preferred plain speech. She couldn't tell her the truth, but she didn't want to lie to her either. "I thought a life at Melness was what I wanted, but it's not right for me," she admitted softly.

"Do ye miss yer sisters?"

Jean nodded, grateful Grace had given her something to cling to.

"Come, lass." Brighde stepped up and took Grace by the hand, drawing her back. "Jean has a long ride ahead of her ... we should let her depart."

Casting Brighde a grateful smile, Jean did a final check of Dusty's saddle before mounting her pony. She glanced back once more at the cook, their gazes fusing, and in Brighde's green eyes, she saw understanding.

Her friend didn't know what had happened between Jean and the laird—yet it was clear they'd fallen out.

Clearing her throat, Jean gathered the reins. She then surveyed the knot of servants that had gathered before her in the barmkin. "All of ye welcomed me to Melness." Her mouth quirked then. "And ye tolerated my bossy ways."

"Aye, well, some of us need bossing around," MacVane replied with a grin. He moved up to Brighde and threw an arm over her shoulders. "I love a bossy woman, don't I, Bri?"

Brighde's mouth pursed. "Get yer hands off me, MacVane."

The captain quickly did as bid.

Jean's escort were all mounted, and the first of them urged his courser toward the gates, making it clear that the farewells were now concluded. Grateful that they were departing, Jean gathered the reins and nudged Dusty's sides with her heels.

And as they moved off, she glanced one last time up at the high tower that loomed above. She hadn't meant to—it was instinct really—but when she did, her gaze alighted upon a broad-shouldered figure standing on the top step of the stairs leading down from the broch to the barmkin below.

Robin Mackay had come outdoors to see her leave after all.

The cool dawn breeze ruffled his hair and tugged at the loose lèine he wore tucked into his braies.

The sight of him made Jean's stomach twist in a blend of longing and hurt.

How would she ever recover from this man?

Meeting her eye, Robin raised a hand.

Jean's vision swam then. Tearing her gaze away from the laird of Melness, she kicked Dusty into a brisk trot and headed for the gate.

31

HARSH LESSONS

"JEAN?"

SHIFTING HER gaze from the view out the window, Jean blinked. She then focused on Neave. "Did ye say something?"

Neave's brow furrowed. "Aye." With a huff of impatience, her older sister lowered the tiny lèine she was sewing—a garment for her unborn bairn. Beneath the loose kirtle she wore, Neave's belly was starting to swell noticeably. "I've been telling ye about my garden at Achness. Did ye hear anything I said?"

Jean sighed. "No ... sorry."

Neave's features tightened for an instant, not in annoyance, but concern. She then put aside her sewing and pushed herself up off the chair, moving across to the window seat.

Meanwhile, Beth and Eilidh looked up from their projects. Only Angus paid Jean no mind: the bairn sat on a rug in front of the hearth, playing with a cloth hedgehog that Beth had sewn for him out of scraps of rag.

"Are ye going to tell us what happened?" Neave asked gently, placing a hand on Jean's arm. "It's not good to keep things bottled up inside."

"Ye know we'd never judge ye, Jeanie," Eilidh piped up. She observed Jean over the top of her embroidery hoop, her lovely face taut with concern.

Likewise, Beth wore a worried expression. "Ye can trust us," she murmured. "Ye always can."

Jean swallowed. Aye, she knew her sisters loved her, and only wanted what was best for her. However, when she'd returned from Melness, everything had been too raw. Just the thought of speaking of what had happened made her pulse spike, made dizziness sweep over her.

But she'd been back at Castle Varrich nearly a fortnight now, and her sisters were clearly getting worried about her distracted silences.

Like Eilidh, Jean had always enjoyed a lively conversation. Yet these days, she sought solitude, and when she did spend time with her sisters, she had little to say.

It was special, to have the four of them together again. When Neave had learned of Jean's return, she'd insisted on making another visit. John had joined her, and he and Niel were off stag hunting at present, leaving the sisters to catch up.

"It must have been awful," Eilidh said softly, filling the awkward pause. "To see yer escort cut down like that … to fear for yer life."

Jean nodded. It had been—but the emotional hurt she'd suffered a few days later had eclipsed that ordeal.

All she'd been able to think about was that awful conversation in the chieftain's solar. Robin had been so detached, so cold.

Clearing her throat, she decided it was time to be honest with her sisters. Neave was right: it wasn't wise to let things fester.

"I'm in love with Robin Mackay," she admitted, her voice catching. Mother Mary, she wasn't going to be able to keep her composure—not when all three of her sisters were staring at her with such compassion.

Beth's full lips quirked, even if her hazel eyes were solemn. "That isn't news to any of us," she replied. "We know why ye offered him yer services as chatelaine."

Jean dragged in a deep breath, feeling a little foolish. She thought Beth hadn't realized, but, of course, she had. "Aye, but I didn't *love* him then," she murmured. "It was just a girlish infatuation in the beginning."

Neave gently squeezed her arm, encouraging her to continue.

And so, Jean did. "Initially, Robin avoided me most of the time. As such, I focused on learning my new role. The laird was reclusive … he took all his meals alone … and didn't spend time with anyone, even his daughter."

"I hadn't even realized he had a bairn," Beth said, shaking her head. "He kept that quiet."

Jean nodded, although she remained close-lipped on that subject. She'd given Robin her word—and she would keep it.

"His wife and brother's betrayal scarred him more deeply than I'd first thought," Jean continued. "He didn't want me as his chatelaine … but I cornered him that day after Samhuinn."

Eilidh snorted. "Aye … the poor man looked like he wanted to bolt from the table."

Jean inwardly cringed at the memory. That was what came from being pushy. It was a lesson she'd now learned. Likewise, Neave wore a sheepish expression— perhaps recalling the hand she'd had in forcing Robin Mackay to take Jean on as chatelaine.

"He kept away from me at first," she said, forcing herself to continue. "But after Yuletide, he started to thaw … and I realized my infatuation for him had merely lain dormant." Jean cleared her throat, looking down at her lap as her cheeks started to burn. "In the spring, we became lovers."

Eilidh's startled gasp filled the women's solar. Yet Jean's two elder—and worldlier—sisters remained silent.

She wondered then if this revelation had come as a surprise to them either.

"Are ye with bairn, Jean?" Neave asked softly, breaking the tense hush that had fallen.

Jean shook her head. She then closed her eyes, and painful memories flooded through her. "No, but Robin asked me to marry him."

"And ye refused him?" Eilidh's voice was incredulous.

"Aye."

"But ye love him!"

Jean's eyes snapped open. "I do ... but I learned ... too late ... that Robin will never feel the same way about me."

"Are ye certain?" Neave asked, giving Jean's arm another squeeze. "Men can be thick-headed at times."

Jean huffed a bitter laugh. "He spelled it out, Neave. He told me he could never trust another woman ... not after what Liosa did to him ... and then offered to wed me out of a misguided sense of decency. Love wasn't to be part of our relationship."

Beth murmured an oath under her breath, and when Jean looked her way, she saw ire smoldering in her eldest sister's eyes. "Where have I heard that before?" she muttered. "Ye aren't wrong, Neave ... men can be clod-headed fools." Beth then rose to her feet and crossed to the window, squeezing in on Jean's other side. She took Jean's hand in hers. "Niel's fear of love ... and his stubbornness ... nearly cost us both dearly."

Jean nodded. With everything that happened of late, she'd almost forgotten the rocky start to Beth and Niel's marriage. A lifetime of keeping his feelings locked deep, and the trauma of a decade in prison, had given Niel Mackay a hard, bitter, shell. It was only when a battle wound nearly ended him that he woke up to what he stood to lose.

Beth was the best thing that had ever happened to him.

Jean's eyelids started to sting, and she blinked rapidly. Aye, there were some similarities between their tales, yet one great difference.

Niel Mackay loved his wife, and he had even when he'd been intent on denying his feelings. It was true that Niel had been through a lot, but the hurt and anger from his father's betrayal—which had sent Niel to Bass Rock for ten years—had eventually healed. He'd let love in and had become a better man for it.

But Robin Mackay wasn't going to heal, or trust.

He had a different nature to Niel—more sensitive, gentler. He was someone who'd grown up wanting to think the best in others. He loved deeply, but if wounded, walled himself off forever.

"So that's it," Jean said, cursing the way her voice wavered. Tears escaped then, and she removed her hand from Beth's gentle hold and wiped at her cheeks. "Now ye all know." She drew in a shaky breath and attempted to smile through her tears. Across the solar, Eilidh was also weeping. "Sometimes life teaches us harsh lessons," Jean concluded softly, remembering the discussion she'd had earlier in the year with Grace on this very subject. Unfortunately, she was no closer to understanding why things happened the way they did. "I just wish this hadn't been mine."

Robin reined in his courser, his gaze narrowing as he took in the charred remains of the fire pit. Wordlessly, he swung down from the saddle and crossed to the fire, kneeling to touch the ashes.

"They're still warm," he announced to his men.

"The rustlers are nearby then," MacVane replied.

"Aye." Robin swung back onto his horse and whistled to the dogs. The wolfhounds, who had been sniffing eagerly around the fire pit, barked excitedly before racing south. "Let's see if we can catch them up."

The party of ten men thundered after the hounds, their horses' hooves throwing up turf behind them.

Taking the lead, Robin leaned forward over his courser's neck, welcoming the sting of the wind against his cheeks and the feel of the horse's muscles bunching and releasing as it settled into a fast canter. He was careful not to push it into a gallop, for the ground was uneven and it wouldn't help their pursuit if one of their horses came to grief.

He also wanted to save his mount's energy for when they spotted their quarry.

Jaw clenched, Robin kept his gaze fixed upon the southern horizon.

They'd had problems intermittently with sheep-rustling over the past years. However, the thieves had gotten bolder over the winter and into the spring. His nearest neighbors were the MacLeods, but they weren't to blame for this. Ever since his marriage to Liosa, relations had improved between the Mackays of Melness and the MacLeods. Liosa's father, Cameron MacLeod, had been embarrassed by his daughter's behavior and had sworn there would be no more raids upon Robin's lands.

But the Sutherlands were a different matter.

Farther south, John Mackay of Aberach had dealt with the worst of it. Melness was too far north to be bothered at first. Yet of late, sheep and cattle had gone missing from Robin's southernmost holdings. The Sutherlands were the culprits—he was sure of it.

Robert Sutherland bore a deep grudge against the Mackays these days, especially against John.

Even so, sheep hadn't been stolen this close to Melness broch before.

Rage smoldered in the pit of Robin's gut as he rode—and he embraced the heat. It was a welcome change from the knot of misery that usually resided there, and the nagging feeling that he'd made a terrible mistake in letting Jean Munro ride out of his life.

Fourteen days had passed since her departure—aye, he'd counted each one—and he'd hoped that with time he'd wake up one morning and tell himself it was for the best that Jean had returned to Varrich.

But so far, that realization hadn't come.

He'd focused on Grace, spending afternoons with her reading, practicing French, or going out for a ride. They were growing close once more, yet even his daughter's love couldn't ease the ache in his chest.

Up ahead, the dogs started baying. Squinting into the distance, Robin spied a knot of riders with a mob of sheep running before them, racing up a heather-strewn hill. "There they are!" he shouted. "After them!"

He let his gelding have its head then. And as if sensing its rider's bloodlust, the courser flattened into a gallop. They flew down the hill, leaped the burn that trickled through the peaty soil, and thundered up the slope in pursuit.

"Flank them!" Robin shouted to his men as they steadily drew closer. "Draw a net about the riders out front."

An instant later, MacVane veered left, racing up the outside of the fleeing group. Meanwhile, another of his men galloped up the right side.

The rustlers, riding upon stocky horses, were shouting at each other, while the mob of frightened, black-faced sheep bleated pitifully.

And then, as Robin and his men closed the net, the sheep panicked—as the creatures were wont to do—and scattered.

One of the rustlers—a big man with wild peat-brown hair—roared an oath. But it was too late. And when MacVane and four other warriors cut in front of them, forcing the rustlers to halt their flight, the game was up.

Breathing hard, Robin pulled up his horse and drew his axe in one smooth sweep. "Thieving whoresons," he snarled. "Did Sutherland send ye?"

The rustlers, a group of six men wearing sweat-stained lèines and braies, watched him, their faces paling. They were surrounded, and Robin wasn't the only one who looked ready to draw blood.

However, despite their fear, all the rustlers remained mutinously silent. None of them wore a clan sash—a wise choice, for they were still some distance from Sutherland territory and wished to travel unnoticed. It was clear they didn't intend to give up their identities.

Fingers clenching around the hilt of his axe, Robin's gaze swept over the band. His pulse hammered in his ears, and the urge to lash out clawed at him. He focused then on the big warrior with wild brown hair—the only one of the group who didn't look as if he was about to piss himself.

Holding the man's defiant gaze, Robin swung his axe in an arc around his head, letting the sun glint off its wickedly sharp blade. "Do I need to ask ye twice?" he growled.

32

I PROMISE YE

"MACKAY."

ROBIN GLANCED up from where he'd been staring sightlessly at his accounts, to see Brighde standing in the open doorway to his solar.

He tensed, surprised to see the cook there. Brighde didn't usually venture away from her kitchen. Indeed, she looked as if she'd been baking, for she wore a flour-dusted apron.

"What is it, Brighde?" he asked, a note of impatience creeping into his voice. "Is something amiss?"

He'd told the servants he didn't want to be interrupted. After Jean's departure, the accounts were his chore once more. He'd put off looking at them, for it was a reminder of his chatelaine, of his lover, but this morning he'd forced himself to retrieve the ledger from the library.

It had been a mistake, for, looking upon Jean's neat handwriting, a pain, akin to being stabbed, twisted deep within his chest.

God's teeth, he missed her.

"Aye, laird," Brighde said crisply. "Grace ventured outside earlier ... and saw that head ye have mounted on a pike outside the gates. She's now sobbing on her bed."

Robin went rigid in his seat. He hadn't meant for Grace to see the severed head of the leader of the sheep rustlers.

In truth, he hadn't thought of his daughter at all when he'd mounted it there.

Yesterday had ended badly for those sheep rustlers. It had taken them a while to admit they were Sutherland's men, but eventually, one of them had blurted it out.

Their leader had lunged for the loose-lipped warrior, but it was too late—their identities had been revealed.

Robin had acted swiftly then, cutting the leader down with one chop of his axe. He'd been tempted to deal with the other men the same way, yet the terror on their faces had cut through the red haze of fury.

The rest of the party had been marched off to Castle Varrich, where the clan-chief would dispense justice.

But Robin had kept the leader's head and brought it back to Melness. A trophy. A warning.

"Chac!" Robin muttered, rising to his feet. "What was Grace doing outside the walls?"

"Going to the morning market as she often does," Brighde replied. The cook's censure was written clearly upon her face. She then placed her hands on her hips and glared at him. "Ye are a decent man, Mackay ... but ye have let bitterness and hurt turn ye blind." She paused then, a muscle in her jaw flickering. With a jolt, Robin realized the cook was upset. "Jean Munro brought happiness back into this broch. Grace has been adrift without her, and I have lost a friend. I don't know what ye did to offend Jean ... but if ye had any wits at all, ye would ride to Varrich right this day, get down on yer knees, and beg forgiveness."

Robin scowled. The cook had been talking to him about Grace, yet now she was scolding him over Jean. He opened his mouth to reprimand her, but Brighde wasn't yet finished.

"Ye have thrown away the best thing to ever come yer way, Mackay," she continued. "I know ye suffered a great betrayal and that ye are afraid to be hurt again ... but I never took ye for a fazart."

With that, Brighde swiveled on her heel and stormed away.

Robin watched her go, surprise rendering him speechless.

His cook had just called him a fazart, the worst kind of yellow-bellied coward.

Drawing in a deep breath, he clenched his hands at his sides. His father would have beaten a servant for talking to him thus, but Robin had never raised a hand to any member of his household.

Shaking himself free of the shock that had momentarily rooted him to the ground, Robin headed for the door to his solar.

He'd deal with Brighde later, but first he had to see his daughter.

He found Grace, as Brighde had described, face-down upon her bed, weeping.

Her thin shoulders trembled, her sobs muffled by the pillow. Throat constricting, Robin moved across to the bed and lowered himself down next to his daughter.

"Grace," he murmured before reaching out and placing a hand on her back. "It's me … Da."

Her sobs eased, and then Grace rolled over. Frightened hazel eyes stared up at him. "That man," she whispered, her voice trembling. "Did ye kill him?"

Robin stared down at her. Curse it, now he felt like a beast. "Aye," he said gruffly. "He was the leader of a group of Sutherland sheep rustlers … sent deliberately to provoke us. I had to make an example of him, love."

"But ye cut off his head."

The horror in her voice stabbed him in the guts. What had he become? He didn't want his daughter to see him as a ruthless killer.

That wasn't who he really was.

Growing up, his father had warned him he wasn't hard enough to assume the mantle of Chieftain of Melness. Gordon had smirked whenever the subject was brought up, for he'd known it to be true. As a youth, Robin had wanted to be everyone's friend. He was an able warrior, yet he lacked that cruel streak his brother had. Liosa and Gordon's betrayal had changed him, forged him into someone he didn't like.

For a short spell, Jean had managed to break through the hard shell he'd grown, but he'd pushed her away.

And now, his daughter looked at him with fear in her eyes.

Something inside Robin gave way then.

He didn't want Grace to view him so, to believe he was pitiless and harsh.

"I'm sorry ye had to see that, lass," he said softly, reaching out and brushing away her tears with his knuckles. "I shouldn't have put his head up there ... for ye to stumble upon. I understand why ye are upset. I promise ye, I will never do something so callous again."

She nodded, her tear-filled gaze never leaving his face. With a pang, he realized she believed him. Just like that—her trust in him was absolute.

Had he once been so easy to convince, so ready to think the best of others? Indeed, he had. Grace had inherited his soft heart; he just hoped she didn't suffer for it as he had done.

Robin's jaw tightened. He would do everything in his power to ensure she didn't.

"Let's go down to the kitchen together, lass," he murmured eventually. "Shall we see if Brighde has any treats for ye?"

Grace nodded. She pushed herself up then, scrubbing at her eyes with her fists.

Robin pulled her into his arms for a hard hug, holding her tight for a long moment. Grace's thin arms tightened around his torso in response. "I love ye, lass," he murmured into her hair. "Never forget it."

"I won't," she promised. Nonetheless, her face still looked wan, her eyes red-rimmed. She wouldn't forget the sight of that severed head in a hurry.

Hand-in-hand, they went down to the kitchen, to find Brighde busy kneading dough.

The cook glanced up, her eyes flying wide at the sight of the laird and his daughter. Her cheeks flushed then, and she hurriedly straightened up. "Mackay."

Indeed, it was rare Robin ever set foot in the kitchen these days. Taking in the large scrubbed table, glowing hearth, and the delicious aroma drifting toward him from the large cast-iron pot suspended over the embers, he realized it was a pity he stayed away from this homely space. As a lad, he'd spent too much time in here, usually pestering the cook—Brighde's predecessor—for treats.

Robin's attention settled upon Brighde once more, and the cook lowered her gaze. Clearly, she thought he'd come down here to reprimand her.

He'd planned to—although not with Grace present— however, he now found he couldn't dredge up the self-righteous rage. Talking to his daughter had drained it from him, like lancing a wound.

Brighde had been bold and cutting, yet he'd deserved her censure. He wasn't going to thank her for it, yet he wanted her to know she wouldn't be punished either.

Robin favored the cook with a rueful smile. "We were wondering if ye have any of those delicious plum cakes left over from yesterday?"

A brisk wind barreled around the barmkin when Robin strode from the broch a short while later. He'd left Brighde and Grace chatting while the cook warmed some milk to make a restorative caudle for the lass. Indeed, there had been some cakes to spare, and the three of them had sat companionably around the table finishing them.

But after a while, Robin had gone upstairs, retrieved a woolen cloak, and headed down to the stables. He was in the middle of saddling his horse when Danny MacVane entered the stables.

The captain's brow furrowed. "Where are ye going?"

"I've urgent business to attend to," Robin replied. "Look after things while I'm away, will ye?"

MacVane's frown deepened. Robin's answer had been deliberately cryptic. "Would ye like an escort?" he asked, his tone cautious now.

Robin shook his head, flashing the captain a veiled smile. "No, this is something I must do on my own."

MacVane's gaze glinted. "The days are long this time of year," he murmured. "If ye ride hard, ye should make Varrich by nightfall."

Robin's smile widened. Aye, MacVane had guessed his destination. "I plan to."

Leading his gelding out of the stables, Robin glanced up at the cloud-streaked sky. It was windy, yet he hoped the weather would hold for his journey. He then swung up onto the saddle, his attention flicking right, to where MacVane had followed him out into the barmkin.

"Take down that sheep rustler's head outside the gates and burn it," he ordered.

The captain raised a questioning eyebrow in reply.

"It's upsetting Grace."

MacVane nodded, understanding lighting in his eyes. "I will see it done."

Robin gathered his reins and urged his gelding forward, heading toward the stone arch leading out of the barmkin. He then glanced over his shoulder at his captain, meeting his eye. "Thank ye, Danny ... I never say it enough, but I've appreciated yer loyalty over the years."

MacVane's mouth curved. "How long will ye be gone?"

Robin flashed him another smile. "As long as it takes."

33

IN THE CHAPEL

"YER SHAWL!"

JEAN made a grab for Eilidh's blue woolen wrap as the wind ripped the garment from her shoulders. However, she was too slow. The shawl fluttered off the path and tumbled across the adjacent field.

"No!" Eilidh wailed, picking up her skirts and giving chase. "That's my favorite one!"

Muttering a curse under her breath, Jean hurried after her sister, basket clamped under one arm. Unlike Eilidh—who raced, heedless, over the rows of cabbages, kale, and turnips—Jean took the narrow path that led through the fields spreading north of Castle Varrich. The sisters had been on their way into Tongue, to market, when a particularly harsh gust of wind had barreled into them.

The cottars working the fields glanced up from their toil, bemused, their gazes tracking Eilidh's lithe form as she sprinted after her shawl.

The wind pixies were intent on having fun with her, it seemed, for every time she neared it, another gust buffeted the shawl just out of reach.

Eilidh's unladylike curses rang across the fields.

Jean hurried on, her gaze tracking the billowing blue shawl as it tumbled into the center of the field—and straight into William Gunn's arms.

The prisoner, who was allowed outdoors daily to help in the fields, had straightened up from hoeing at the sound of Eilidh's cursing. Dressed in a sweat-stained lèine and braies, Gunn's ankles were shackled in iron.

However, there was no need for him to shuffle sideways to catch the shawl, for it came straight to him.

Eilidh rushed up to Gunn before abruptly halting a few feet away from him. Jean arrived moments later to see the prisoner and her sister staring at each other.

Misgiving pitched within Jean.

Mother Mary, she'd seen Eilidh eye the clan-chief's hostage a few times now—often in a bold fashion. She wasn't sure what her sister was up to, but no good could come from looking at Gunn in such a way. It was unseemly.

But Eilidh didn't seem to care about propriety. She just stared, wide-eyed, at the wild-haired man holding her shawl. Likewise, Gunn held her gaze with an odd, poleaxed, expression.

Jean cleared her throat then, breaking the spell. "Thank goodness ye caught that," she said, louder than was strictly necessary. "Otherwise, my sister's best shawl would have ended up in the kyle."

William Gunn's mouth kicked into a half-smile. "We couldn't have that, could we?" he murmured, his voice low yet powerful. His gaze never left Eilidh's face as he stepped forward and handed her the shawl. "Here ye are, lass."

Jean's sister took her garment, smiling back at him. "Thank ye … my name's Eilidh."

"Ay-lee," he repeated her name slowly, almost as if he were committing it to memory. "I'm Will."

"I know who ye are."

Jean tensed, her grip on her basket tightening. Her sister's manner was going from bold to impertinent. Yet Gunn didn't seem to mind. If anything, he appeared to enjoy her directness, for his own smile widened.

"Well, we thank ye again for catching Eilidh's shawl," Jean interrupted briskly, stepping forward and linking her arm through her sister's. "We shall leave ye to yer work." She then drew Eilidh away. Her sister didn't want to go, and resisted her pull, but Jean was stronger. Trying not to trample the rows of kale they'd traveled over to reach the center of the field, Jean towed Eilidh after her.

"What's the hurry?" Eilidh muttered, trying to extricate her arm from Jean's. "The man's not carrying the plague."

"No, but he *is* the clan-chief's prisoner. Ye shouldn't be talking to him ... or flirting with him."

"I wasn't flirting!"

"Aye, ye were. Ye were staring at him ... and he was looking at ye as if ye were a tasty morsel he longed to devour." Jean glanced over her shoulder then, to see that Gunn hadn't resumed his hoeing, as she'd hoped. Instead, his gaze tracked Eilidh's departure. "Ye mustn't encourage him."

When they reached the path once more, Eilidh ripped her arm from Jean's. "God's teeth, Jeanie, ye have turned into such a bore!" She stalked away toward the wooden bridge that led them into Tongue. "We weren't doing anything wrong. He caught my shawl, and I was trying to thank him."

Grinding her teeth, Jean followed at her sister's heels. "I'm not a bore," she bit out, her temper simmering. "I just know what comes of reckless behavior."

Eilidh halted, swiveling around to face Jean with such suddenness that the sisters nearly collided. "Listen to ye. Do ye know how bitter ye sound?"

"I'm not bitter, just realistic. Ye can't trust men, Eilidh ... especially ones like William Gunn."

Eilidh heaved in a deep breath, her own temper close to boiling over. "I know ye mean well, but ye need to stop telling me how to behave," she said, her voice unusually sharp. "When ye went away to Melness, I missed ye terribly ... but I've gotten used to being my own person over the past months. Beth doesn't criticize me the way ye do."

Jean flinched. "I don't criticize ye."

"Aye, ye do ... ye are two years my elder, but sometimes ye act like my mother." Eilidh's expression softened then. "Ye grieve Robin Mackay ... and there's nothing wrong with that. Why don't ye just let yerself feel sad about what happened at Melness, instead of trying to put me to rights?" Her oak-colored eyes glinted, and she folded her arms across her breasts. "I don't need mending."

Robin rode up the winding path to Castle Varrich just as the last of the light faded from the western sky. The wind, which had harried him all day, finally died with the settling of dusk.

His destination now loomed before him.

Robin gazed upon the high curtain wall of the castle, his belly tightening in a blend of anticipation and dread.

He'd had a lot of time to think on the journey from Melness—much time to dwell upon the impulsiveness of his behavior.

Yet now, as he guided his gelding toward the stone arch leading into Castle Varrich's bailey, he started to worry about the reception he'd receive.

Many things had been said between him and Jean, things that could never be taken back.

Could she forgive him?

Could she ever trust him?

What if she refuses to see me? Robin clenched his jaw, pushing aside the worry. He'd find out soon enough.

Riding into the bailey, his gaze alighted on two women standing together near the steps before the keep. Robin recognized them instantly: Beth and Neave. The former carried a bairn on her hip, while the latter was noticeably pregnant. It looked as if they'd just come inside from a stroll.

Neither woman wore a friendly expression when Robin drew up his courser and dismounted.

"Beth ... Neave," he greeted them with a smile. "Good evening."

"Robin," Beth replied coolly. "This is a surprise ... Niel didn't tell me ye were paying us a visit."

"This wasn't planned," Robin replied, favoring her with a respectful nod. "I apologize for not sending word ahead so ye could prepare for my arrival."

"We've already had supper," Beth answered, "but I shall have a chamber readied and food brought up to ye."

Robin noted that Beth, who was usually so warm and welcoming, hadn't yet smiled. Next to her, Neave was frowning. His stomach sank. It didn't surprise him that Jean had confided in them about what had happened. However, his pulse accelerated at the thought of what Jean might have told them.

He wasn't proud of his behavior.

"Thank ye, Beth." He had to find a way to get Jean's sisters to thaw toward him. "Ye have always been welcoming to me ... even now."

Beth's gaze widened, although her expression didn't soften. "Ye are one of Niel's loyal chieftains," she replied. "It is expected."

A heavy silence fell then, stretching out for a few moments until Neave broke it, addressing him for the first time. "Are ye here to see Jean?"

Robin met Neave's eye, holding her stare. "Aye."

"Ye broke her heart," Neave went on, her voice hardening. "Ye know that?"

Robin swallowed. "Aye ... and I'm here to make amends." His gaze shifted to Beth then. "Can I see her?"

Beth's lips thinned as she hiked her son higher on her hip. Meanwhile, the bairn watched Robin, his expression curious.

Drawing in a deep breath, Robin dug deep for patience. He understood that Jean's sisters were only being protective. Nonetheless, he hadn't ridden all this way to be thwarted now. Stubbornness hardened in a knot under his breastbone. No matter what it took, he'd find a way to see Jean.

Perhaps sensing his mood, Beth shared a look with Neave. After a long moment, her sister gave a slight nod.

Glancing back at Robin, Beth sighed. "Ye will find her in the chapel."

Favoring the women with a nod, Robin handed his gelding to the lad who'd just emerged from the stables and headed in the direction of the chapel. The small stone building with a peaked roof crouched between the keep and the curtain wall. At this hour, it lay in shadow.

Robin climbed the steps to the oaken door before gently pushing it open. The greasy odor of tallow, blended with the musky scent of incense, wafted over him, and he stepped into a cool, shadowy space. Banks of candles lined the walls and either side of the altar, illuminating the small figure that knelt at one of the pews.

Dressed in a grey-blue kirtle, her hair tumbling loose down her back, Jean Munro was a lovely sight.

Head bowed, Jean was deep in prayer. She was oblivious to his presence.

Heart pounding, Robin made his way down the aisle between the rows of pews. When he was a few feet away from Jean, he halted, drinking her in.

How he'd missed her. Melness broch was a drab, dull place without Jean's presence. She breathed life into any space she inhabited. Jean was everything in this world that was good and pure. Her soul was light—untroubled by guilt, hate, or bitterness.

He couldn't bear to think of returning home without her.

Dragging in a deep breath, he clenched his hands by his sides. "Jean."

34

HERS

JEAN'S HEAD SNAPPED up, the words of the prayer she'd been reciting dying on her lips. Eyes opening, she swiveled left, her gaze alighting upon a strong, broad-shouldered figure.

She blinked. "Robin ... what are ye doing here?"

The chieftain of Melness's mouth lifted at the corners, even as his hazel eyes bored into her. "Looking for ye, lass."

Heart pounding, Jean rose to her feet, dusting off her skirts. "Well, ye have found me." Her calm response belied the turmoil within. The sight of Robin standing before her made her feel light-headed, panicked.

It hadn't been the easiest of days. Her argument with Eilidh, after the incident with William Gunn, had left her on edge and troubled. The sisters had continued to the market before returning to the castle with a basket of treats. By the time they re-entered the keep, Eilidh was chattering as happily as usual. But Jean's thoughts had turned inward.

Once supper was over, she'd sought solitude, leaving Eilidh at her weaving in the solar. Beth and Neave were going out on an evening stroll, but Jean didn't join them. Instead, she took refuge in the chapel.

Attempting to keep her equilibrium, Jean cleared her throat. "I didn't expect to see ye again," she admitted softly. "Not so soon anyway."

Robin took a hesitant step toward her. "These past two weeks have been the longest of my life," he replied, his voice husky now. "But they have given me time to reflect on what really matters in life."

And then, to her shock, Robin sank down on one knee before her.

"I made a mess of things last time I asked ye to marry me," he said, his gaze never leaving hers. "But now I shall do it properly." He paused there, his chest expanding as he inhaled sharply. "Jean Munro ... tha gaol agam ort."

I love ye.

Stunned, Jean stared down at him. They were the words she'd longed to hear, yet events were moving so swiftly that she didn't know what to say, how to feel.

"So ye can trust me after all?" she asked, her voice barely above a whisper.

"Aye," he said roughly. "I was afraid, Jean. Ye see, I knew from the moment I agreed to take ye on as my chatelaine that my heart was in danger." He paused, pain flickering across his rugged features. "That's why I was such a cold bastard in the beginning. I was doing my best to keep away from ye ... but in the end, it was futile." He broke off then, running a hand through his short hair, leaving it in spiky disarray.

The urge to reach out and smooth it broke over Jean, but she quashed it, instead folding her arms across her chest in a protective gesture. She still carried the bruises from the last time she'd locked eyes with this man; she wasn't yet ready to let her guard down.

"I used to be like ye, Jean," he continued huskily. "I loved openly, fearlessly ... but Liosa changed me. I used her as an excuse to reject all women." He grimaced then. "Brighde took me to task over my behavior a few days ago. She called me a fazart ... and she was right. I was a coward." His gaze held hers steadily. "But for ye, I shall lay myself bare. Ye are the best thing to come into my life, Jean ... and I will fight for ye."

Jean stared down at Robin, her pulse thundering in her ears.

Swallowing hard, she stepped forward and reached out, offering him her hands. Silently, he took them, his grip warm and strong. However, she felt a tremor, evidence of how brutally honest he was being. He was still scared, yet he'd let her see into his soul, nonetheless.

"Ye are not a coward or a fool, Robin Mackay," she said, gently squeezing his hands. "Ye just chose the wrong woman as yer bride … and paid dearly for it. I know life has left its scars upon ye … but I've wanted ye since the day we first met. Do ye know why?"

He stared back at her, his eyes glittering, before he shook his head.

"Because right from the beginning, I saw the man beneath the hurt and bitterness." Jean's throat ached now, as tenderness for this man threatened to overwhelm her. "Please believe that I would never hurt ye. I would take a dirk to my own breast before I did so."

"Aye," he replied huskily. "I trust ye … as does Grace. The lass adores ye. I want for the three of us to be a family."

Jean's breathing caught. "Robin," she whispered. "I—"

"God, how I love ye, Jean." The words tumbled out of him. "Will ye be my wife? Will ye share my bed, my life? There will be no separation between us, lass. I promise I will give ye all of me … until my dying day."

Jean's vision blurred then, tears trickling down her cheeks. "Aye," she whispered.

Still grasping her hands, Robin rose to his feet and hauled her into his arms.

Heedless that they were in a holy place, he kissed her, his lips searing hers in wordless passion. Jean melted into his arms, her hands splaying against his strong chest. His pulse pounded hard against her right palm, his body trembling against hers.

And at that moment, the last of her hurt, her fears, dissipated like mist on a summer's dawn. Indeed, there was no barrier between them now. In laying himself bare, he'd exorcised his demons. The past couldn't control him any longer.

Jean's mouth opened to Robin, her tongue tangling with his. The rasp of his stubble against her skin, the taste of him, made her feel giddy, as if she'd just consumed a cup of strong wine.

Is this really happening?

It was.

Robin was here. He was real. And he was hers.

Robin Mackay wed Jean Munro on the steps to Melness kirk three days later. It was a warm day in late spring, and Jean wore a crown of wildflowers, skillfully woven by Eilidh for the occasion.

Niel and Beth Mackay had traveled from Varrich to attend, as had Eilidh. Neave and John Mackay were present too. Neave's pregnancy was steadily advancing, yet she'd insisted on making the trip.

Back at Varrich—when Robin and Jean had emerged hand-in-hand into the bailey, their eyes gleaming with joy even though their cheeks were wet with tears—Beth and Neave had been waiting for them. Both women had worn tense expressions, yet their worry dissolved as soon as they witnessed the joy on Robin and Jean's faces.

Fortunately, Father Malcolm was in a sweeter mood today. The priest even managed a smile as he concluded the ceremony and unwrapped the ribbon of Mackay plaid that bound the bride and groom's hands.

Robin pulled Jean into his arms for a hungry kiss, and the crowd of kin, servants, warriors, and villagers that filled the kirkyard roared their approval.

Standing at the front of the crowd—with Brighde, Fiona, and Kenna—Grace squealed, her young face flushed with excitement. And as her father and his new wife made their way down the steps of the kirk, the lass threw rose petals over them.

A day of festivities followed. The market square in the heart of Melness village turned into an outdoor feasting hall. The marriage had been hastily arranged, and the entire village had banded together to help Brighde with the necessary preparations. Sides of mutton had been spit-roasting since dawn, and Brighde had spent the past day baking a variety of breads and cakes. Wheels of cheese lined the tables, as did platters of spring greens. Seated at the head of the table, at her husband's side, Jean couldn't stop smiling.

They shared a goblet of wine, before eating off the same platter, while guests feasted at long trestle tables under the warm sun. Laughter and conversation rose high into the air, blending with the strains of a harp—for a woman sat upon a stool at the heart of the square, playing for them all.

Wishing this moment could last forever, Jean took it all in.

"Are ye happy, lass?" Robin asked, drawing her attention once more.

Jean met his eye, warmth spreading over her at the love, the pride, she saw in his eyes. "Aye," she whispered. "If I was any happier, my heart would burst."

The meal drew out, ending with fresh strawberries and thick cream, before the villagers pushed the trestle tables back and a piper joined the harpist. They played song after song as the guests danced around them.

Robin led Jean out for a dance.

It was the first time they'd danced together, for Robin had always made his excuses in the past. However, Jean was surprised to discover that he was a good dancer. Gazes locked, they twirled around and around. And the joy on Robin's face lifted the cares and worries from him, erased the grooves around his mouth and nose. When they'd first met, he'd appeared older than his thirty-four winters—but today he looked years younger and carefree.

Grace joined them for a dance, gripping Jean and Robin's hands as the three of them spun around in a circle. Afterward, Jean returned to the wedding table while the laird continued to dance with his daughter.

Jean watched them, a smile curving her lips.

Robin made time for his daughter every day now. Jean was always careful not to intrude: the two of them needed time to get to know each other again.

Shifting her attention from Robin and Grace, Jean saw that Danny MacVane had approached Brighde.

"Just one dance, Bri?" he asked, splaying his hands wide in a helpless gesture as his men teased him mercilessly. "I beg ye."

Meanwhile, the cook viewed him with a jaundiced expression, her fingers clasped tightly around the stem of her pewter goblet.

"Go on, Brighde," Jean piped up, unable to prevent herself. "Put the man out of his misery."

She knew Brighde had her reasons for keeping men at a distance, yet in her time at Melness, Jean had observed MacVane keenly. A swaggering exterior couldn't hide a good character. She'd seen how loyal he was to Robin, and how her husband relied on him.

He was persistent too. Jean wished for his tenaciousness to be rewarded, today of all days.

Muttering a curse under her breath, Brighde slammed her goblet down and rose to her feet. "Very well," she growled. "If this means ye shall leave me alone afterward, MacVane ... let's get this over with. Just one dance, mind."

Undeterred by her lack of enthusiasm, MacVane held out his hand to the cook before favoring her with a wide smile. "I'll be sure to make it count."

35

OUT OF THE DARKNESS

SOMEONE HAD SCATTERED rose petals across the floor and the bed in the laird's chamber. Jean smiled at the sight before breathing in their sweet, spicy scent. "How romantic," she breathed. Her gaze shifted from the petals then, surveying the room for the first time.

In all her months living at Melness, she'd never seen inside Robin's bed-chamber.

It was a huge space, taking up the entire top floor of the tower. A great hearth dominated one side, and a large oval window, currently shuttered, lay opposite. Tapestries depicting stag hunting scenes covered the stone walls. A large canopied bed stood in the center of the flagstone floor, with a full-length looking glass standing opposite, against the wall.

Jean's attention rested upon the bed, heat blossoming in her lower belly in anticipation of what was to follow.

The wedding festivities had gone on late. It was now dark outside, and while some of the guests were still drinking downstairs, many had retired. All the guest chambers inside the tower were occupied, filled with their visitors from Varrich. They'd even turned the library into a temporary bed-chamber so that Eilidh and her maid would have somewhere to sleep.

"Yer chamber is fine indeed," Jean murmured. "Those tapestries are beautiful."

"My mother made them," Robin replied from behind her. A gentle thud followed as he closed the door. "They were projects that took her years."

"I'm sure they did," Jean agreed. Her gaze then alighted upon the looking glass. "Heavens, that's magnificent." Her prized hand-held looking glass was tiny compared to this. The glass, which was six-foot high and at least three foot wide, stood upon an intricately carved wooden stand.

"It was my gift ... to Liosa," Robin said, his voice turning gruff. "After she departed, I considered ridding myself of it ... but couldn't bring myself to."

"Grace told me of it," Jean replied, remembering now. "She said ye had it made specially?"

"Aye, but if ye wish, I will have it taken away."

Jean turned, her gaze meeting his. "The looking glass doesn't bother me," she assured him. "It can stay." She spoke the truth. She wasn't insecure where Liosa was concerned. Nor did she associate the looking glass with her.

Robin frowned. "Are ye sure?"

Jean smiled. "Aye, why don't ye come here and kiss yer bride?"

It was a saucy request, and it had the desired effect as a grin split Robin's face, chasing away the shadows. "Yer wish is my command, wife," he murmured, approaching her.

Cupping Jean's face with his big hands, he lowered his mouth to hers, giving her a slow, sensual kiss that made her toes curl inside her slippers.

"Ye have been driving me to distraction all day," he murmured, drawing back slightly so that he could trail kisses down Jean's jaw to her neck. "That *kirtle*."

Jean gave a soft laugh, even as a mix of nervousness and anticipation fluttered within her. She'd already lain with Robin—a few times now—but not since their relationship had taken this turn.

Not since he'd admitted his love.

"Do ye like it then?" she asked lightly.

He growled softly, low in his throat, giving his response, as his lips trailed to the hollow of her throat before dipping to the swell of her cleavage.

The kirtle, a shimmery moss-green, was one of Beth's. The two sisters were of nearly identical size and height. In the past, Jean would have balked at Beth's suggestion she wear the kirtle that had long bell-sleeves, a daring neckline, and flared skirts, accentuating the dip of her waist. But that was the old Jean—the lass who hid her figure under loose, plain clothes, who wanted to blend into the background.

These days, Jean wanted to stand out. She loved wearing beautiful clothes now, but she wanted to make her husband proud too. Pleasure shivered through her then as Robin's tongue darted between her breasts. "This dress is coming off," he said, his voice rough with desire. "Now."

Jean's breathing quickened, although she made no move to loosen the laces on her bodice. Instead, she let her husband do it.

They were both breathing fast now, the air inside the chamber becoming charged, as if a storm were about to break. A low fire glowed in the hearth, despite that it was a mild night. Nonetheless, Jean found herself shivering as Robin slowly peeled her clothes off.

Finally, she stood before him, naked except for the crown of flowers in her hair and her silk slippers. Kicking off her slippers, Jean reached up to remove Eilidh's beautiful wildflower wreath. However, Robin put out a hand to prevent her. "Leave it on," he commanded softly. "Ye look like a faery lass with flowers in yer hair."

Smiling, Jean complied before she reached out and pulled the fine dark-blue lèine he wore out of his chamois braies. "Yer turn, Robin," she whispered.

His mouth lifted at the corners, his hazel eyes darkening, as she pushed the lèine up, over his muscular torso. He pulled it off, tossing the garment carelessly aside as Jean unlaced his braies and pushed them down.

His shaft thrust out to meet her.

Breath catching, Jean lowered herself to her knees before him and took the swollen head of his rod in her mouth. She sucked him eagerly, heat pooling between her thighs when Robin's long, sensual groan filled the chamber.

"God's blood, Jean," he rasped. "Ye'll make me lose control."

Power thrilled through Jean. Aye, she wanted to see him unravel. The times they'd coupled had been exciting, lusty, and passion-filled, but there had always been a reserve in Robin. He'd held a part of himself back. Things were different now.

Robin was hers, and she'd undo him.

Jean's tongue explored the rounded head of his shaft, flicking gently against the sensitive underside. One of her hands stroked its hard length, and the other caressed his heavy bollocks.

And to her delight, his shaft grew harder and bigger still as she worked him.

Murmuring an oath, Robin tangled his hands in her hair, stilling her. He then drew Jean up and hauled her against him.

Their mouths fused, the kiss hot and wild.

Jean writhed against Robin, desire spiking through her. His tongue invaded her mouth, and she sucked it, hard, mimicking how she'd sucked his rod. A deep groan rumbled through Robin's chest—the sound exciting her further. She writhed against him, welcoming the feel of his hands cupping her buttocks, pushing their loins hard together. His member was like a rod of hot iron pressed against her belly.

Wildness exploded within Jean, and she clutched at him as if she were trying to climb his strong, heavily muscled form.

Sensing her desperation, Robin walked her backward to the bed. There, he tore his mouth from hers and pushed her down across the scattered rose petals. Breathing hard, Jean stared up at him, her gaze raking over where his rod twitched, eager to bury itself deep inside her.

Yet, instead, Robin crawled over her and began to kiss and lick his way down her body, from her greedy mouth to her neck. He cupped her heavy breasts and lifted them to his mouth, suckling them hard.

Ragged groans filled the chamber, and with a jolt, Jean realized those animalistic noises were coming from her.

And when he lowered himself between her legs, spreading her wide so he could pleasure he there too, her groans became cries. Thighs locked around his shoulders, she arched up toward his wicked mouth, seeking more.

Eventually, when she was a molten pool of want, he released her.

Jean was panting, her limbs trembling as he rolled her over and lifted her up onto all fours.

"My darling, Jean," he growled. "Just look at yerself."

Raising her head, Jean glanced left.

A gasp escaped her when she stared back at her own reflection. Shock and excitement shivered through her. She'd forgotten the looking glass stood against the wall, a few feet back from the bed. She barely recognized the sensual woman who looked back at her. Both her and Robin's bodies gleamed with sweat. Her hair was a mess, her crown of flowers askew. A flush marked her cheeks and chest.

"Ye are so bonny," Robin murmured, stroking the length of her back with slow, sensual reverence.

Jean watched him, need tightening deep in her womb. Groaning, she arched her back like a cat, pushing her bottom toward him.

It was an eager invitation.

Gaze riveted upon the mirror, she watched him take his shaft in hand and position it behind her. She felt the blunt head nudge her entrance, and then, with delicious slowness, he pressed into her.

The feeling of being stretched made Jean groan once more. She sank down onto her elbows, her swollen nipples brushing the counterpane.

However, her attention never wavered from the looking glass.

Robin sank to the hilt inside her and halted, letting her adjust to him. Their gazes met in the reflection and held. His lips were parted, his gaze hooded. Like her, a flush stained his cheeks.

Still holding her gaze, he gripped her hips and slowly withdrew—almost to the tip—before gliding deep inside once more. "Ye are a goddess," he rasped, as he resumed moving, taking her in slow, even strokes. "And ye are mine."

"Robin!" His words, the sensations he was provoking within her, were eroding Jean's self-control. She'd wanted to undo him this eve, but the opposite was happening.

With each thrust, each murmured endearment, he was pushing her closer to the brink.

She could barely think now. Her lower belly clenched as she clawed for something just out of reach.

His gaze continued to trap hers, even as he lifted her hips even higher, altering the angle of his thrusts. He drove into her now, and Jean's womb turned molten.

Crying his name, she bucked back against him, welcoming him deeper still—and when he reached underneath to stroke her where their bodies joined, Jean's thighs started to tremble. Her arms collapsed completely—her cheek pressed against the coverlet.

Robin's groans entwined with hers. Then he gripped her tighter still and plunged into her once more, rolling his hips as he did so.

He touched a place deep inside her—a place that caused a wet rush of heat—and Jean shattered around him. She clawed at the coverlet, shaking as her climax drew out.

"Jean!" Robin thrust wildly once more. His fingers bit into the soft flesh of her hips. An instant later, he went rigid against Jean, spilling deep inside her, his shout shaking the walls of the chamber.

Sprawled across her husband's sweat-damp chest, Jean sighed. Her womb still throbbed in the aftermath of her violent peak, the sensitive flesh between the thighs tingling.

"That ... was ... magnificent," she eventually murmured against his chest. In truth, she was struggling to think coherently, and those words weren't enough to describe what she'd just experienced. What they'd *both* experienced.

Eventually raising her head, Jean's gaze settled upon Robin's face. His eyes were closed, his skin gleaming in the light of the lantern next to the bed. "We will most *definitely* be keeping that looking glass," she informed him.

Robin's eyes flickered open at that, his mouth curving as their gazes met. "Saucy wench." His voice was rough in the aftermath of their passion, and the rawness of it made heat tremble in Jean's core once more. She still hadn't gotten enough of him—she wondered if she ever would.

Tonight was a new beginning, and she couldn't wait to continue her exploration of the erotic, emotional connection they'd forged.

Their gaze drew out, and Robin's smile widened. "Aye, we shall keep it," he assured her. "I intend to explore a few new positions where I can watch as I take ye."

Excitement quickened Jean's breathing as lusty images filled her mind.

Smiling down at him, she laced her fingers through his on the counterpane. The sweet yet spicy scent of rose surrounded them, for they still lay atop the scattered petals. "I love ye, Robin Mackay," she whispered. "Yer strength, yer kindness ... yer passion ... all the things that are uniquely yers." She paused then, recalling their stilted conversation at Samhuinn—and how he'd virtually fled her company. Her smile faded, and she pulled a face. "Although I admit I shouldn't have forced my way into yer life the way I did. I've always been too pushy."

Robin huffed a laugh. "If ye hadn't, we would never have ended up together, mo ghràdh."

Jean swallowed. "I never dared dream I'd find love like this," she admitted softly. "I saw how much Niel and John love Beth and Neave yet didn't believe any man would lose his wits over me."

His expression grew soft, his eyes gleaming with sudden emotion. "Ye were made for me, lass," he answered. "Whenever ye are near, I feel … whole. If ye hadn't come into my life, I'd have likely continued to live as an angry and bitter man. Grace would grow up resenting me … and I wouldn't blame her."

"That's all behind ye, mo ghràdh." Jean's gaze misted as she squeezed his hand tightly. "Ye are out of the darkness now … it's time to embrace the light."

EPILOGUE

TRULY BLESSED

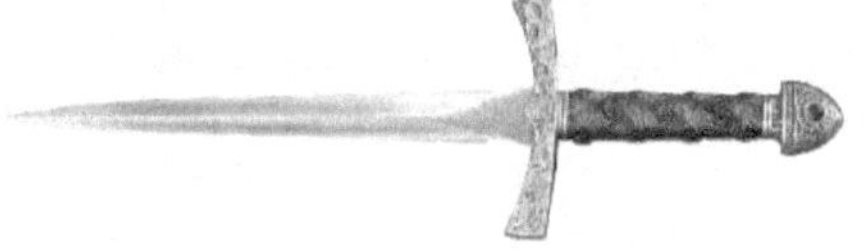

Three months later ...

JEAN PLACED THE last of the bread at the center of the display beneath the altar and stepped back to admire the finished effect. "What do ye think?"

"It's perfect," Grace replied, excitement in her voice. "Will we be able to eat some of this food?"

Jean glanced over at where the lass stood behind her, empty basket in hand, and grinned. "Aye."

"Ye will have to wait until mass is over, Lady Grace." A terse male voice intruded then, and they both turned to see Father Malcolm approaching up the aisle between the pews, a scowl upon his face. "Ye shall not touch the bread until then."

Jean forced herself not to scowl back at the priest, hunched in his dark robes like a bad-tempered magpie. "Of course, Father," she replied, taking Grace by the hand. "We're both well aware of the Lammas Day tradition."

"Jean has done a fine job of the display, has she not, Father?" Grace chimed in, motioning to the selection of plaited loaves—some studded with dried fruit, others with boiled eggs woven into the braids—that sat amongst sheaves of oats and barley.

Father Malcolm harrumphed, his gaze roaming over the display. "It isn't *bad*," he finally grumbled.

Deciding that was the closest to a compliment she could expect from the priest, Jean flashed him a tight smile and moved away from the altar. "We shall see ye for mass at noon then." Without waiting for his reply, she strode off down the aisle, towing Grace after her.

"Aye," he called out. "Don't be late."

"Surly auld curmudgeon," Jean muttered as she and Grace exited the kirk into bright sunlight.

It was the first day of August, Lammas Day—a yearly celebration that heralded the start of the harvest and gave thanks to nature's bounty. Lammas was Jean's favorite festivity. Among her sisters, Neave loved Yuletide, Beth Beltaine, and Eilidh Samhuinn—but Jean preferred the earthy Lammas Day to any of the fire festivals. Harvest was a special time of year.

"Why's he so ill-tempered?" Grace asked, falling in step with Jean.

"I've no idea, lass," Jean replied. "Perhaps he's lonely … some priests marry and have families … but others live more like monks. Father Malcolm is one of the latter. He's pious, indeed."

Grace's brow wrinkled as she considered this. "Da was a bit like him … before ye arrived at Melness." She paused then. "Maybe I should give him one of Willow's kittens … for company."

Jean smiled before reaching out and stroking Grace's head. The lass was such a kind soul, with a naturally happy disposition. Willow was the broch's mouser, a lazy brown and black striped cat. Grace was in love with her—and spent all her spare time playing with Willow's kittens. "I don't think Father Malcolm wants a kitten, lass." Her smile widened then as she imagined the horror on the priest's face as Grace eagerly handed him a mewling bundle of fur and claws. It was almost worth it to encourage her.

Leaving the kirk behind, Jean and Grace made their way through the village toward the broch. It had been a warm summer, with a bountiful harvest. The locals all had the day off work; everyone they passed wore a smile.

"See ye at mass, Bessie," Grace called out to one of the village lasses of a similar age. The girl nodded vigorously, her face lighting up in delight.

Watching their exchange, Jean's chest constricted. She and Grace spent many hours together, and Robin's daughter enjoyed her company—but it wasn't the same as having friends of her own age.

"Do ye want to invite Bessie up for supper one eve?" she asked Grace as they left the village behind and made their way up the slope toward the stone arch that led into the barmkin of Melness broch. "I'm sure her parents wouldn't mind."

Grace's face lit up like a candle. "Are ye sure?" She paused then, frowning. "Da won't mind?"

"Of course not."

"I shall ask Bessie when I see her at mass then," Grace replied, doing a little skip. "Thank ye, Jean!"

Smiling, Jean led the way into the barmkin. Her gaze swept over the familiar surroundings before it alighted upon a couple standing in the open doorway to the kitchen annex, next to the towering stone broch.

Danny and Brighde.

As Jean looked on, the captain leaned in, murmuring something. The cook then laughed and gave him a playful shove. In response, MacVane pulled her into his arms, embracing Brighde for all to see.

"Did ye see that!" Grace squealed. "He's kissing her."

"Don't stare, lass," Jean replied, averting her own gaze. "Let's leave them be."

Even so, she was delighted to see Danny and Brighde so happy together. Apparently, things had changed between them on Jean and Robin's wedding day.

"There ye two are." A low male voice filtered over the barmkin, and Jean glanced up to see her husband standing in the doorway to the broch.

"We've finished decorating the altar, Da," Grace exclaimed, rushing up the steps toward him, her empty basket swinging at her side. "Jean says I can invite Bessie to supper!"

Robin tilted his head, brow furrowing as he tried to make sense of the excited words tumbling out of his daughter's mouth. "Bessie ... the miller's daughter?"

"Aye!"

His mouth curved. "A fine idea, lass. Now go in and get yerself ready for the Lammas festivities ... Kenna will have drawn a bath for ye in yer chamber." With a nod, the lass rushed off, her feet pattering up the stone steps behind him.

"I hope ye don't mind me inviting Bessie without discussing it with ye first?" Jean said, alighting the steps. "It just struck me that Grace misses seeing bairns of her own age."

"Of course, I don't mind," Robin replied. He moved down the steps to meet her before taking Jean's hand and drawing her against him. His head lowered then, and his lips brushed across hers in a tender kiss. Pulling back, he then favored her with a boyish smile. "I should have thought of that myself."

Jean watched his face, her belly fluttering. Lord, he was handsome. The three months since their wedding day had passed in a blur. Every morning, she awoke with a smile on her face, a deep sense of contentment filtering through her when she rolled over and viewed the man sleeping beside her.

Her husband. Her love.

True to his word, Robin hadn't retreated from her again. Instead, he'd thrown himself into ensuring she felt involved in every part of his life. Jean had continued her role as chatelaine, duties she enjoyed, and still tutored Grace. However, Robin took her with him when he visited his tenants, and she sat at his side whenever he held audiences in the hall of Melness, helping him settle disputes.

They were a team.

Things had been so busy, that Jean had even forgotten to miss her sisters. Although she corresponded regularly with Beth, Neave, and Eilidh, she hadn't seen any of them since the wedding. Neave was just over a moon away from giving birth now, and Beth had gone to Achness to see how she was faring. Meanwhile, Eilidh sent Jean chatty missives, yet there was nothing personal in them. Ever since their argument that day, after Eilidh had spoken to William Gunn, the two youngest sisters weren't as close as in the past. Jean knew it was just part of life, yet it saddened her a little.

Still smiling, Robin reached out and traced Jean's cheek with his fingertip. "Ye look so serious all of a sudden, Jean," he murmured. "Is something amiss?"

She shook her head. Robin was so attuned to her these days; he noticed the moment her mood changed. "I was just thinking about Eilidh," she admitted. "We used to be inseparable ... but I suppose I just have to let her forge her own path now."

"And she is," Robin replied with a wink. "During our clan meeting last week at Varrich, Iver Mackay serenaded yer sister. The man got down on one knee and sang *The Maiden in the Rye* to her ... in front of us all."

Jean squealed. "He did?"

Robin grinned. "Aye ... Eilidh blushed like an ember."

"I can't believe ye didn't tell me!"

"Sorry." He favored her with a sheepish smile. "It slipped my mind. We were so focused on discussing what to do about the Sutherlands, I thought of little else on the journey home."

Jean frowned. She understood her husband's worry. The situation with their neighbors was beginning to escalate. Niel had ordered the arrested sheep rustlers to be flogged and sent back in shame to Sutherland territory—and ever since, raids along the Mackay-Sutherland borders had increased.

A clash between the two clans was brewing, and there was little anyone could do to prevent it.

Mulling this over, Jean linked her arm through her husband's. "If only I hadn't been so busy with the harvest ... I should have gone with ye to Varrich," she said, deliberately steering the topic of conversation back to her sister—it was less troubling than feuding. "Eilidh never mentions Iver in her letters."

Robin favored his wife with an arch look. "Perhaps she wishes to conduct her affairs in privacy."

"Privacy? We Munros don't know the meaning of the word." Jean's mouth curved then. "I only want Eilidh to be as happy as I am."

Her husband smiled down at her, his eyes crinkling at the corners. "Ye bring me such joy, Jean," he murmured, his voice husky now. "I didn't know happiness like this was possible ... I'm truly blessed, mo chridhe."

And with that, he drew her into his arms for a passionate kiss.

The End

FROM THE AUTHOR

I hope you enjoyed the third installment in the COURAGEOUS HIGHLAND HEARTS series.

Jean and Robin's story was a real journey for both characters. I'm a bit of a sucker for a wounded hero. Robin really had a rough deal. If a man ever deserved a HEA, it's him! I also love how Jean starts as a bit of a 'plain Jane' but discovers her confidence as the book progresses. I adore reading a good 'make-over' scene in books, so decided to add my own to this story!

There's a lot of pain and healing in this book—it was an emotional and complex one to write, that's for sure, but when Jean and Robin overcome their obstacles to love, I couldn't stop smiling. This really is one of the stories where love conquers all.

Get ready for Eilidh and Will's dramatic story, up next!

Jayne x

HISTORICAL NOTES

I usually have lengthy historical notes with all my books—not so with this one!

Unlike Niel Mackay and John Mackay of Aberach—my previous two heroes, who were actual historical figures—Robin Mackay is entirely fictional. There aren't any real battles or historical events in this story either, although the tension between the Mackays and the Sutherlands did exist during this period.

However, the Mackays of Melness were an actual branch of the Mackay clan. Their holding is long gone, so I created Melness broch, using details from strongholds from the same period that still exist.

Melness (Gaelic: Taobh Mhealanais), which boasts a fine sandy beach, comprises a group of small remote crofting townships, lying to the west of Tongue Bay on the north coast of Scotland. In the 15th Century, this area was part of Mackay lands, although it now sits within Sutherland territory.

The novel also takes you back, briefly, to Castle Varrich. This fortress was the seat of the Mackays. Built out of sandstone, the castle perches upon a high point of rock, overlooking both the Kyle of Tongue and the village of Tongue. The castle's precise origins and age are unknown, although some historians believe it is over a thousand years old, and the medieval castle may have been built atop a Norse fort. The original castle had two floors, plus an attic. The ruin is located around one hour's walk away from the village of Tongue. It has views of the mountains Ben Hope and Ben Loyal.

I hope you have enjoyed my notes—brief as they are! I really enjoyed researching the history and landscape of this wild and beautiful corner of Scotland.

COURAGEOUS HIGHLAND HEARTS CHARACTER GLOSSARY

The Mackay clan

The Mackays of Varrich
Beth Mackay (neè Munro—Niel's wife)
Niel Mackay (Mackay clan-chief)
Angus Mackay (Beth and Niel's son)

The Mackays of Farr
Connor Mackay (Mackay chieftain—laird of Farr Castle), married to Keira (they have three children: Rose, Rory, and Quinn)
Morgan Mackay (Connor's brother), married to Maggie (they have one daughter, Tara)
Jaimee Mackay (Connor's sister), married to Alexander Gunn (they have two children, Anice and Aodhan)
Kennan Mackay (Connor Mackay's cousin), married to Cait (they have two sons, Blake and Logan)

The Mackays of Loch Stach
Hugh Mackay (Mackay chieftain—laird of Loch Stach)

The Mackays of Aberach
John Mackay (Mackay chieftain—laird of Achness—Mackay clan-chief's cousin)

The Mackays of Melness
Robin Mackay (Mackay chieftain—laird of Melness broch)
Grace Mackay (Robin Mackay's daughter)
Liosa Mackay (Robin's estranged wife)
Gordon Mackay (Robin's brother)

The Mackays of Balnakeil
Breac Mackay (Mackay chieftain—laird of Balnakeil broch)
Janneth Mackay (Breac's wife)

The Mackays of Dun Ugadale
Iver Mackay (Mackay chieftain—laird of Dun Ugadale)

The Gunn clan
Tavish Gunn (clan-chief)
Roy, Blair, Evan, and William Gunn (Tavish's younger brothers)

The Munro clan
George Munro (Munro clan-chief)
Laila Munro (the clan-chief's wife)
Fionn Munro (the clan-chief's son)
Neave Munro (the clan-chief's daughter)
Jean Munro (the clan-chief's daughter)
Eilidh (pronounced Ay-lee) Munro (the clan-chief's daughter)

Other characters
Father Malcolm (priest at Melness)
Ewan Reay (captain of the Varrich Guard)
Daniel MacVane (Captain of the Melness Guard)
Evan Pollard (man-at-arms, Melness)
Brighde Nielson (cook at Melness)
Fiona and her daughter Kenna (servants at Melness)
Brian (servant at Melness)
Ian (healer at Melness)

DIVE INTO MY BACKLIST!

Check out my printable reading order list on my website: https://www.jaynecastel.com/printable-reading-list

ABOUT THE AUTHOR

Multi-award-winning author Jayne Castel writes epic Historical and Fantasy Romance. Her vibrant characters, richly researched historical settings, and action-packed adventure romance transport readers to forgotten times and imaginary worlds.

Jayne is the author of a number of best-selling series. In love with all things Scottish, she writes romances set in both Dark Ages and Medieval Scotland.

When she's not writing, Jayne is reading (and re-reading) her favorite authors, cooking Italian feasts, and going on long walks with her husband. She lives in New Zealand's beautiful South Island.

Connect with Jayne online:
www.jaynecastel.com
www.facebook.com/JayneCastelRomance
https://www.instagram.com/jaynecastelauthor/
Email: contact@jaynecastel.com

www.ingramcontent.com/pod-product-compliance
Lightning Source LLC
Chambersburg PA
CBHW021110110726
47900CB00007B/2122